FALLING FOR MY RIVAL

AN ENEMIES TO LOVERS ROMANCE

DAKOTA DAVIES

SAVAGE CREEK PRESS

Falling for my Rival
A small town enemies to lovers romance
Book 2 in the Falling Hard Series
by Dakota Davies

Cover Design: Coverluv

Cover Photography: iStock

Editing: Jana Stojadinović

1

WYATT

I pace behind my desk and try to calm my thumping heart. "I, uh, don't know what to say," I say into the phone to the man who, as of an hour ago, is my new boss.

On the floor of my office at the Mountain Gazette, my six-year-old nephew is completely consumed by the hot-glue-and-twig project I set him up with a half hour ago so I could put the Monday edition to bed. Normally my sister Annika babysits, but her mutt Juney ingested another sock and needed to be rushed to the emergency vet.

"Don't sound so scared, Wyatt," my new boss says. "This is a good thing for your paper."

My paper. He's wrong there. I just work here. For another five months and ten days. Not like I'm counting down or anything.

The man lists all the benefits of "my paper" being bought by Jensen and Thorne Media: access to resources, financial security, blah, blah, blah. Why do I care? In five months, I'll be working for the L.A. Times. Finally starting my life. At least that's the plan.

"Are you going to cut jobs?" I ask as my younger brother Caleb steps into my office.

"Daddy!" Taylor cries and jumps into his arms.

I tune out their chatter to listen to the man's reply.

"Funny you ask that," he says with a chuckle. "I'm sending someone from our Denver desk to partner with you. A journalist who is ambitious and extremely insightful."

So, he's implying that I'm not ambitious or insightful. "We don't have a need for another reporter right now, sir," I reply, my voice edged with frustration I fail to hide.

"I disagree," the man says, his voice taking on a steely tone that makes the hairs on the back of my neck prickle. "And since I now sign your paycheck, you don't have a choice."

A tense silence stretches into seconds while I process what's happening. He's right. I don't have to like this plan, but then again, it's not my paper.

"Yes, sir," I say. Before I can ask anything else about this big city reporter who's coming to show us small-town hacks how to do our jobs, he replies with a "I'll be in touch," and hangs up.

I set the phone down and inhale a slow breath.

Caleb is watching me from the floor, where Taylor is demonstrating the many accolades of his twig-and-eraser car. "Everything okay?" he asks.

I rub the back of my neck. "No."

One of the sticks has come off Taylor's car and he pounces on the glue gun to fix it.

I huff a sigh at the ceiling. "Our paper just got bought by Jensen and Thorne Media."

"Is that bad?" he asks.

I force my fists to unclench. "Yeah, it's bad. They'll want to restructure. Maybe even cut jobs. Cut our budget."

"What budget?" he asks with a smirk.

A laugh escapes my lips, but it's dry. "Exactly." I gaze out the window, over the tops of the buildings to the jagged Sawtooth mountains dusted with autumn's first snowfall. "The worst part is they're sending someone from their Denver office. To partner"—I put air quotes around the word—"with me."

Caleb crosses his arms. "Sounds like they want to spy on you."

My blood heats. "See what I mean?" I lean over my desk, my

2

fingertips pressing firmly into the scuffed wood. "Shit, I forgot to ask when they're sending that journalist."

"Uncle Wyatt," Taylor warns, deep in concentration reconstructing his car.

I give him a puzzled look, then it registers. "Right." I slide my wallet from my back pocket, pluck a single dollar bill from its folds, and slide it across the desk. Between Caleb and me, this kid's going to be rich by the time he's driving.

I walk to the window and gaze down at the dusty street, trying to picture how we're going to make room for another journalist at the Mountain Gazette. We employ only two other writers besides me. We occupy a small space on the second floor of a hundred-year-old building. Ike and I are the only ones with our own office.

"I don't even have a desk available right now," I say, mostly to myself.

A noise from the doorway pulls me from my thoughts. I blink several times because standing there is a petite brunette holding a laptop case and a tall paper cup.

Not just any brunette. *That* brunette. The one I spent nearly twenty-four hours devouring last July. The one with the pert, soft lips and perfect curves. The one who never told me her name. The one I've pushed out of my mind because I would never see her again.

"Then I'll just take yours," she says, lifting an eyebrow.

An uncomfortable silence fills the space. Even Taylor is still.

The woman's face breaks into a sly smile. "Hello, Wyatt," she says, striding into the middle of the room. She's wearing a black-and-white striped blouse that flutters around her small frame when she moves, black slacks that hug her tight curves, and black heels.

I'm vaguely aware of Caleb collecting Taylor's project and leading him toward the door.

I suffer through a moment of panic until I remember that *I'm* the older brother. That *I'm* the one who's supposed to be supporting him, not the other way around. Caleb gives me an amused expression and disappears through the door, Taylor's chatter echoing down the hall.

What is my one-night stand doing in my office, threatening to claim it?

Then, it hits me.

Oh fuck.

She's who they sent.

I swallow my unease and square up to the woman. She shouldn't be making me nervous. She's...like...five foot three, tops. I'm six two and can swim four hundred meters in under four minutes, fast enough for a silver medal in Rio, if I'd had my shot.

"I, uh, didn't...catch your name," I manage.

"Brooke Henderson," she says, and steps forward to shake my hand.

Her small palm is smooth and cool inside mine. A shiver passes through me as memories flash like lightning. Her delicate hands stroking me. Her fingers white-knuckling the sheets while she begged me not to stop.

Holy freaking hell.

"Nice to meet you, Brooke," I say, hoping she doesn't notice the tension in my voice or the sudden bulge in my pants.

I need to sit down before I make a damn fool of myself, so I indicate for her to take the chair across from my desk and I settle into mine.

Brooke. I like the sound of her name on my lips. And up close like that, I caught her spicy floral scent, like mountain heather and cloves. Whatever it is, it smells really fucking good.

Stop.

I shouldn't drink in her tight curves and luscious lips painted an even more luscious shade of pink, or the way the afternoon light catches the honey highlights in her hair as she moves the few steps to the chair and sits down. But I do.

God help me.

She props her laptop against the chair leg then sips from the contents of her cup. Watching the way her lips part and darken the lipstick stain on the cup's rim has me mesmerized.

"So," I say after clearing my throat. "I'm still not quite sure why you're here."

"Mr. Freeman didn't inform you?" She licks her lips and leans in. "I've been sent to rescue the Gazette."

A shock wave erupts from the hollow behind my navel. "Excuse me?"

"Jensen and Thorne media are debating reducing the Gazette to online only." She sips from her cup and brushes back a lock of hair that's fallen in front of her shoulder. "Mr. Freeman offered me an opportunity that'll help save it."

I realize my jaw is hanging open. "Save it? You?" I manage, which is a dick thing to say but what the hell?

She doesn't flinch. "I have a lot of experience."

Right. She must or Mr. Freeman wouldn't have sent her. "So, last summer," I say, quickly fast-forwarding through the memory of her panting in my ear as I took her against her hotel room dresser. "That was, what, you doing recon for your boss?"

"Something like that," she replies, her smile making her sky-blue eyes sparkle.

I grip the edge of my chair. "You lied to me."

"No," she says, her lips forming a prim pucker that shouldn't make my cock ache. "As I recall, we didn't exactly discuss our personal lives."

Do I detect a flicker of heat in her expression?

"You should have told me."

Her gaze flicks to the cup in her hands. "Why complicate things like that?"

"So you just...used me?"

Both of her silky eyebrows shoot up. "Didn't you use me just as easily?"

Oh did I. Again and again and yes, damn it, again. Would anyone blame me? For the last six years, I've been too busy raising my three younger siblings to enjoy many nocturnal adventures. That night with the woman sitting across from me broke a seven-month dry spell.

And when I say, "broke," I should say shattered. My dick was sore for days.

"I'll be straight with you," Brooke says after a sip from her cup. "That night was just an escape for both of us, nothing more." A pink blush runs up the side of her face. "Let's just forget it."

She can't be serious. How can I forget the way her soft, ripe tits tasted or her keening cries when I made her come?

Her face tightens into a firm expression, as if she's gearing up for battle. "So we can do our jobs."

I grip the edge of my desk. "How long is this...partnership... supposed to last?"

She crosses her slender legs. "Until the end of the year."

I fight my rising panic. Three whole months? "And then you'll just...go back to Denver?"

There's that little pucker again, this time with a tilt of her head, like she's debating something. "Hopefully only temporarily," she finally says.

I watch her a moment longer, trying to read the subtext. Does she travel around gobbling up small-town newspapers? "And how do you propose saving the Gazette?"

Her chin lifts. "You need deeper stories. People don't buy the paper to read about the school board meeting or the golf course closing for the winter."

Something gnaws at the inside of my stomach. "And you think an outsider like you is going to dig up cutting edge news here?"

"Maybe not," she says, sipping again from her cup. "But that's why I have you."

She sets her cup on the edge of my desk and lifts her laptop to her knees. "What's your deadline tonight for the Monday edition?"

"Eight o'clock," I reply as she unzips her case. "Why?"

She checks the slender, silver watch on her wrist and shakes her head. "That's not much time, but let's see what we can do, shall we?"

"But I've already gone through it. It's ready."

She glances up from her screen with a determined glint in her eye. "Let's have a peek anyway."

Inhale. Exhale. So this is how it's going to be, huh? "Fine," I growl.

"Login please?" she asks, her slender fingers poised over her keyboard.

Three months of this. Of not knowing if I should argue with her or bend her over my desk. I straighten my spine, disgusted with myself. She might be smart, but I'm a fighter. Hell, I've put up with a landslide of shit for the past six years. Three months will be a walk in the park.

She wants to throw down?

Game on.

2

BROOKE

On a Sunday night, Penny Creek might as well be a ghost town. To top it off, I've arrived on the verge of a season they call "slack." Summer ends after Labor Day and the tourists and vacation homeowners all go back to Scottsdale or Seattle for school and jobs and their regular lives, reducing the population of Rogue Valley by half. While the locals likely enjoy having their town back, it means they roll up the sidewalks by nine o'clock; some businesses close completely from October until Thanksgiving when the town fills back up.

At least it's made finding a hotel room easy. And cheap. Tomorrow I'll hunt down a room to rent. For now, I need a glass of wine and a hot bath. I wish it wasn't so late or I'd call my dad and give him the update he's been waiting for all day. Tomorrow I'll make time in the afternoon, when he's done teaching. I can already hear his praise, which is almost as good as hearing it from him.

I purchase a bottle of Cab from the IGA and smuggle it into my hotel room. As I run my bath, I open the bottle and fill half of a plastic cup. Though it won't taste nearly as good, I take a slow sip, appreciating the nuances all the same, then release a slow sigh.

I'm able to relax, but only a little. Wyatt Morgan and his dangerous good looks won't allow more than that.

Seeing him again was harder than I thought. Our one night was months ago. I've hardly thought about him since then.

Ha. If only that were true. My one night in Penny Creek was supposed to be just that. Or I never would have gotten so...carried away with a certain sexy journalist. The one with the storm-blue eyes and the chiseled jaw who walked toward me with that half-smile on his face, like he already knew he had me.

Did he ever.

I never planned to return to Penny Creek, but Mr. Freeman offered me this opportunity before I knew it was the Gazette he wanted to save.

I remember the way he beamed when I accepted.

"Then you'll take this position in Penny Creek?" he asked.

My eyes must have bugged out of my head, because his benevolent expression changed to one of concern. "Is something wrong?"

Penny Creek?

I tried to quiet my racing heart. Penny Creek = sexy journalist I thought I'd never see again.

"Your assessment of the region and the Mountain Gazette last summer gave me critical information I used to make the sale," Mr. Freeman continued, his brow furrowed. "It's only fair I offer you this opportunity."

"I appreciate that," I said, pasting on a bright smile that felt as fake as it probably looked. "And it's no problem at all."

"Good," Mr. Freeman said, then nodded to my editor. "Set it up and send the bill to me," he told him.

I stood to shake Mr. Freeman's hand. "Thank you, sir," I said, my mouth suddenly dry. "I won't let you down."

"I'm sure you won't," he said, his eyes twinkling.

The roar of the bathwater brings me back to my simple room with the watercolor print above the bed and the floral-patterned carpet. I made sure to avoid the same hotel I stayed in during my last visit, but the memory of Wyatt's urgent kisses against the wall fills my mind anyway.

I take another sip of my wine then set it down and undress, hanging everything neatly on the hangers—real ones, I notice.

The cool air hits my bare skin, making it erupt with goosebumps. Just like the ones I got in Wyatt's office when I surprised him this afternoon. It's almost funny the way he stammered and gaped. It was worth making him angry. I wonder what make up sex would be like with Wyatt Morgan. The idea of it makes me groan.

I top up my wine and bring it into the bathroom. After turning off the faucet, I step into the hot water and sink down with a long sigh. There's a lot to do in three months, and I don't mean riding Wyatt Morgan like a bicycle. I mean research and interviews, and probably plenty of battles with Wyatt about how things need to be done.

After my bath, I slip on my nightgown and crawl under the thick comforter, wishing there was a warm body waiting for me to heat me up.

I have to stop thinking like this or these next three months are going to break me.

Or maybe that's exactly what I want Wyatt to do to me. Break me into little pieces so he can make me whole again with those intense, possessive kisses and those dirty words he whispered in my ear. A shiver runs over my skin. Nobody had ever talked to me like that, touched me like that, made me *want* like that.

I suppress another shudder and force images of his firm pecs and trim hips and his expert mouth from my mind. The only way I can be successful here is to keep my mind on the job and my libido locked away. What Wyatt and I shared is in the past. It's over, and what I want now is too important to jeopardize for something as inconsequential as another one-night stand.

THE NEXT MORNING, my alarm goes off at six thirty. I fumble for the orange snooze button on my screen then snuggle back under the covers. As per my usual, I repeat this snooze pattern until I finally crawl out of bed at 7:00. If I want to get in a workout, I have to get up now, so I get dressed and pack my gym bag. After stumbling bleary-eyed to the lobby, I pass the sideboard with the Keurig, bananas, and packaged muffins without a second glance. Workout first, then food, and God please let this cowboy town have decent tea.

Outside, the early morning chill makes my throat clamp shut. It's only October but the cold is already this bone-deep? Ugh. I thought Denver was bad. But if I do well here, I'll be trading my winter boots for flip flops and selling my snow tires soon enough.

I shiver inside my long winter coat and hurry to my rental car. I have to yank on the door because it's frozen shut, then sit for five minutes while the defrost clears my windshield. I drive the two miles to the community pool in total darkness, the stars bright overhead. The schedule I read online before leaving Denver listed lap lanes from 5:00-6:00, which is completely insane, and again from 7:15-9:00, which is still early but after my travel day and late night, a hard swim will get the day off to a productive start. That, and it will hopefully banish the last of my cravings for Wyatt's kisses.

As I reach the door, it swings open and a flock of tall, teenaged boys saunter out, their hair wet and loud voices bursting with confidence. They ignore me, too caught up in some story about Friday night. I try to catch the gist of it—all intel is good intel—but their rapid banter and jeering is a mystery to me, so I slip past them to the pool lobby.

The chlorinated steam bathes my cold skin in a welcoming cloud. After a life of swimming, I've been in countless pools and they all have the same vibe: cold concrete and that mix of cold air pumped in with the humid breath coming off the water.

I'm about to step up to the window to buy a punch card from the young woman behind the register when a man emerges from a door behind her. He's dressed in jeans and a blue hoodie with "Rogue Valley Beavers Swim Club" logo on the front. My mouth goes dry.

Wyatt.

"Beavers?" I blurt before I can stop myself.

He eyes me. "Good morning to you too," he says in a voice way too cheerful for this early. "And I'll have you know that beavers can swim five miles per hour, can hold their breath for fifteen minutes, and have transparent eyelids, allowing them to see underwater."

"But they're still beavers," I say, unable to stop the memories of what we did in a hotel room last July from heating my blood.

He laughs. "True."

"So, you're a swim coach?" I ask as the pieces fall into place.

He crosses his arms. "Yes, ma'am. Regional Champions four years running." He steps closer to me, his eyes flashing playfully. "You here to dig up all the deep, dark secrets of the community pool?"

The surprise factor from my announcement yesterday must have worn off. That or he's one of those infuriating people who are bright and bushy-tailed in the morning. Either way, I'm screwed, because a cocky Wyatt is way harder to resist than the argumentative, walled off Wyatt I worked with last night.

"Stories are everywhere if you know how to look," I say, raising an eyebrow.

A skinny man in his sixties steps past me to the register and the woman behind it punches his proffered card. The man disappears into the men's locker room.

I step up to the window and slide my debit card toward the young woman. "A month punch card, please," I say.

Out of the corner of my eye, I catch Wyatt's frown.

The young woman completes my transaction then gets called into the pool deck behind her, leaving us alone in the lobby.

"You swim?" Wyatt asks.

Punch card and my debit card in hand, I face him. I could rattle off my record times that still grace the wall of my high school swim center, my four years of varsity swimming at Colorado College, my national title in the 200 Breaststroke. "Yes," I say instead, and tuck my punch card and debit card into my wallet.

"You should come a little earlier," he says in a teasing tone, lifting an eyebrow at the word "come." "I'm here every morning at five."

Before I can stop myself, I place a hand on my hip. "What, you think you can take me?"

His eyes light up with a playful spark. "Oh, sweetheart, I know I can."

A smile tugs at my lips but I bite it back before he can see and hurry into the locker room. The door thumps shut behind me, and I release a shaky breath. How can he be so maddening and sexy at the same time? Why is it so surprising I swim? Why is it so surprising I can save his paper?

Why does being called "sweetheart" by him make me want to grab him by the hair and kiss him senseless?

As I undress I imagine Wyatt's hands sliding my clothes from my body. Goosebumps erupt on my arms and torso, followed by an electric buzz that tightens my nipples. Blood starts to pump harder through me, creating an urgent pulse between my legs.

"No," I groan, my voice as tortured as I feel right now.

I can't let these stupid cravings into my mind like this. Sleeping with Wyatt is a bad idea. Penny Creek is a small town. Word gets out that I'm involved with Wyatt and my credibility goes out the window. I made a promise to myself long ago to make it in this business. It's the same pledge that's kept me going since I was sixteen. My dad gave up his dream of being a writer for me. I won't deny his sacrifice by hooking up with my coworker.

I tuck my long hair into my cap and grab my goggles, then exit the locker room. After a quick rinse under the deck shower, I choose a lane and hop into the frigid water.

Though my teeth start to chatter, I welcome the cold. It grounds me. Reminds me of my purpose, which is to overdeliver for Mr. Freeman so he can recommend me for the job opening at the L.A. Times this spring. I'm sure they have outdoor pools in L.A. and lap times that are not so obscenely early.

I push off the wall, the water enveloping me in a silky, cold embrace. With each reach and kick of my legs, Wyatt fades further from my thoughts.

But I know it's only temporary. The minute I see him again my cravings will ramp up to full power.

How am I going to resist him for three months?

3

WYATT

After shrugging into my puffy coat, I grab my keys and lock my office, all without sneaking a peek into the pool deck in the hopes of seeing Brooke emerge from the locker room.

That night at the city council meeting last summer, I pegged her as an athlete. Her toned arms in that sleeveless shirt and her sleek, muscular thighs made that clear. But a swimmer? From her small frame, I assumed yogini or maybe a former gymnast. As I discovered, she was quite flexible. What's her stroke? I'm betting breaststroke. Imagining the powerful sweep of her thighs as she propels down her lane sends a hot prickle over my skin.

Fuck, I'm already hard and I haven't even had breakfast.

When I exit the pool, my sisters are waiting for me in their fleece-lined deck coats and sweats, both nose-deep into their phones. We walk to the Suburban and climb in so I can drive us home for the second half of our morning routine.

But driving away from the pool brings on a sense of longing, like I should have changed back into my suit and jumped into Brooke's lane for a second workout, just to mess with her. Something in her look told me she's not a recreational swimmer. She's in it to win.

I exhale a slow breath and use the stunning sunrise to ground me.

Soft pink light bathes the Sawtooths, lighting up the patches of snow and the pale granite.

After the short drive through the center of town, I turn west on Cold Springs Road and ascend the short rise, following the creek. Bright sun rays peek over the White Cloud mountains behind me, turning the pale sky into a robin's-egg blue. I savor this moment of peace before turning up the driveway to the home my parents built when I was seven years old. My dad was a master carpenter and all-around pro at fixing anything. He never paid a mechanic or plumber, preferring to do things himself. A pang of grief mixes with gratitude in the place behind my breastbone as I pull the rig to a stop in front of the wrap-around porch. Though Dad wasn't always easy to be around, he taught me a lot, and as a family, we had some crazy adventures. Special memories that will live inside me forever.

I climb the wide steps and slip through the screen and front door. Vonnie and Leah hurry up the stairs to get ready for school. Gideon, my sister Annika's part-psycho cat, curls around my ankles. After a tentative scratch behind the ears, I feed him in the kitchen, satisfied it's spotless, then continue down the hall to my room to change into an oxford and chinos. When I took over parenting duties six years ago, the twins were twelve and Dylan was fourteen. They were living in what I've come to understand as a state of denial. Dad had died the year before in a kayaking accident, and mom was slowly unraveling. None of my three youngest siblings still living at home with her stepped up to be responsible. As if they thought that by waiting for Mom to reclaim her role—making lunches, driving them to their various activities, enforcing their chores, homework, and family obligations—they could pretend that everything was okay. But Mom got worse, and finally, us older siblings made a decision.

"So how are we going to do this?" I asked that fateful night after we checked Mom in and reconvened at the mothership.

Pete, my oldest brother who once was my closest friend, frowned at the senior members of the Morgan clan—me, Annika, and Caleb. "Someone has to take over for mom while she gets help."

"I'll do it!" Annika said, practically jumping out of her chair.

Pete crossed his arms. "No way. What about college?"

"I can go back," Annika protested. "After Mom's better."

"You really think you can handle this, Annika?" I asked. Though she had always been the most nurturing of the eldest Morgans, this was too big a job for a nineteen-year-old. At least this Pete and I could agree on.

Annika blinked away her tears.

"Caleb certainly can't," Pete said, cocking his head at my younger brother.

Weeks before, Caleb's life had been turned upside down with the news he was going to be a parent with his unstable ex, Delaney. Overnight, he broke up with Lori, the love of his life, quit his plans to move to San Diego, and enlisted in the fire academy.

Caleb ran a hand through his hair. "Why not? Just combine all the crazy under one roof."

Pete shook his head. "No, you're going to need help. Add in what's going on with Leah right now and..."

Everyone paused as this sunk in. Leah was going to need special help to get her through, and Caleb could hardly provide that while coping with fatherhood and Delaney.

"You're right," Caleb said with a sigh.

"That leaves me," Pete said with a grimace that whitened his cheeks.

Annika gasped. "But what about medical school?"

Pete swallowed, the motion looking painful. "I'll just defer a year."

"But you're almost done!" Annika said, her gaze flicking to the rest of us.

My gut soured like curdled milk. I couldn't let Pete do this. There was no telling how long Mom would be out of commission. What if she never got better?

"I'll do it," I said as a painful quiver tightened my stomach muscles.

"What?" Annika cried.

"No," Caleb said at the same time.

Pete's mouth hung open for an instant. "Wyatt, you...can't...you've worked hard."

Our eyes met. Even though we hadn't been close since the disaster that made us enemies, there was still a bond there, an understanding.

"I know," I say.

Annika started to cry. "But the Olympics," she said. "Your dream since you were ten years old."

From the top of the stairs, I spied two pairs of eyes watching us—scared ones. My sisters and brother deserved better than what they'd been through. Waiting for mom to get better. Wondering why she was pulling away, drifting from them. They deserved someone to love them and care for them, to set them on the right path. Leah especially. Shoplifting, skipping school. The other two were faring better, but Vonnie had been chronically sick with strep throat or allergies for months, with no one to care for her, while Dylan had thrown himself into hockey and practically lived at the ice rink.

Anger surged through my veins at my mom's neglect. How could she give up on them? Give up on herself?

"Dreams change," I said, forcing my balled fists to relax.

From the top of the stairs, Vonnie cried into Leah's shoulder as she and I locked eyes. Hers were fierce, challenging, but behind all of that was relief.

It was then I knew I'd made the right choice.

"Besides, someone in this family is going to have to make money," I said to Peter. "You're our best bet."

Pete paced in front of the river-rock fireplace. "Fuck," he groaned.

"You know it's the only way," I said, watching him grapple with this plan.

"We'll use the inheritance to pay off your loans," Caleb said to Pete.

"No," Pete and I said together.

"That money's for Mom," I said. "So she can get the care she needs."

Caleb muttered something under his breath, but I let it pass. It was no secret Caleb had already given up on Mom. Probably because she had long since given up on him.

"You really think she can get better?" he asked, and the hope in his voice nearly broke me.

"It's going to take time," I said, judging by the detox and therapy plan drawn up by the social worker at the hospital, but I didn't want to tell them that. "But if she's willing to do the work, yeah, she can get better."

But that's all in the past. As for the "work" Mom needed to do, well, the jury's still out on that.

With a sigh, I tuck in my shirt and buckle my belt, then slip on my street loafers and walk back to the kitchen. While I whip up eggs, my thoughts turn to the editorial meeting I'll be sitting in soon. The one where I'll be introducing Brooke and her new role. Just the thought of seeing her, even though I can't touch her, makes shivers cascade over my skin. What will she wear today?

As I pour the eggs into the hot pan, my daydream is shattered by the shouts coming from upstairs.

"It's my hairbrush, Vonnie!" Leah's muffled voice booms. Likely, they're both in the bathroom vying for time in front of the mirror.

"You stole it!" Vonnie replies. "You lost yours, remember?"

"I did not!" Leah shrieks.

"Let's go, you two!" I shout while folding the eggs around the pan with more force than necessary.

As usual, they ignore me.

Vonnie hurries down the stairs, her cheeks flushed and eyes blazing. Only her twin can put her in this state. Normally Vonnie is the one to back down, to say she's sorry, to try to fix a problem, even one that's not hers. But not when it comes to Leah.

"I swear I'm going to kill her in her sleep one of these days," Vonnie grits out as she hurries past, her sandy blonde curls falling over one shoulder.

"I heard that!" Leah cries from upstairs.

I turn off the burner and scrape my eggs onto a plate. "I hope you're going to be ready to go in five!" I call out to Leah.

"Kiss my bass, Wyatt," Leah says with a groan.

"Just for that it's an extra two hundred meters tomorrow!" I fire back.

Leah groans. "I hate swimming!"

With a chuckle, I grab a fork and pour a cup of coffee. "Keep dissing the sport that turned your life around and it'll be four hundred," I call out.

Leah mutters something I can't hear, which is probably for the best. My blood pressure can only tolerate so much.

While I dig into my breakfast, Leah stomps down the stairs.

"You have a serious power trip issue, don't you?" she says.

"Only with you," I say, though this is a lie. I do have a definite... penchant for control in certain situations.

"See!" she says. "I knew it. You're harder on me than anyone else."

I give her a steely glare. "Because I know you can take it."

From the other side of the kitchen, Vonnie looks up, a pained look in her eyes.

"Shit, sorry, Vonnie," I say, regret dropping over me like a lead blanket.

Vonnie shrugs. "Whatever."

Great, now I've managed to upset Vonnie, the sweet kid who begged me not to compete anymore when she was fourteen because it made her too nervous.

Leah gives me a wicked grin, as if claiming some kind of victory.

Oh, how I will enjoy it when I am no longer their parent and they can be free to make their own choices.

"Let's roll, ladies," I say, refilling my mug and gulping down my last bite of eggs. Vonnie hands one of the bagels she'd made to Leah, who flashes her a look of thanks. We all tuck into our thick winter coats. Leah tugs on a black beanie while Vonnie slides on a pair of wool mittens and matching fleece-lined hat.

"What's with the lucky shirt today?" Vonnie asks as we leave the house. "Is someone famous coming to Penny Creek?"

Damn. I hadn't even realized I'd chosen my blue plaid dress shirt, the one with the yellow and orange accents. The same one I wore to interview Dave Mathews when he came to town for a show at Buck Creek Cabin two years ago. I side-eye Vonnie, wondering if she can read my thoughts, but her eyes are open with curiosity.

"No, just an editorial meeting," I reply as we climb into the rig.

Leah gives my shoulder a punch. "Who are you trying to impress at this meeting?"

I fire up the engine and cruise to the end of the long driveway. "I have to introduce a new journalist to the team, but I'm not trying to impress her."

"Her?" Leah asks, ignoring everything else I said. "Who is it?"

"Where's she from?" Vonnie asks at the same time.

"Is she hot?" Leah asks.

"She's totally hot or he wouldn't be wearing his lucky shirt," Vonnie adds at lightning speed.

I put up my hand to stop them from bombing me with any more questions and to simmer my raging anticipation at seeing Brooke again before they notice.

I swear, the two of them together are like barracudas.

We reach the junction with the highway and I pause to look both ways, then turn south. Before us, the toffee-colored valley opens to the forested hills on the east and west that rise steeply to mountains. Though I will miss the peaceful beauty here when I leave, I will not miss having no personal life, no privacy.

"Come on," Leah groans. "You know we're going to find out anyways."

She's right. Half the town knows about Brooke by now. "She's from Denver. She's here for a few months. For...an assignment."

"And you're going to show her the ropes?" Leah says in a snarky voice.

"Can we meet her?" Vonnie asks.

"No and no," I say as I slow to the 25-mph speed limit in the town's center.

Leah groans and looks out the window. "If you ask her out, we definitely get to meet her."

"Yeah, we have to give her the Morgan stamp of approval."

"Enough, you two," I say. "I'm not asking her out and you don't get to judge her even if I was."

Leah grins wickedly. "Then why are you getting all stiff-lipped?"

"It's twenty-two degrees outside," I say, my fingers tightening on the wheel. "My lips are cold just like yours are."

"Wyatt's got a crush!" Vonnie sings.

I ignore her as I navigate the mayhem of cars at the high school's drop off, waving to the other parents and the staff I've befriended throughout my tenure as elder in chief.

"Out, both of you," I say as I pull to a stop.

"Have a nice meeting," Leah says before sliding out of the car.

"Go learn something," I reply as both of them slam the doors and race off.

"Assholes," I mutter as I watch them go. They're wrong. I'm not crushing on anyone, least of all a big city journalist who thinks she can run my paper. A big city journalist who happens to have the most expressive blue eyes, the most luscious curves, the softest lips.

Nope, I'm not crushing at all.

4

WYATT

I climb the stairs, steeling myself for seeing Brooke. I will not stare at her perfect lips. I will not bait her into a fight so I can enjoy that spark in her eyes. I will focus on the work and not the memory of her taste, her moans.

My preparation crumbles to dust the minute I see her. She's stepping out of my office, her highlighted hair tied back in some kind of twist, exposing her slender neck, her lips a glossy red sheen that stops me cold. That, and she's wearing a pale blue shirt the same color as her eyes, dark pants that look made for her perfect curves, and matching dress shoes. Under one arm is a thin laptop, and in the other hand is a tall white paper cup.

I fight my annoyance. Nobody dresses up in Penny Creek. Then I remember Leah teasing me about my choice of shirt, but that was a total accident. I was distracted.

Yeah, distracted by *her*.

"Good luck getting around in those shoes when it starts snowing, city girl," I say as I come up alongside her, my travel mug of coffee and notebook in hand.

Brooke startles, then seems to recover because she replies, "Thank you for being so concerned with my well-being."

Her clove-and-honey scent makes my taste buds start to water. "I'm thoughtful like that," I reply as we both enter Ike's office.

"Good to know," she replies, settling into the chair at the end of the row facing Ike's desk. Because I've followed her in, I have no choice but to claim the seat next to her. Ike's office isn't exactly large, so the arms of our chairs are only an inch apart. Her scent mixed with the spicy contents of her cup invades my senses. I attempt to lean away but bump into Quinn, our science and environment reporter, who has settled in next to me. I swallow another gulp of coffee.

Ike turns from the white board on the side wall where he had been scribbling and greets us.

Samantha, our events and outdoors writer, and Jenny, in charge of ads and obituaries, enter, their chatter ceasing when they see Brooke.

I take the lead and introduce her. "Guys, this is Brooke Henderson, from the Denver Post."

"She's going to be with us for a few months, while the Gazette merges with Jensen and Thorne Media," Ike adds in his grizzly tone.

Samantha jumps forward, hand extended. "*The* Brooke Henderson?"

Quinn glances at me as if to ask what the hell is going on.

Brooke smiles through a blush that colors her cheeks the exact same shade they were when I had her back arching off the bed.

I shift uncomfortably in my chair, but it doesn't relieve the forceful throb in my dick.

"That's me," Brooke says, standing to shake Samantha's hand, then Jenny's and Quinn's.

"I read your series on that plastic surgeon, and that story about the illegal game park. That must have been so amazing to crack stories like those." Samantha settles into her chair. "You sure you're in the right place? Nothing big ever happens here."

Brooke's smile is tight. "I'll bet plenty happens here."

"Well, I'm sure you don't need any assistance," Samantha says with a quick wink. "But if you do, I'm in the middle cubby."

"That's very nice of you, thank you," Brooke says.

Ike clears his throat, startling Samantha. She turns to see us all staring at her.

"Shall we get on with our meeting?" Ike says.

"Eek, sorry," Samantha says with an embarrassed grimace.

We settle in, notepads at the ready, though Brooke's using her sleek little laptop. How nice for her. I wonder if that's a perk from her big-city job in Denver. Did they buy it for her? Like a signing bonus? My laptop is the same one I had in college and so slow that half the time I just dictate stories into my phone then send them to the computer at the Gazette. I was going to replace it last year, but both Vonnie and Leah needed computers for school.

"Welcome, Brooke," Ike says with a kind smile before eyeing the rest of us over his bifocals. "This gal has more awards than I can count, so don't be a pigheaded asshole around her, got that?"

"Agreed," I mutter with the rest of the team.

Brooke's gaze darts about the room, her cheeks flushed, as if Ike's little speech has made her uncomfortable. Is she trying for modesty? I did some digging. Not only did she earn a Blythe Miller, but a Poe and one for journalistic achievement as a woman. I should be downright impressed, but instead, her accomplishments make me feel like a schmuck. For the past six years, I've been lucky just to keep up with the workload at the paper, running our family's raft guiding company in the summer, coaching year round, and parenting three teenagers. Conjuring the kind of energy required to write crackling, investigative pieces like the ones Brooke's won awards for makes me want to lie down and take a nap.

Brooke inhales a deep breath and smiles. "I'm looking forward to working with you all."

Ike turns back to his giant white board. He picks up a blue dry erase pen and taps the list of running ideas we keep for developing stories. At the top are the words: "CJ Parks/Sawtooth wolves," the story I've been tracking since July when a local rancher tried to frame a biologist for poisoning his sheep in order to get rid of her and terminate her research. It's very personal to me—the biologist who was framed is my brother Caleb's girlfriend, Lori, and is the reason he now spends a lot of time in Missoula, where she's earning her PhD.

"All right," Ike says. "Let's talk story."

We spend the next thirty minutes hashing out ideas for the next edition--high school sports, a hunting accident in the Lost River basin, a house fire last night, and our tiny airport's new de-icing equipment, bought by one of our resident billionaires so he can fly off to Florida whenever he needs to thaw out.

Brooke's fingers fly over her keys, like she's taking notes on all of the stories, even though she doesn't need to. Unless she really is a spy.

"Could that fire be arson?" she asks.

Ike purses his thin lips. "You want to find out?"

"On it," she says, then types something, her face rapt with focus.

"I can get the intel faster," I say.

Both Ike's and Brooke's gazes swing my way. I shrug off the feeling I just stepped in dog shit. "What? It's true. Caleb wasn't on shift last night but he'll know what happened."

Ike lifts a bushy eyebrow. "Introduce Brooke to your brother."

I fight the urge to ball my fists. "Sure," I manage.

Next to me, Brooke's shoulders give a little satisfied wiggle.

To ignore this, I cradle my coffee cup and doodle on my notepad.

"I'll take the hunting accident," Samantha says. "My cousin knows the guy."

Quinn lifts his pencil. "And I've already studied up on the de-icing," he says. "It's actually really cool technology."

Ike scribbles "Q" on the board beside "airport," then turns to me. "Any updates on our rancher?"

"Since the DNA test came back with a match and he posted the million-dollar bail?" I say. "Not much. They're setting the trial date on Thursday though."

Ike crosses his arms and furrows his brow. "Let's run a couple of inches rehashing the story and get a quote from his lawyer."

"That'll be fun," I grunt, making a note in my pad. His lawyer is a cold-blooded jackass.

"Where's the court appearance?" Brooke asks.

"Boise," I reply.

"Don't you think we should be there?"

I give her a sharp look. "That costs money we don't have."

Brooke purses her lips, but glances at Ike, as if searching for confirmation.

"I can get a report from my contact at the Sun," I add.

"It's not the same. This is the biggest story you've got," Brooke warns. "Congress is voting on the Sawtooth Wolf Pack's Endangered Species status soon, right? That makes the stakes even higher."

I hold back from telling her how complicated this story is for me, this town, and my family. CJ Parks and my dad used to be friends. They made a handshake deal about a land use policy that unraveled when Lori challenged him regarding the wolves he perceived as a threat to his livelihood. Then CJ married Caleb's ex, Delaney, Taylor's mom. At the time we were fighting to protect Lori from CJ's crazy plot, Delaney tried to kidnap Taylor. Though Caleb didn't want to press charges, she's been banned from getting anywhere near him. So, yeah, complicated doesn't even quite cover it.

"Maybe we can scrape some funds together when it goes to trial," Ike says, letting me know with a look that he understands my struggles. We argued about it when the story first broke. He wanted to give it to Quinn, said I was too close to it. But I have better stamina for a story like this—I'm like a bulldog that won't let go, and I need to be the one to protect my family.

"I noticed your events page is looking a little thin," Brooke says, batting her dark lashes as she sips from her paper cup.

"It's winter," I say with a snort. "It's always thin."

Brooke sets her cup down on Ike's desk, the lid stained red by her lips. I get a shock of memory of how those red lips looked sliding down my cock and practically choke on my spit.

Get a grip, asshole.

I coax in a slow breath and count to five the way I used to as a teenager in math class with a boner I desperately wanted to hide.

"What about the arts? The library?" Brooke asks. "Book signings? I would think that in winter, people need things to look forward to more than ever."

"That's the fuckin' truth," Quinn mutters.

Ike points at Brooke. "I'm glad you brought up the calendar because I got a tip from my wife. She's in the Art Guild. Guess who's coming to Penny Creek for their Artist in Residence this winter?"

I gulp the last of my coffee and move on to my to-do list. The Artist in Residence program is nothing newsworthy and isn't my beat.

Ike's gaze sweeps the room. "Hazel Gunn."

My throat closes around my gulp of lukewarm coffee. I start choking and have to clamp my hand over my mouth. Someone hands me a napkin. Someone else hands me a bottle of water.

"Need me to call 9-1-1?" Quinn asks, clapping me on the back.

I wave him off and manage to get in a breath between spasms. I wipe my face and the front of my coat, which is spattered with coffee. At least my shirt was spared, but I'll have to grab my extra coat from home if I leave the office for any interviews.

"You okay?" Brooke asks, her silky eyebrows furrowed.

"Fine," I say in a garbled tone. I swallow a long drink of water, then look around at the concerned faces. "Really guys, I'm fine. Wrong pipe."

Fuck. Hazel Gunn, coming back to Penny Creek? All these years, I've kept her secret, even though it destroyed my relationship with Pete. I heard she became an artist, but I had no idea she was famous enough to land the Artist in Residence.

Ike taps the white board pen against his desk. "All right, let's get to work."

Everyone gathers their things and shuffles for the door.

"Wyatt," Ike says when I'm halfway there.

I stop and let Brooke pass, her enticing scent following her.

Once the room has emptied, Ike regards me with concern. "I got a call from the editor at the news desk at the L.A. Times."

That was fast.

"You sure about this?" he asks.

I nod. "Yeah," I reply, smoothing the front of my coat. "I hope you'll support my decision."

He eyes me, his watery blue eyes like a hawk's. "I've decided to retire in May," he says. "You're the best qualified for my job."

I clench my lips together. "Thank you, that means a lot."

"But you're still set on leaving?"

"Yes," I say. "I've waited a long time for this."

Ike tilts his head. "True."

A tense silence stretches between us. Ike has been with me every step of the way at the Gazette. He's mentored me with patience while also challenging me, pushing me. And he's been a friend when things were hard. I'm definitely in his debt, but I'm not going to take a job I don't want just to please him. It's high time I took care of myself.

"All right then," Ike says, then gives me a slow nod. "I'll do what I can to help you."

5

BROOKE

I stand frozen just outside Ike's door, my heart tapping hard against my chest. I didn't mean to overhear, but I've always had "elephant ears" as my dad calls them. This skill has definitely come in handy—I can hear things most people can't. When I was a kid, I was able to memorize the stories my dad read aloud after hearing them only a few times. And now, as a journalist, when I interview someone, I only need to write down a few cues to recall what was said.

But I'm not sure I wanted this knowledge about Wyatt. There's only one job opening up at the Times this spring—a reporter is taking a year-long sabbatical to write a book. Even though the job to fill his position will only be temporary, it's a foot in the door. A foot I've earned.

I force myself to continue walking, and enter Wyatt's office, my mind spinning. Wyatt thinks he can steal this job from me? I grit my teeth. Let him try.

"You okay?" Wyatt asks from the doorway.

I take a second to regain my composure. "Yes, why?"

He hangs his coat over the back of his chair, then settles into it. "Why the hell do you take so many notes? Ike only assigned you two stories."

"It's called paying attention," I reply, my voice too sharp.

In one instant, his eyes turn from concerned to challenging. "There's a coffee shop in the building across the street," he says. "It's a nice place to work sometimes."

"Are you kicking me out?" I ask.

He cocks his head. The feisty gleam in his eyes makes my ovaries flutter.

"Are we having our first fight?" he asks, linking his hands behind his head and leaning back.

I force a breath through my nose. How can he just sit there watching me like I'm his next meal? "Why? So we can skip to making up?"

Heat flashes in his eyes. "My favorite part."

I grab the reins controlling my raging lust and pull back. Hard. "Sorry, I didn't mean that."

He barks out a laugh. "Liar."

My heart is beating a hundred miles an hour as I try to navigate us back into the "friendly rivalry at work" zone. "I can't...work like this," I manage.

Wyatt pushes off from his chair and approaches. "Work like what?" he asks, stopping just inches from me, his voice deep and firm in that commanding way that turns my willpower to jelly.

Does he know what that voice does to me? His body heat fills the narrow gap between us, making my skin tingle. My fingers itch with the need to glide up his chest. I long to lower my lips to his collarbone and plant kisses to his shoulder, then down his muscular arms. Good Lord, how am I going to withstand this kind of torture for three whole months?

I coax in a steadying breath. "I can't think when I feel like I'm seconds away from kissing you."

He walks to his door and shuts it, then returns to pierce me with his sharp blue eyes. "What would be so bad about kissing me?"

"Everything," I say, my chest tightening.

"Don't give me a shit answer like that, Brooke," he says, as if he's angry. Which makes me want to breathe fire.

But the sound of my name coming from his lips does something to me. Mixes the anger and pent-up frustration with a decadent heat, forming a lusty, raw craving that makes my toes curl inside my shoes.

Someone please take me outside and shoot me because I'm in so much trouble.

"I have a job to do," I say, forcing strength into my tone. "One that's very important to me."

"And letting me cure that little ache building inside you is going to somehow get in the way of that?" he replies in a low purr.

It's as if he's talking directly to my body, because the empty, achy place he's speaking of, the same he filled so expertly months ago, responds with a throbbing pulse that shoots sparks to the roots of my hair.

"Yes, Wyatt," I say, breathing fast now. I need to get out of this room, before I do something I'm going to regret. "I think it's best if we try to be colleagues."

His eyebrows shoot up. "And that's going to work when what you really want is for me to bend you over this desk?"

My mouth drops open, but at the same time, heat surges into my core. I step back, managing not to trip on my heels—a shock considering how off-balance I feel right now.

Quinn leans into Wyatt's office, a reminder that this a public place, our voices loud enough to be overheard. "Hey, I got the photographer set up for shots of the airport, you need him for anything else today?"

Wyatt shakes his head.

"No, thank you," I reply, and scoop up my laptop.

Quinn disappears.

"Maybe I will check out that coffee shop," I say because I have to get out of this room. "Thank you for the recommendation."

"Wait," Wyatt says as I'm turning away.

He grabs his coat. "Stay, okay? I have to go out anyway." He indicates the speckles of coffee he sprayed on the fabric of his shirt.

"So we're good?" I ask like the needy side of me takes the reins.

He slides his laptop and notepad into a messenger bag and slings it over his shoulder. "Sweetheart, you know we're good," he croons, his eyes glittering playfully.

I can't help but smile at this, then clamp my lips shut and shake my head at him.

With a wink, he strides for the door.

"Tell me why you choked when Ike said that artist's name," I say to his back.

He pauses, but only for a split second, then reaches for the door. "It's a name I haven't heard in a long time, is all," he says, glancing only halfway back so I get his profile. And then he disappears into the hallway.

I collapse into the extra chair, feeling like I've just sprinted a 200 IM. Will every day with him be this exhausting?

An hour later, I have the fire chief on speaker while I jot down notes about the house fire the night before.

"We don't have a fire investigator here," Chief Houghton says with a chuckle. "If something big happened, the state would send someone from Boise or Pocatello."

"Arson isn't big enough?" I ask, adding a reminder to get Wyatt to introduce me to his firefighter brother.

"Hold on, I never said this was arson."

"But you said it burned hot," I counter. "Doesn't that indicate the use of an accelerant?"

He utters an uneasy sigh. "Could be there was something highly flammable inside the kitchen. The guy is a mechanic, after all."

"You think he was repairing engines in his kitchen?"

"Honestly, it wouldn't surprise me. I've pretty much seen it all, Ms. Henderson."

"Okay," I reply with a sigh. "When will you know if arson is involved?"

"Hopefully in a few days, maybe a week."

I resolve myself to a few inches recapping the facts. Not the splash I was hoping for on my first byline. "Have you had any other suspicious fires recently?"

"No," the chief replied.

We end the call and I cross my legs, bouncing the top one as I think. My phone chimes. It's a text from Wyatt. His brother Caleb's contact info is below a simple message:

Coffee?

I stare at the screen while my pulse accelerates. I could use more caffeine after my early start today, but getting it with Wyatt is a bad idea. Especially after his "bend you over my desk" comment.

My fingers move before I can stop them. *Where?*

You think you can handle walking a few blocks in those shoes?

I'm capable of more than you'll ever know

I'd like to see that in action

I slam my phone down before I can reply *I'll bet you would.*

I cannot take his bait like this.

That empty place inside me, the one he so easily knew how to satisfy, begins to throb again.

Resist.

I shake off the way my core has begun to tighten, and slip into my full-length down coat, the one I'll never need again in L.A.

The realization grounds me and is yet another good example that I need to squash my yearning to strip Wyatt Morgan naked in order to rock this opportunity. I won't let him steal what's rightfully mine. Fluttery ovaries be damned.

I pack up my laptop and slide it into my leather satchel, then leave the office, using the distance to the downstairs exit to build another layer of armor.

I expect him to text me an address, but he's leaning against the side of the building outside the leaded glass doors. When he sees me, he smiles, his soft lips curling upwards just enough to make his eyes sparkle. He pushes off the wall and begins walking. I join him but keep my distance, determined to show him my strength.

"You're either breaststroke or long-distance freestyle," he says, eyeing me.

His gait is unhurried, but his legs are much longer than mine so I'm practically speed-walking to keep up.

"Breaststroke," I say. "Middle distance."

A car passes by, the studs in the snow tires ticking on the pavement. We turn a corner and pass a line of small shops. A wine and beer store, a curio shop with a family of stuffed moose and quirky t-shirts in the window.

"Where'd you go to school?" Wyatt asks.

"Colorado College," I reply, my heels grinding against the fine grit coating the sidewalk.

"Is that where you grew up?" he asks.

"Wait, what are you doing?" I ask, giving him a sharp look.

He pretends to look offended. "I'm getting to know you, isn't that what colleagues do?"

"Not if the end goal is office sex," I say, increasing my pace.

"Come on," he groans. "I get that you're...conflicted...but—"

"There is nothing conflicting about this," I say.

He slides his hand around my bicep and steers me into a narrow walkway between two buildings. "Okay, whoa," he says in a stern tone. "I'm getting this feeling like I'm the enemy here, and I don't like it."

"You don't have to like it," I say, my skin prickling from the way he's touching me. It's not forceful, but it's demanding, firm. I tell myself I'm reacting to the cold, not the way his eyes are lit with that mix of determination and lust.

"I'm only reading your signals," he says. "Why does that make me the bad guy?"

I huff a sigh. *Because you make me want things I shouldn't.* "Because I can't trust myself when I'm around you."

I expect his eyes to light up with greed or hunger, but instead, what I see is compassion. "Maybe there's a reason for that. One that needs addressing."

My blood thumps thick in my throat. "Wyatt."

He lets go of my arm but moves closer. I take a step back but find the solid brick wall of the building.

"We don't have to start anything serious," he says. "You're leaving, right? And I..." he trails off.

My curiosity surges to life. "You're what?"

34

He lifts his chin, as if coming to some kind of decision. "I'm busy with my family, and coaching."

I had thought he would tell me about the Times job. That he doesn't hurts somehow, though I have no claims to feel this way. "So you're saying we can just pick up where we left off."

His eyes light up and he taps his chin. "What a brilliant idea."

"It's a terrible idea," I say in a stern voice. Especially now that I know that we're both competing for the same job, one I won't back down from. "I can't get distracted."

"Wouldn't you be less distracted if I made you come right now?" he asks. "I know it would do wonders for me."

"Right now?" I ask, glancing in either direction, but the narrow walkway is empty. We're five feet away from the sidewalk and street. There's hardly any traffic, but there's no way he's serious.

Wait, is he?

"How?" I ask, my chest heaving inside my coat.

His left eyebrow arches. "How would I make you come?"

I swallow but the thick feeling in my throat doesn't go away. "Yes," I breathe.

He places a hand on the wall next to me and leans close. "First, I would kiss you right behind your ear. Softly at first, until you start making those needy little sounds."

"What sounds?" I ask.

His lips are so close to my ear that if I turned, we'd kiss, but I force myself to be still. He's just talking. Maybe if I let him work through this, he'll be satisfied and leave me alone.

"Those sounds that tell me you want more."

I clench my eyes shut to block the image of how I begged him. I've never been like that with anyone, so desperate, so unhinged. It felt so good to let go that way, to give in to the secret desires I've kept inside for so long.

"And then I'd glide my fingers up the inside of your thighs and touch you. Barely. Rubbing back and forth. You'll want me closer. You'll want it harder. So I'll slide my fingers inside your panties where you're wet and trembling. I'll touch you, stroke you. I'll play with your hard little clit, rubbing it until it's so achy and needy that you think you're going to burst. And then I'll dip my fingers inside you and suck right here—"

His lips wrap around the tip of my earlobe, sending a shock wave of desire straight to the throbbing hollow between my thighs.

"Stroking that place inside you that's begging for my touch. That needs to be fucked. You'll ride my fingers until you come. And then I'll suck every last drop of your taste off me."

Oh my God, it's so dirty. So dirty but so hot. I release a shuddering breath but my whole body is tingling, burning, my empty core pulsing. For him.

"And then what?" I ask, my heart thumping fast inside my chest.

I can't see his face, but I can hear the smile in his voice. "And then we can get back to work, and we can both concentrate."

"You're not actually serious," I say, still trying to get my breathing under control.

He chuckles. "Why don't we try it and find out? Call it...research."

I give an anguished moan. "Not here," I say, then try to take it back. What am I doing? I cannot hook-up with Wyatt Morgan, aka my sort-of boss and as of this afternoon, my rival. "I didn't mean that," I say.

"Then why are you panting in my ear?"

"Damn it," I grit out, turning away. "If you think I'm throwing away my opportunity for another night in the sack—"

"Another night in the sack?" he asks, his eyes narrowing. "You make us sound like two people who had some casual fuck. That's not what happened, and you know it."

I blink. He's right, though I had assumed I was casual to *him*. That it meant more makes my resolve that much harder to defend.

But I can't show him that.

I lean in so my lips are an inch from his ear. "Okay, cowboy, let's say you're the best I ever had," I say, savoring the way his shoulders jolt. "But there's no chance in hell I'll let it happen again."

To my complete fury, he laughs. "You are so cute when you're worked up. I'm going to remember that."

I glare at him. "You can remember all you want, you disgustingly chipper morning person who is way too handsome for his own good." I put my hand on his chest to push him back, or maybe to steady myself. But before I can push him away, he covers my hand with his and holds me there. Beneath his clothing, his chest is solid, sculpted, and brings back the stolen moments when I touched him there, kissed him, caressed every inch of him.

He reaches up and tucks a stray hair behind my ear. I should slap his hand away, but my body betrays me, just like it has since I stepped into his office yesterday.

"Go ahead and resist me," he says in a soft voice. "It will only make this worse."

"Make what worse?" I ask, my voice pained.

He smiles. "That little need inside you. You'll try to shut it down but it won't work because you know I'm the only one who can make it better." He stares me down. "Let me make it all better, Brooke. Let me make it all go away."

I want to scream "uncle!" because he's right. Nobody has ever made me feel so good. But there's no way I can give in and still accomplish my goal. Losing the Times job would be a disaster I can't afford. I need all my sacrifices to finally mean something. I let my guard down with Hugh and I'm never doing anything that stupid again.

"No, Wyatt. If anyone found out we—" I barely stop myself from using the present tense. "—were together last summer, it would make my job impossible. I'm already an outsider. I can hardly expect the community to open their souls to me if they think I open my legs for the first guy I meet."

My face flushes with heat because isn't that exactly what I did six months ago?

He laughs in that rich, hearty tone, as if this is actually funny. "Is that what you're so afraid of?" He slides a hand over my hip. I remember those hands. Big and firm, his fingers wickedly skilled. "What if we kept it a secret?"

I ignore the tingling in my core ignited by his touch. "Secrets have a way of leaking out," I say. "You know this as well as I do. Our jobs depend on it."

His lips tighten into a grimace. "You're right," he says, his shoulders relaxing in what looks like defeat. "Fuck."

"So, are we through here?"

6

WYATT

"Yeah, we're through," I say, sucking in a breath of the dusty, cold air of the breezeway. Maybe I misread her, or maybe she's changed her mind.

But I get it. This is a small town. No secret is safe.

I indicate with a sweep of my hand for her to lead the way out of the alley. "Do I need to warn them to hide the knives or can we have that coffee in peace?"

"I don't drink coffee," she says as we exit the alley.

I steer us to the crosswalk. "Seriously? What kind of journalist doesn't drink coffee?"

"The kind that drinks tea," she says.

"I guess I'll be performing an intervention, then," I say as the light changes. "Come on."

She doesn't budge, instead fixing me with a sharp glance that's edged with fear. "You don't get to be right about everything."

I cross my arms. "I'm right when it counts."

She gives me a narrow gaze.

"I'm sorry," I say, though I'm only sorry she's so torn up. I'm not sorry for making her feel something. Our spark is still there, the way she looked at me in that alley is proof. "You know what you have to do to make it stop."

Her shoulders slump. "Please," she whispers.

The defeat in her tone gets to me. "I'm not going to stop wanting you, Brooke. I'll be ready for you when you change your mind."

"I won't."

I need to back off. "Okay, then, *colleague*, let's get that coffee."

"Tea," she says as the color returns to her cheeks.

So she doesn't hate me enough to want to completely avoid spending time with me. There is hope.

We cross the main street and head toward the west side of town. I fight back the craving to take her slender hand in mine.

"What's your stroke?" she asks as we wait to cross another street.

"The four hundred free," I reply as a car whizzes past. "And the eight hundred. I was also the anchor on a medley relay."

She tilts her head. "Where'd you go to school?"

"University of Oregon," I reply, and name the elite club I also swam with.

Her eyes widen in surprise. "Wasn't that the same club that sent an entire relay team to the Olympics?"

I chew on my lower lip. "Yes."

"Did you know them?"

I become aware that I'm walking faster and try to slow down. We turn left at the next block and I steer us towards the Growly Bear, the single-story log house that's been a bakery for more than thirty years and is now owned and operated by my sister, Annika.

"Yeah, I know them." Two of them will likely never talk to me again. The third is my friend Marshall and is the reason I know about the upcoming opportunity at the L.A. Times—he works in their HR department.

"Wow," Brooke says as we reach the gravel pullout leading to the wide wooden steps so weathered in the center the varnish is practically white. "I made it to Nationals my senior year of college, but I only placed into the top twenty."

The top twenty is still an incredible achievement. How does she do it? She's so tiny. "I was gone by then," I say. We climb the steps and I push open the door for her.

She gives me a startled look, but it passes.

Because we're smack dab in the middle of Slack and it being late morning, the Bear is mostly empty. The calico curtains are drawn back to let in the sunlight, and although it's pale compared to July's, the dark wood interior glows. To our left is a counter with four built-in stools facing an espresso machine. Behind it, a broad window gives a view of the bakery. Annika isn't present, but two of her minions buzz around, opening bins, unloading pans from the oven, mixing dough.

"It smells heavenly," Brooke says as we walk up to the register. Her stomach growls and she laughs softly. "Maybe it's time for breakfast."

"You haven't eaten yet?" I ask, my mouth hanging open.

"I never eat in the morning. Tea is all I need."

How I'd like to challenge that. "By the time I get home after practice, I'm coming unglued."

She frowns. "I wondered why you weren't in your office when I got in."

"Yeah, I have to go home not just to eat, but my sisters need to get ready for school."

She gives me a quizzical look. "How old are your sisters?"

"Seventeen."

Before she can ask her questions, the young woman behind the counter smiles at us. "What can I get you?"

I order drip coffee and the last almond butter-tahini power ball.

Brooke orders English Breakfast tea with steamed milk, a smoked ham and provolone sandwich, and a Cowboy Cookie the size of a small plate—Annika's specialty.

Damn. I do like a woman with an appetite. I reach for my wallet but Brooke has already slid her card across the counter.

"No way," I say, giving the young woman about to slide Brooke's card through the reader a sharp look.

"What?" Brooke asks. "It's the least I can do for barging in here and forcing you to take orders from me."

"Who says I'm taking orders from you?" I ask. Though if we were naked right now, my answer would be much different.

The young woman watches both of us, unsure what to do.

"Here," I say to her, extending my card.

"I'm trying to do something nice, Wyatt!" she says, exasperated.

"I appreciate the gesture, but just…no."

The young woman takes my card and swipes it, then slides both cards back.

With a huff, Brooke tucks her card into her leather wallet, then drops it into her oversized purse. Seeing her flustered is worth making her frustrated. Her cheeks redden and her eyes flash, like she's about to set the place on fire with her eyes.

I sign the receipt and scoop up our number and my mug of coffee. "You can pick the table," I say.

Brooke strides to my favorite, the one with a giant window looking out to the jagged Sawtooths rising above the foothills.

"How's this?" she asks, turning back to me.

I drink in her tight curves and the way her hair catches the light. "It's perfect," I say.

If she detects the lusty tone in my voice, she's good at hiding it. We unzip our coats and settle into the booth. I try not to get caught watching her by raising my mug to my lips. The coffee here is just the way I like it—not too strong or burnt, just good, solid, and dependable. The kind you could drink all day. Like if you were gearing up for an all-nighter with a spry and sassy little brunette.

I almost laugh out loud. Like I would need caffeine to stay awake for another night with Brooke.

The woman from the counter comes to the table carrying Brooke's tea. "Your order will be right out."

Brooke blows across the surface of the mug, her red lips forming a delectable pucker, the heat from the tea turning the tip of her nose a rosy pink. Something so simple should not make my skin itch, but fuck, I want to touch her. I want those lips on mine.

"Why are you in charge of your sisters? Do your parents work?" she asks, finally taking a tiny sip of her tea while I drool.

I run my index finger around the rim of my cup. "My dad passed away when they were eleven and my mom's...not here."

Brooke takes another tiny sip, her blue eyes watching me thoughtfully. "I'm sorry to hear that," she says softly.

"Thanks," I say.

An uncomfortable silence stretches between us. Before I can fill it, a server brings out Brooke's food and my snack.

"That's all you're eating?" Brooke asks, tucking her napkin onto her lap.

I take a bite. "They don't call it a power ball for nothing. There's almond butter, tahini, honey, protein powder. One of these babies and I'll be good for a few hours. When the team travels, I have Annika make me a Tupperware bin of them for my swimmers."

"Who's Annika?" she asks.

"My sister. She runs the show here."

Her eyebrows rise. "How many sisters do you have?"

"Just three." I sit back and cross my arms. "But I also have three brothers."

"Wait. Seven kids?" she says, her tea mug poised halfway to her mouth.

I nod, bracing myself for the usual onslaught of comments, but Brooke tilts her head, a compassionate expression in her eyes. "That must have been intense."

I sip my coffee. "It was at times."

"Coaching must be sort of natural for you, after having so many siblings growing up," she says before taking a bite of her sandwich.

I hadn't really thought of it like that before, but she's right. "I needed an outlet when I moved back. Swimming was always what grounded me. When I quit competing, I thought helping others might help replace it. The club coach was moving at the end of the year, so I offered to take over."

A blob of mustard smears onto her finger. She gives it a lick with the tip of her tongue.

Thankfully, I catch the groan before it leaves my throat.

When she glances up for my answer, her eyes freeze.

43

Busted.

I pinch my lips together and look away. Is it my fault that watching her lips and fingers and tongue is completely fucking fascinating?

"Why did you give up competing?" she asks with a curious look.

I keep forgetting that she's a journalist. That her hungry mind will dig deep down for every last shred of detail. I don't have to know her well to understand this about her. She didn't earn those awards by leaving stones unturned. It reminds me of her questions about Hazel, and I quickly shove my memories down in case she has X-ray vision. I swore to keep Hazel's secret. It's hers to reveal, not mine.

That's going to get complicated when Hazel shows up in Penny Creek.

"It was just time," I reply.

She looks like she's about to ask more, but doesn't. After a sip of her tea, she asks, "Why not coach high school?"

At least I have a good answer for this one. "When I returned home, my sisters and I all needed swimming. They weren't old enough for the high school team, plus it's seasonal and I wanted them in the pool year-round." Or rather, I wanted Leah in the pool full time. She needed structure and a way to reconnect with herself. Swimming has helped Vonnie too, though in more subtle ways. I know it's definitely helped me, being able to give back to the sport that molded me into the person I am now.

"So you forced them to join the team?"

"Go ahead and call me a barbarian, but things were pretty fucked up when I returned home. Swimming has always grounded me. I figured it might work for them."

Brooke pauses, as if sensing the mental gymnastics I'm doing. "Has it worked?"

I cross one leg over the other and tap the rim of my mug. "So far, yeah. But it ain't over till the fat lady sings," I say.

She raises a slender eyebrow, creating a sultry kind of glimmer in her eyes. It makes my pulse throb deep in my gut, creating a low buzz that makes the air seem electric, like I could create a spark with a snap of my fingers.

"They both have to graduate in May for me to claim it as a success," I explain.

"Winning or going to Junior Nationals doesn't count as a success?" she asks, then takes another bite.

"Nope. I care that they commit and try hard. That they learn discipline. Vonnie likes swimming but competing makes her anxious, so she comes along to meets as my assistant. Leah's in it to win and she does locally, but she's never wanted to compete beyond that because she knows she'll lose."

Brooke tilts her head to peer at me. "And she's not discouraged by that? I think I'd quit."

I shrug. "Quitting's not an option and she knows it."

"Huh," Brooke says, gazing into the cup in her hands.

"Go ahead and judge," I say, my jaw hardening.

She looks up, surprised. "No, I'm not judging you at all. I was more, I don't know, impressed." She sets her cup down. "You seem to care very much for your family. I guess I wasn't expecting that."

I can't help but smile. "You'd rather think of me as the asshole coworker, huh?"

Her shoulders slump. "I don't think that either."

I'm about to ask what she does think of me when she says, "Thanks for introducing me to your brother. The firefighter."

"Sure," I say, gulping down a sip of my now lukewarm coffee. "Do they think it's arson?" I ask, popping the last of my snack into my mouth.

She grimaces and sets her sandwich down, then wipes her hands on her napkin. "They won't know for a few more days, maybe as long as a week."

I nod. Things move slow in Penny Creek. It's good she's learning that now. "What else are you working on?"

She sips her coffee, looking thoughtful. "I'm curious about Hazel. Guess how much one of her paintings costs."

At least this time I manage to keep my coffee in my throat. "Enlighten me."

"Her last gallery showing, she sold four of them for over fifty thousand. Each."

I gaze beyond Brooke to the ripsaw ridgeline of the Sawtooths as a pulse of gratitude washes through me. Thank goodness Hazel got out of Penny Creek. Thank goodness she had a chance to start fresh. I don't want to think of the alternative. "That's amazing," I say.

Brooke rattles off more Hazel facts she's likely found from Google. I nod with encouragement, but my mind returns to the confusing night I found Hazel curled up in my car, her face a tear-stained mess.

"I wonder why it's taken her so long to come back to Penny Creek," Brooke is saying. "I mean, so many of her paintings seem to have been inspired by the landscape here."

I shrug. "Sounds like she's been busy."

"You knew her," Brooke says, eyeing me curiously.

My spine stiffens. She caught me off guard. "Sure, Rogue Valley High isn't very big."

She gets a pensive look on her face, like she's chewing on a detail she can't quite place, but then it's gone. "She moved away in the middle of her junior year. That seems like a strange time to change schools. Why not stay until she graduated?"

"Are you going to ask her that?" I say, keeping my voice casual.

Brooke nods vigorously. "I tried to reach her for an interview, but her agent says she doesn't do them."

"Huh." I sip my coffee.

Brooke's eyes narrow like a cobra's. "I'll get through to her. I want to know why she disappeared in the middle of her junior year. What if there's a story there?"

My gut flips. "I'm sure it's no big mystery. Maybe one of her parents got a job."

"In San Luis Obispo?" Brooke asks. "There's, like, zero industry there."

"Her parents probably got sick of the cold here. It happens."

She sets her coffee down. "I can definitely relate to that one."

Relief at the change of subject makes it easier to breathe. "Really? Colorado's plenty cold."

"Not like this," she says with a tiny shiver. "And supposedly it's only going to get worse."

"Maybe you just need someone to warm you up," I say, then remember I'm supposed to be her *colleague*.

She gives me a warning look. "You ever think about leaving?"

"Every day," I say as a tightness stitches my ribs together.

"You seem so at home here."

"I grew up here," I say. "It is home. Always will be. But once the twins graduate, there's no reason for me to stay."

"Where will you go?"

I'm not jinxing my shot at the Times by blabbing about it. I'm not even supposed to know there's an opening. "Not sure," I say, staring into my empty coffee cup.

She lifts her tea and takes a slow sip, then licks her lips.

That flick of her little pink tongue is impossible to look away from. "What about you?" I ask to refocus. "You surely have big plans. The Denver Post isn't your end game, I'm betting."

"Jensen and Thorne own many media outlets."

I suppose I should know this, but keeping track of stuff like this seems pointless. Unless you're a hotshot journalist wanting to impress your boss. Realization dawns on me. "That's why you're here," I say softly. "Your assignment at the Gazette is a bargaining chip, isn't it?"

She swallows, her slender neck tensing. "Yes."

"You do a good job here, and you get to write your ticket to wherever you want."

"It's...not quite that simple."

"Where do you want to go, Brooke?" I ask, imagining her behind a big, glossy desk in some corner office with a huge window overlooking a sprawling city. She hates the cold, so...Honolulu? Phoenix?

Her eyes flash with a steely resolve. "The L.A. Times."

7

BROOKE

"Good for you," Wyatt says, leaning back. He looks away, a tiny muscle in his jaw flexing. Gone is the playful spark, the teasing edge to his voice.

"Well, I better get going," he says, and slides out of the bench.

I should say something to smooth things over, but what would that be? Maybe this is the perfect solution to him hounding me. He'll really think I'm the enemy now. I should feel relieved, but I don't—it's much more complicated than that.

"Ike and I do a wrap at four," he adds, sliding on his coat. "I'm sure you'll want to be there."

"I will be," I say, my voice so soft I wonder if he hears me.

With that, Wyatt scoops up his plate and mug and walks to the bus tub. I don't watch, but I hear his dishes clank into the tub, then the squeak of the door to the porch. Through the window, I watch him descend the steps and walk down the street with long strides, his shoulders tight.

I can't help but feel bad. He obviously wants the job in L.A. From the sound of it, he gave up a lot to help raise his siblings. Now that they're grown, he's ready to spread his wings. I get it, but I can't get soft. I've earned my shot too, and I'm going to take it.

After asking the server to wrap up the rest of my sandwich and the half of the cookie I'll save for this afternoon, I push through the door to the chilly sunshine and breathe the crisp fall air deep into my lungs.

It's time to refocus. Wyatt will leave me alone now and that's what I want.

Story ideas begin to unfurl and an excited little flutter tickles my belly. Purpose floods my veins and I march down the wide planks, my to-do list growing with every step.

IT'S late afternoon and I'm typing furiously to meet the four o'clock deadline. Though I still don't have an interview with Hazel Gunn, I did some research, and then I was lucky enough to land a story about a helicopter crash in the White Clouds. I could have used Wyatt's local knowledge for the story, but he's been gone all day. I have the feeling Ike would have given him the assignment if he was here. But that's okay. I'll prove my worth, just like I always do.

My phone rings just as I type out the final sentence on the crash piece.

I pounce on my phone when I see the caller ID.

"Dad!" I say.

"How's my girl?" he asks in his smooth, easy voice.

Warmth fills me. "I'm good. I just put my last story to bed."

"Way to go, tiger," he replies. In the background, the tea kettle whistles. The longing to be back in our kitchen having tea together after work catches me off guard, but it's there, an achy throb in my chest. "Settling in okay, then?"

"Yes, so far so good."

"They giving you a hard time?" he asks.

I slide off my shoes and pull up my knees in Wyatt's chair. "No, everyone's been great." I'm not sure Wyatt's behavior qualifies as "great" but there's no sense in sharing that.

"If they want to keep their paper, they'll treat you like royalty."

"No way," I say. "I don't want special treatment."

The rattle of his teaspoon against the rim of the mug chimes through the phone lines.

"Well, they'll soon realize what a gift you're giving them."

"Dad," I groan. My screensaver slideshow flashes to life on my laptop. The first is an image of palm trees and pale sand facing a crystalline blue ocean. The first thing I'm going to do when I move to L.A. is go to the beach. Because of competing, I've traveled to both coasts, but it's not like they gave us free time to lounge at the beach between events.

"How was class today?" I ask him.

"Oh, the usual. Senior comp had a big essay due so I've got plenty of grading. Freshman English is still a disaster. They can't even write complete sentences. What the hell are they teaching them in middle school?"

"They're likely too busy keeping them in line to teach them very much," I reply. This makes me think of Wyatt trying to keep his twin sisters in line. It's no surprise he turned to swimming.

My dad gives a tired sigh. "Better them than me, that's for sure."

"How's your book coming?" I ask. "Did you get any writing time this weekend?"

"Nah," he says with an evasive huff. "Your mother and I hiked Lincoln Peak, and then well…the trees needed pruning."

I hold back the disappointment in my tone when I reply, "There's always next weekend." I keep telling him it's not too late to finish the novel he's been tinkering with since before I was born, but he's as stubborn as I am.

"Exactly," he says. "So what are you writing about? Penny Creek's pretty small, isn't it?"

"Yeah, but there's enough going on."

"Enough to keep their paper edition?"

"I don't know yet. Winter is much slower, but it's also an opportunity for deeper stories. I've skimmed the archive collections. In the summer, there's so many things happening. Music festivals and fly-fishing demonstrations and wildfires and conflicts over land use." The screensaver flashes a picture of my parents and me smiling and hugging each other outside of Giorgio's, the fancy Italian restaurant where we celebrated my promotion at the Denver Post three years ago.

"Do you know the artist Hazel Gunn?" I ask.

"Hmm. Isn't she supposed to be the next Georgia O'Keefe?"

"That's what they say," I reply with a chuckle. "She's coming to Penny Creek for an Artist in Residence program."

"Why? Doesn't she have enough money that she doesn't need a handout like that?"

"The winter residence program is very prestigious. They've offered it to her before, but she's turned it down."

"Any idea why?"

"No, and I won't until she talks to me."

"Attagirl," my dad replies.

"We'll see. Supposedly, she doesn't talk to journalists. Wyatt thinks she's just really private."

"Who's Wyatt?" my dad asks.

My face floods with heat. "He's the writer I've been partnered with at the Gazette."

"You don't need a partner," my dad says in his no-nonsense voice.

"It's not like that," I say quickly, fighting the sensation that I've been here before—Hugh and how I gave up the promotion in San Francisco.

"Just so long as he knows you have the upper hand," my dad replies.

"He understands, Dad," I say, my voice shaky.

"Good." My dad slurps his tea. "I remembered something about that town today. A guy disappeared there. A youth pastor. Must have been six, seven years ago? Anyway, last month, some kids found his bones in an old mine shaft."

My pulse accelerates and a familiar itch awakens in the back of my brain. "That was Penny Creek?"

He chuckles. "He was found closer to a little town called Garnet, so the story would be easy to miss," he says after another sip of his tea. "Plus, I seem to recall that you had your hands full at that time."

"The plastic surgeon piece," I say. For three months I lived and breathed that story.

"Anyways, the case never closed. They thought he just took off, but now they're not so sure. The bones are being examined by a forensic anthropologist."

"What, they think it was foul play?" I say with a shudder.

"They don't know. He was wearing hiking clothes and boots, or what was left of them anyway."

"Thanks for giving me nightmares," I say.

He laughs. "Anyways, I wonder if that story might be an opportunity."

A shiver races down my spine. "Heck yeah."

The office door opens, and Wyatt leans in, his handsome features stiff. "Meeting's starting."

Immediately, I sit up. "I gotta go, Dad."

"Good to hear your voice, tiger," he says.

"Say hi to mom for me," I reply, and we hang up. Wyatt's already left, so I snap my laptop shut and tuck it under my arm.

"Have a nice day?" Wyatt asks when I catch up with him in the hallway. His tone is flat and distant. Guilt washes over me, but I refuse to let it linger.

"Yeah," I reply. "You?"

"Great," he says.

He holds the door for me to Ike's office. The gesture unnerves me. If we're going to be enemies, why is he being such a gentleman?

Ike stands with his hands on his hips. Once we're all seated, he taps the whiteboard list with a dry erase pen. "Updates," he says, and looks to me because "chopper crash" is the first story in his list.

"Search and rescue crews rescued two victims," I say, then grimace. "One is in critical condition, the other was sent to surgery."

"Did you get photos?"

"Yeah, one of the rescue crew members offered them."

Wyatt side-eyes me. "Boy, you've been busy today," he says under his breath.

Ike nods. "Good. I want that on page one."

I resist the urge to do a little dance in my seat. Next to me, Wyatt shifts away and crosses one leg over the other.

Ike and Quinn hash out the airport story, which Ike's already previewed and declared too long. We toss out headline ideas, but every one I offer, Wyatt shoots down. In the end, Ike chooses Wyatt's idea over mine.

Ike dismisses us, and the room empties. Still stewing, I return to Wyatt's office to collect my coat, then fall in behind him and Ike as we head for the door. I guess I shouldn't be surprised that Wyatt's being so difficult, and I did land a page one story.

"That little brother of yours did well in contract negotiations, I hear," Ike says as we file down the open stairway. "Two million, that's a decent start. Is he liking L.A?"

Wyatt laughs. "Are you kidding? It's a good thing he's so committed to getting off the bench or he'd probably play beach volleyball every day and have the clap by now."

Ike roars with laughter as he and Wyatt push through the double doors at the bottom of the stairs, muttering a quick goodbye before Ike tugs a blue beanie onto his head and strolls in the opposite direction.

"Big plans tonight?" I ask Wyatt. We're both heading toward the parking lot in the back of the building. I can live with him being frosty when we're collaborating, but it's going to be a long three months if he won't talk to me when we're not.

He gives a snort. "Let's see, yeah…I've got twin wrangling until six, then dinner from six to seven. After that, it's laundry and homework."

Relief seeps into my core. "Sounds…busy."

He shrugs. "How about you? You gonna paint the town red?"

"Not much to paint in this town on a Monday night," I say with a sigh.

He digs his keys from his pocket.

"But I'm checking out a few places to rent. Hopefully one of them will work out."

"I'm sure it will," he says, and turns toward his Suburban, the same one I remember him parking outside my hotel.

"Wyatt," I say, unnerved by the distance he's pushed between us.

He turns, a tight expression on his face.

"Is there something you want to tell me?"

A glimmer of fear passes through his eyes, just for a moment. "No, why?"

"It was nice talking with you, at the bakery today. I'd really like us to get along."

"We are getting along," he replies easily.

Why am I challenging him right now? This is what I want, right? For him to leave me alone so I can do my job.

"So you shooting down my ideas in there was just...friendly sparring?"

"Colleagues push each other," he says.

"That works both ways, you know."

His eyes narrow, letting me know he's read my challenge. A tingle races down my spine.

"Good luck with the housing search," he says with a lift of his eyebrow.

"Good luck wrangling your sisters," I manage.

This earns me a smirk. "Thanks."

He turns away, leaving me with a sense of loss I can't explain.

TWO HOURS LATER, I'm signing a three-month lease agreement with Mrs. Genesee, a retired librarian and bona fide cat lady. From the looks of her garage, which was open when I arrived, she's also a cross country skiing fanatic. I counted four pairs of skis hanging from their hook along the wall and two electric boot driers set up on the floor. She also has old jerseys pinned up with thumbtacks, and posters of what I'm guessing are famous skiers, some signed in loopy black ink.

"Here's the rules," Mrs. Genesee says, sliding another piece of paper under my nose.

A white cat meows at her ankles and leaps up to the counter to walk across the paper I'm trying to read. He sits down and immediately starts licking his crotch, one leg extended at my face. His rough tongue makes almost no sound as his head bobs furiously.

I slide the paper from under his rump and scan the list: No loud music after nine, no drugs, I have to park my car in the alley behind my cottage so I don't block her view, access to her washer and dryer in her basement is only on Sundays and Wednesdays after four o'clock, and when it snows, I have to shovel the driveway. Oh, and if I want wood for the fireplace, I have to chop it myself with the axe out back.

I scribble my signature on the line and hand it over. The rules may be quirky, but the cottage is better than the moldy single wide or the cement-shingled house next to the sewage treatment plant I visited earlier. It's only for three months. Quirky is fine.

"Are you married, honey?" my new landlady asks, glancing at my bare ring finger.

My diaphragm quivers. "No," I say.

"Then I won't expect to see visitors late at night," she says with a steely gaze.

Hot prickles erupt on the back of my neck. Why am I thinking of Wyatt?

"It's better for you, and better for me."

She's absolutely right. "It's no problem."

"Good," she says curtly, then hands me a set of keys. "You can move in tomorrow."

I force a smile. "Great."

Back in my hotel, I eat the rest of my sandwich and cookie while reading everything I can about the youth pastor who disappeared from Rogue Valley seven years ago. After Jonah Rundell failed to show up for his Sunday youth group activity, a geocaching game, police were alerted. They searched his house and found some of his personal items missing, including a suitcase. Pastor Fredrickson, his boss, had no idea he was planning to leave town. There was a rumor that Jonah ran off with a rich widow, but I don't find any follow up or proof that this was the situation.

The case stalled, and police assumed he'd wanted to disappear.

Then, last month, a group of kids found Jonah's skeleton inside an old mine shaft near Garnet, a hamlet at the north end of Rogue Valley.

I tap another link, this one from the Mountain Gazette, then sit back, blinking at the byline.

Wyatt.

The first of his two stories rehashes the circumstances of Rundell's disappearance, with several quotes from the local police about the bones. Originally, when he disappeared, police thought he had left town instead of setting up for the geocaching game he'd planned for the next day with his youth group. When his bones were found, police changed their tune. "He either had some kind of medical emergency while placing his clues or got lost. A storm moved in that night. If he was unprepared, the exposure could have killed him."

I read the article again, turning the story over in my mind. Why had it taken them so long to find him? If the pastor drove up there to hide items for the geocaching activity, and hadn't come home, why hadn't someone seen his car in the parking lot?

The next story answers my question. Once the body was found, they did a search for Rundell's vehicle. Turns out his Grand Cherokee had been recovered from a meth bust in Laramie, Wyoming a year after he disappeared. But nobody connected the Cherokee with the missing Rundell because it had stolen plates.

"The lot for that trail system has been vandalized before. If his car was left out overnight, it would have been an easy target," Officer Tucker stated.

A thrill tingles down my spine. It's the same tingle that alerts me of an opportunity. What if there is more to this story than an accidental death? Ultimately, my goal is to increase subscriptions, and there is no better way than with a juicy story that uncovers a hidden truth.

I have the urge to call Wyatt, gauge his reaction, then shut that thought down. I need my own stories, with my own byline. Mr. Freeman is counting on me to increase subscriptions and I can absolutely do that on my own. So maybe it's time to dig up a little more about these bones.

Alone. I don't need a partner.

A twinge of longing tightens my core. Someday, I hope to meet the right guy and build a life with him. Someone I can talk to, someone who can make me laugh, but most of all, someone who will look at me and see his dreams reflected back, someone who will cherish me and love me for who I am.

Wyatt was just a good lay.

Okay, a great lay. A surge of heat fills my body, making my thighs clench.

I snap my laptop shut and exhale a shaky breath.

No.

I needed to forget about my night with Wyatt, forget about the way he kissed me, touched me. *Better for you, better for me*, Mrs. Genesee had said.

Indeed.

8

WYATT

I'm familiar enough with the waiting area outside Vice Principal Kris Baker's office, but I focus on the details anyway. The Halloween decorations on the secretary's desk, the soft tapping of her computer keys, the ringing of a phone from the attendance line across the room, my wood-frame chair with the thin fabric cushion. One I've warmed on countless occasions, though it's been almost a year since my last visit.

I thought we were through this. I thought Leah was making better choices.

Kris, a kind but strict woman in her fifties with short blonde hair, exits into the hallway and spots me waiting.

I stand and walk into her small office. The space is set up for conversations, with two couches, lit by three large lamps instead of the glaring overhead lights.

We take our usual places, her on the couch facing the door, and me on the adjacent one facing the wall that's covered with pictures, poems, and cards from students. I wonder if it helps her find meaning in such a difficult job.

"Leah's skipped two classes this month already," Kris says. "Both days, it was after lunch."

I curse under my breath. Kris doesn't flinch. As the hammer at an alternative high school, she's heard far worse from parents and students. Plus, the two of us are long past upholding etiquette.

"Do you think she's drinking or using drugs?" Kris asks.

It's not a surprise question. "No," I say.

"That's the biggest reason kids don't come back after lunch. They get too intoxicated to come back."

My gut wriggles like a bag of worms. "I see her every day after school. I think I'd know if she was wasted."

A month before I moved back to Penny Creek, Leah had been caught shoplifting cough syrup. She'd planned to drink it with a couple of her derelict friends. It wasn't her first time doing so. Pete and I debated what to do. I mean, cough syrup isn't heroin, after all. Kids mess up, try things. Especially a free spirit like Leah. But Pete and I were both worried. Once cough syrup stopped being fun, what would be next? Everclear? Pot? Something worse? She was only twelve. It felt ominous. So we did something drastic. We enrolled her in an alternative program that included a wide selection of specially designed classes and physical challenges like a ropes course and rock climbing and backcountry skiing.

Her intense love for skiing is what finally turned Leah around.

"Fair enough," Kris says.

"I think her off-campus lunch privileges should be revoked."

"Agreed," Kris says.

I rub the back of my neck. "Interesting that she's cutting right before ski season," I say, trying to keep my voice calm.

Kris gives me a kind smile. "Almost like she's trying to get your attention."

I shake my head. Typical Leah. Instead of coming to me with a problem, she finds some self-destructive way to shove it in my face. "I've been…toying with the idea of leaving in the spring," I say.

Kris gives me a thoughtful look. "Leaving how?"

"For a job," I say as my chest tightens. The rivalry between me and Brooke is alive and well, and she's a worthy opponent. If I want the Times job, I'm going to have to fight hard for it.

I force my eyes to meet Kris's. "In Los Angeles."

Her face brightens. "Sounds like a splendid opportunity."

My gut flutters again. "It could be," I say, because if Leah fails to graduate, I'll be turning it down. That or taking her with me, and Los Angeles is the last place for a kid like her.

"Sounds like Leah's experiencing some feelings about that."

I laugh because Kris knows Leah almost as well as I do. "That's a very distinct possibility."

Kris and I share a long moment that feels peaceful. I let it wash over me. Fuck, it's been a long road, with the finish line finally in sight.

"I'll talk to her, remind her of the consequences of any more missed days this semester." Leah's going to blow a gasket, but she brought it on herself.

"Did you ever think you'd have to learn so much when you took on being her parent?" she asks as we stand.

I chuckle. "Nope. I thought it'd be girl scouts and carpool and science fair projects."

Kris laughs.

I resist the urge to hug her. She's been my mentor, my guiding light. She's listened to me rant, hashed out solutions, but most of all, she cares about Leah and wants what's best for her. Even if it means thinking outside the box. If only all school administrators were as creative and caring, maybe less kids would get washed out by the system.

As I wave goodbye to the secretary on the way out, a pang of an emotion I can't place tugs at my insides. It's not until I'm inside the Suburban that I realize what it is: loss, which is crazy. I'm not going to miss coming here. I'm not going to miss meeting with Kris about Leah's constant need to test the limits.

I sigh and start the engine, telling myself that the sense of melancholy is just a sign that change, no matter how welcome, isn't easy. This has been my life for six years. It's natural that I should have second thoughts.

Panic floods me. No. I don't have second thoughts. I paid my dues and now I get my life back, my freedom. I'm getting that job in L.A.

I grimace at my frosty windshield when Brooke's voice floats through my mind. *Is there something you want to tell me?*

Does she somehow know about L.A? The only people I've told are Ike and Caleb. I briefly wonder how Leah heard about it, or maybe it's a coincidence. Maybe Leah's acting out because she's scared to move on.

I get it. It's a big world out there.

However, Brooke can't possibly know my plans. Not that it matters. She wants to fight me for the job? I grit my teeth.

Bring it.

I put the truck in gear and drive toward the IGA where Leah works after school as a stocker. The whole way there I'm mentally rehearsing what I'm going to say. One would think that after six years of this, I'd be a pro. Nope. Every time I have to confront her my gut aches and my fingers shake. But damn it, someone has to be the asshole. I just hate that it's me.

These are the moments that are hardest, where the bitterness at my mom and dad rises to the surface.

I gave up my dreams for this, I want to yell at them. *Because you're not here.*

After parking at the back of the store, I walk to the loading dock and hop up to the ground level. Inside, the back room is dark, with shelves full of boxes. From down one of the rows, I hear a box being sliced open.

"I just came from a meeting with Vice Principal Baker," I say to Leah as she unloads boxes of cereal into a shopping cart. "Do you want to tell me what's going on?"

She freezes for an instant. "Not really."

I glance up at the vast ceiling with its wires and dim lights for a two-second cooling-off. "I can't help you if you won't talk to me."

"I don't need your help," she replies, her tone sharp.

"You're not going to graduate without it," I reply, crossing my arms.

"I hate school," she says. The look on her face changes, but only for an instant. She's standing in profile, but I know her well enough to catch the anguish in her expression. "It feels like I'm never going to get out of here."

A pulse of empathy flutters through my gut. Fuck do I know this feeling. But I can't share that with her. *Show no weakness.*

"Talk to me, Lee," I say, my voice tight.

Leah cuts the bottoms of her boxes open with a retractable blade, then flattens them. "I'm handling it, okay?"

"How is cutting class 'handling it'?"

"God, you never even try to understand!" she says.

My gut hollows. I could remind her that I was the one who got her into Ridgetop Alternative. I was the one who lets her do online home-school in the winter so she can focus on skiing. If Mom had been left in charge—in the state she was in then—Leah would have dropped out long ago and either be in jail or rehab right now.

"Ski season's off unless you get your grades up," I say instead because we need to focus on the goal.

She clenches her eyes shut. "That's not fair."

"Oh, but it is. Our deal hasn't changed, Leah. You make an effort in school, and the winter is yours. I think that's pretty fair."

Leah's look could melt steel. "Fine."

"No more lunch off campus," I say. "And you're serving detention this Saturday."

"But I work," Leah protests.

"You'll have to adjust your schedule."

"He's going to fire me," Leah says.

I resist the urge to offer to talk to Stan Hobuck. Leah has to figure this out.

"I know it's tough," I say.

Leah turns her back and adds her flattened cardboard boxes to the top of a flatbed cart. Then she pushes it down the aisle, away from me.

I let her go. I've learned that giving both of us some space is a good thing.

. . .

I ARRIVE at the Gazette and I'm still so consumed with worry that I'm going to have to hire a tutor for Leah to get her GED next year that I almost forget why I'm here—our four o'clock meeting.

Brooke is behind my desk again. Today she's wearing a loose-fitting V-neck sweater in a raspberry color that complements her creamy skin. It's fallen slightly to the side of her shoulder, revealing the edge of a matching satin bra strap. Her hair is piled up on the top of her head in a messy pompom, revealing its many shades of brown.

And she's wearing a sexy pair of reading glasses. Fuck me.

Brooke looks up from her laptop, surprised. "Hi," she says.

"I didn't know you wore glasses," I say, frozen in the doorway.

Quickly, she lowers them. "Sometimes my eyes get tired."

"Maybe you should work less," I say.

Her pink lips tighten.

I unzip my coat and throw it over the back of the chair facing my desk. "You coming?"

Her eyes flash.

Damn it. "To the meeting," I say, my voice harsher than I intend. What I wouldn't give to make her come right now. I could sure use the satisfaction. At least one thing I know how to do right.

But I wouldn't be able to stop there. I suffer through a fleeting fantasy of laying her on my desk and kissing up her bare thighs so I can taste her.

"Yes," she says, breaking my train of thought. I open the door for her, inhaling her captivating scent as she passes.

I close my eyes and shut down my craving to yank her back into my office and pin her against the door. I tell myself I'm just worked up about Leah, that I need to stick with my plan: ignore Brooke so I can write my best work of my life and prove I deserve the job in L.A.

Ike meets us in the hallway. "You two got a minute?"

"Of course," I tell him. Then, with a sinking feeling in my gut, I notice that the newsroom is empty.

9

WYATT

Ike shuts the door behind us and we all settle into our seats.

Ike peers at both of us, tenting his fingers. "Nice job with the Artist in Residence piece, Brooke," he says. "I'm moving it to page one, so I need a revised headline."

Ignoring Brooke's happy little wriggle, I splutter a protest—I have the hero section tomorrow with the story of CJ's trial date—but Ike shuts me down with a flash of his palm. "There's something missing in yours."

"Missing? Like what?"

Brooke leans forward. "He needs another source, doesn't he?" She glances at me, her eyes bright with challenge. "It's CJ's word against Lori Grant's. You need more than that. Or at least a quote from CJ."

"Are you serious?"

"Maybe you're too close to this to see it, but you're biased," Brooke says. "You've got a grudge against CJ Parks and you want to see him fry."

"How the hell do you get that from my story?" I fire back, shifting to the edge of my chair to glare at her. "I only want what we all want, a fair trial for him and justice for everyone."

"I'm all about the big story, but not if it's sensationalism, Wyatt," Brooke says.

"She's right," Ike says with a grimace. "I want you to go over it again, make it more balanced."

"You don't actually think CJ is innocent?"

"That's for the courts to decide, Wyatt," Ike says sternly.

I force a calming breath into my lungs.

"Since my piece is ready, I can rewrite Wyatt's," Brooke says, her spine ramrod straight.

"Whoa, hold on there," I say. This series on CJ Parks and his conflict with the Sawtooth Wolf Pack is my ticket out of here. No way am I going to let some big-city hotshot steal it.

"I'll...take another look, but it'll be late tonight," I add. After I go home and cook dinner and monitor chores and the twins' Friday night plans.

"You're asking us to hold the production because you got sloppy?" Brooke says. She crosses her legs and settles back in her chair, which might as well be her throne right now. "You should just pull it," she says to Ike.

"God, you're infuriating," I say as my veins burn hot.

"Maybe, but I'm also right." She tilts her head. "Do you want to save this paper or not?"

A part of me doesn't give a shit, but the deeper part, the one that loves this paper and everything I've invested in it these past six years, does.

"You busting my balls isn't the only way to save it," I say.

Her lips form a tight line. The tension between us draws tighter, like a rubber band stretched to its breaking point. "This paper has needed a good ball busting for years."

Ouch.

Ike stands, which has the effect of making me feel very small. "Send it to Brooke for proofing by eight o'clock, or we set it aside until it's right," he says.

I suppress my shock by rubbing my chin. When did Brooke become honorary editor here? "Fine," I grit out.

Ike opens the door and Brooke prances out. I follow, trying to understand what just happened. Ike squeezes me on the shoulder when I step past. I try to take it as the reassurance it is, but my pride is too wounded.

Inside my office, Brooke is packing up her laptop, but doesn't look up when I enter. "I was right in there and you know it," she says.

I lean my back against the wall and cross my arms. "You may have won awards and cut your teeth in the big city, but you're still an outsider here."

"I think in this case, it's a good thing," she says. "It's called perspective. Something you've lost."

"So I'm supposed to thank you?"

She shakes her head. "You know, If you'd just listen to me, I might actually be able to teach you something."

A switch flips in my brain, and before I can stop myself, I take a step closer. "I can listen just fine, sweetheart. We can start right now."

Anger flashes in her eyes. "Stop. I didn't mean it like that."

The frustration and desire to let her teach me everything about her needs mixes with a new emotion that throws me further off balance.

Fuck! First she meddles with my story, now she's somehow turned up the heat between us so high that I can't think. How many more weeks of this?

"Call me if you need help with rewriting," she says, and breezes out of my office.

I wait for the exterior door to shut, then snatch my coat from the hook on the door. Minutes later, I'm jumping into the Suburban, my muscles pulsing with pent-up fury. Before starting the rig, I force a series of full breaths into my lungs.

Before a big meet, I used to do a ten-minute meditation. It was something one of my coaches taught me to help quiet my jittery mind. I got pretty good at it. Even in a busy pool arena, with buzzers sounding and bodies hitting the water and people cheering, I turned my back to everyone, put a towel over my head, and checked out. It allowed me to find a space inside my mind where everything was still.

My best events always coincided with a good mental reboot. If I was distracted, or I told myself I didn't need it, my time reminded me that I did.

"Shit!" I hear from the other side of the parking lot.

My quiet mind jolts, and I blink. In my rearview, I see Brooke frantically digging into her purse.

"No," she moans, sounding distraught.

I consider ignoring her, then realize how ridiculously petty that is. What am I, ten? I may hate the way she pushed my buttons tonight, but I'm not an asshole. I step out of the rig. "You okay?"

She turns, startled. "Jeez, you scared me."

"Sorry," I say, walking to where she's standing next to her driver's side door. "What's wrong?"

A tight look passes over her face. "I locked my keys in my car."

I frown. "How is that even possible? Most cars won't let you do that."

"Yeah, well, my car isn't one of them."

I glance inside her late-model VW Bug. Sure enough, a set of keys is dangling from the ignition. "Interesting choice of vehicle for snow country," I say.

She gives me a haughty glare. "I like my car."

"Do you have a spare set of keys?"

She stops digging in her purse. "Yes. At my place."

"Come on," I say, nodding at my rig. "I'll give you a lift."

"I can walk," she says. "It's not that far."

"Brooke," I say sternly. She doesn't have a warm hat or gloves and her fancy shoes aren't exactly made for walking. "Get in."

She gives me a look I can't read. "Okay," she finally says.

Even though this is such a small thing, I can't help but want to pound my chest in victory. Maybe she likes my authoritative tone. I'll have to remember that.

Stop. I'm just giving her a ride. We're still enemies or colleagues or whatever the fuck we are.

We walk to my Suburban and I open her door for her. Because

she's so short, she has to reach up for the handle above her head. The motion tugs at her coat and outlines the shape of her breasts. Her nipples make tiny buttons against the fabric. I remember how those pert little peaks tasted between my lips, and how she arched her back, begging for more.

And now she's in my truck.

I close her door and walk to my side, using the ten seconds to tell my erection to fucking take a hike. It's a good thing my coat is long enough to cover my lap.

"Thanks," Brooke says once I'm inside and starting the engine.

"Where's your place?" I say, trying to keep the edge from my tone but the conflicting needs—punish her or kiss her until we steam up the windows—are making that extremely difficult.

She gives me the cross street.

"Wait, are you staying in Mrs. Genesee's cottage?"

Her eyes sharpen. "Yes. Why? Is that bad?"

I suppress a chuckle. "I hope you like cats. And shoveling snow."

She shrugs. "I don't mind."

"She's probably the nosiest person in Penny Creek. Back in high school when she was the librarian, I used to catch her eavesdropping on my conversations with my friends when we'd study there."

Brooke laughs. "So far she's left me alone."

"That'll change," I reply.

"Maybe it's best if you park at the end of the block. I can walk the rest of the way, and then walk back to my car."

"No," I say, with more vehemence than is warranted. What is wrong with me? I should have let her walk in those heels and no gloves. Serves her right for coming here and trying to ruin my life.

"Okay," Brooke says, her eyebrows arched.

I drive in silence for several blocks, until I can't hold my curiosity back any longer. "So, did Hazel Gunn finally talk to you?"

Brooke blinks at me, as if trying to switch gears from wherever her thoughts just were, which of course, makes me wonder. Was she thinking about what I was thinking?

"No," Brooke says. "But she will."

"What are you hoping she'll tell you?"

There must be something in my tone that alerts Brooke because her focus on me sharpens. "The Art Guild has been encouraging her to apply for years. Cavendish Gallery has been selling her paintings since she started. She has a huge following here. I want to know why she's waited so long to come back."

Shit. Why did I open this box?

Brooke gazes out the window while stroking her bottom lip with her index finger, something I've noticed she does when she's thinking. "I'm going to try to run into her."

"Like a stalker?" I ask, shifting in my seat.

She waves me off. "Of course not."

It's none of her business why Hazel Gunn is ready to return to Penny Creek. I can't help but want to call Brooke off, but I have a feeling it will only make her more curious.

I park in front of Mrs. Genesee's peach-colored house. Immediately, the curtains in her kitchen window part and her narrow, weathered face peers at us.

I give her a wave.

She peers sharply back, watching Brooke exit her side. I keep the Suburban idling while I wait, resisting the urge to watch Brooke fast-walk to her cottage because seeing her hips sway is not what I need right now. But as soon as Mrs. Genesee's curtains fall back into place, I sneak a glance and catch Brooke bending over to pick something from her stoop.

Lord help me.

I press the heels of my hands against my eye sockets to black out the image of her bent forward on the hotel bed, her hands gripping the headboard while I stroked her from behind, then kissed my way slowly down her spine.

My passenger door creaks open. "Got it!" Brooke says, jumping into the seat.

Black circles cloud my vision when I release my grip on my eyes, but I'm quick to blink them away.

Her cheeks are flushed from the cold air and her eyes are

sparkling. For this rare moment, she's let her guard down, something I'd like to see more of.

Am I the reason she's always scowling?

We drive back to the Gazette's parking lot in silence. When I pull up next to her car, she turns to me and smiles. "Thanks."

I keep my hands firmly planted on the wheel. "You're welcome."

Then her stern look returns. "I'll be waiting for your edited story."

I don't reply, and she slides from the rig. I wait until she's safely inside her car and has it running before I back the Suburban out of the lot.

AFTER DINNER AND CHORES, I get the twins to tell me their exact plans for the rest of the night. I used to try to ground Leah, but it only made her hate me and it didn't change her behavior. And by grounding her, it meant I had to give up *my* plans. I've learned that she needs her friends as much as I do, so instead of sitting home with her tonight— which would just piss both of us off—she'll have to skip sleeping in tomorrow to complete an extra workout for me then pick up litter with the crew from the Environmental Resource Center.

After I send the twins off with a reminder of their midnight curfew, I'm blissfully alone in the house. On my way to the living room with my laptop and a beer, my phone buzzes in my pocket.

I set everything down on the coffee table and glance at the screen. My friend Tanner and I sometimes meet up for beers on Friday, and I've been waiting to see if he can muster the energy after a week of teaching and coaching wrestling.

Tanner: *I'm free after 8:00. Sourdough's?*

I reply with a thumbs up, then set my phone aside. My younger brother Caleb's band is playing there tonight, so that's my first pick, too.

After cracking open the beer, I open my laptop. First, I read the article straight through, pushing through all my internal protests that this story is perfect, thank you very much, and try to be objective. For years, sheep and cattle ranchers CJ Parks and his brother, Michael have been at war with the Sawtooth Wolf Pack, one of the last wild wolf populations in the lower 48 and federally protected by the Endangered Species Act. The Parks brothers claim the wolves stalk and kill their livestock. This is bullshit because there's been only one case of a Sawtooth wolf killing a sheep. CJ caught him in the act and shot him, which under the agreement in place between the federal officers and the collection of ranchers flanking the wilderness area, he was permitted to do. But if the wolves were delisted from ESA protection, CJ wouldn't need a reason to shoot them.

Last July, wildlife biology graduate student Lori Grant was in the Sawtooths studying the wolf pack for her thesis project. To get rid of her and shut down her research, CJ Parks got her wrongfully accused of planting tainted lamb meat in the wolves' territory. For several nerve-wracking days, things looked pretty bad. CJ is a powerful figure, and connected. But the evidence against Lori was thin, and the Forest Service officer who came to investigate the charges let her go. Then he turned his attention to CJ.

My ongoing series is telling the story that started over a decade ago. The pact between ranchers and the federal biologist that allowed CJ to shoot a wolf if it threatened his flock. The mysterious killings of the wolves over the years: two poisoned and the one he legally shot for supposedly attacking a sheep. The hundreds of thousands of dollars CJ paid a lobby group to influence Congress's decision whether to uphold or delist wolves from federal protection under the ESA.

My article for tomorrow's edition rehashes Lori's testimony about stumbling onto a poisoned carcass, watching CJ ride away, then picking up the cigarette butt imprinted with his DNA, and ends with the details of his court appearance and trial date in March.

The pictures Lori snapped of CJ riding away unfortunately don't nail any distinct markings that identify him. A search of his stables for the horse he rode—a spotted Appaloosa with white fetlocks—turned up empty. But the image did show a partial of the horse's branding.

What's visible matches CJs pattern, but it's not complete, so could be someone else's.

I take another pull from my beer and scan the article again, paying closer attention to the quotes from the lawyer, who claims the whole thing is some giant hoax.

"This proves nothing," CJ's lawyer said to me. "Cigarette butts can last years. My client rides up in those mountains all the time. That's no crime."

In the article, I bring up the missing horse and the panniers prosecutors never found, the ones he would have used to transport the poisoned carcass. Is this where Brooke thinks I'm inserting my bias?

I heave a sigh and take another sip of my beer. Brooke's issue aside, me sticking it to CJ Parks effectively ends the pact he made with my dad over twenty years ago with a handshake. Dad wanted access to the Rogue River, which is on CJ's property. In exchange for sharing the river and his roads, my dad agreed to overlook CJ's cattle killing off the salmon that spawned in the headwaters.

Now that the agreement between CJ and my family is off, maybe I'll write that story.

In the meantime, I need to back off on CJ in this article until I have another source to back up CJ's guilt, or a conviction from the courts. And yet, I'm torn. If I don't push the limits a little bit, take a risk, how can I get readers to care? I've had a few hate letters from townsfolk over the years, but it doesn't bother me. If I'm not riling people up, then I've failed to do my job.

Grudgingly, I agree with Brooke. It's Lori's word against CJ's right now. I've been leaning too hard on my easy access to Lori. I need another source.

But who? I get up and grab my notebook, the one I use for ideas and interviews. I keep it by my bed so when I wake up with a story, I can write down the pieces before I forget. When the twins were younger I could only work when they were asleep, and I wonder if it rewired my process so that my best ideas now come in the nighttime hours.

But after flipping through my notes, nothing stands out. Who else would talk to me?

I tone down my story, read it one last time, then send it. After shutting the lid of my laptop, I drain my beer and grab my keys.

My phone dings with a message. It's from Brooke.

Thanks for getting this to me on time. Have a good weekend.

I slow to a stop in the middle of the living room. Most of the time, Ike takes care of the weekend edition, so our team won't need to meet again until Monday, which means I won't see Brooke for forty-eight hours. A part of me is relieved—two days where I won't be constantly tortured by her presence. But the other part doesn't like this one bit.

Not like I could tell her this. I type back: *You too. Try to have some fun.*

I'm zipping up my coat when her reply arrives.

Yeah, right. It's too cold for fun.

The thought of her sitting alone in that chilly cottage surrounded by cats makes me wince. I could say something cheesy about how fun it would be to keep her warm, but instead I do something stupid.

Whiskey can help

I wait for her reply, my stomach twisting into knots. Why am I baiting her like this? Hating her is the only thing keeping my head on straight.

Too bad I don't have any

She drinks whiskey? I grin at the phone. *I just happen to know a place*

I thought liquor stores closed at five

They do. That's why we have Sourdough Gil's

Thanks for the tip. I'll have to check it out

This is where I should tuck my phone away and forget her for a night. I need to blow off some steam with Tanner and the usual suspects who will likely join us.

But I can't get the image of her surrounded by a gang of unruly cats out of my head.

Me: *I'm heading there now if you want to join.*

What am I doing?

My chest tightens, but I force myself to relax with a hard breath. Our work day is done. What's a harmless drink between colleagues?

Brooke: *I'll think about it. Thank you*

I step onto the porch and descend to the sandy driveway. Even though it's not exactly a rejection, my belly still empties like a deflated balloon.

10

BROOKE

I ignore Wyatt's invitation for a full ten minutes, then call my cousin and best friend, Maggie. She's the only one I told about my tryst last summer, and how I was going to have to confront Wyatt when I accepted the position this fall. But she and I haven't talked since the night after Wyatt cornered me in that alley.

"I'm in a bit of a crisis, Mags," I say, rubbing my forehead as I pace behind the tan fabric loveseat.

In the background, hangers click and slide along a metal rack. Maggie must be reorganizing her collections at French Kiss, her boutique. "Whatever it is, I hope you decked him."

I laugh, but my throat feels tight. "No, this doesn't warrant a left hook. He asked me out for a drink."

"Oh," Maggie says. "Why is this a crisis? You said yes, right?"

"I said I'd think about it."

"Hang on, I gotta put you on speaker so I can steam these trousers," Maggie says, followed by the slight shift in the sound quality. "So you want to go, but you're afraid you won't be able to stop yourself from jumping his bones."

"Something like that, yeah."

"Why do you want to go?"

I slump onto the couch. "Because it's been a really long week and I have ten more of them ahead of me. And...tomorrow's Halloween."

Maggie makes a soft hum of sympathy. "You're better off, girl, you know that."

I inspect my nails for chipped polish, finding none. "I know," I say. "It just might be nice to ...forget about it a little bit."

"Sounds like you've made up your mind already," Maggie says.

I stare at the ceiling's cracks in the plaster, making patterns. There's a giant rabbit, a football, and a five-legged insect.

"Maybe."

"So go have fun," Maggie says.

My belly jolts upwards. "This is harder than I thought it would be."

"Forgetting Hugh or resisting Wyatt?"

I laugh because it sounds so dramatic, and that's definitely not me. "I'm over Hugh," I say, which is completely true. This last year has given me the perspective I couldn't achieve when I was in the thick of it.

"It's Wyatt," I say with a sigh. "He's like sex on a stick. Every time I see him my blood starts to pound."

"That could be a medical condition. You might want to see someone about that."

I groan. "He's applying for the same job in L.A."

The line goes dead silent. "Whoa. How do you know?"

"I overheard him talking to Ike."

"Don't tell me you're worried about this? I'm sure lots of other journalists will apply. You'll beat them all, Brooke."

Her confidence sends a pulse of warmth through me. "Thanks, Mags."

"It's true. How many awards has he won?"

I'm ashamed that I looked. "None."

"See? This changes nothing."

Doesn't it though? "He's been here for six years raising his younger siblings. I get the feeling he gave up a lot for them. That the job in L.A. is sort of like his reward for the sacrifices he's made."

"What about your sacrifices?" Maggie says in a firm tone.

She means the many late nights I spent in college at the newspaper, cranking out stories while my friends were out having a good time. About how I poured myself into the job at the Post. About the job in San Francisco that I gave up to stay with Hugh in Denver.

"It just makes this more complicated," I say.

"I disagree. If anything, this should fuel that mighty little engine of yours even more."

I huff a giant sigh because the truth is too complicated to explain over the phone. "He thinks I hate him."

Maggie snorts. "Doesn't sound like that's a deterrent. You know what they say about that fine line between love and hate."

"You did not just say the L word."

"Oh, did I?" she says, her voice hitching. "Oops, must have slipped out."

I glare at the empty, cavernous fireplace across from me.

"I just meant that hating him might not be the best strategy for turning off your sex drive."

What if I don't want to turn off my sex drive? Nobody has ever made me feel that way. What if Wyatt is the only one who can?

"Does he know you're applying for the L.A. job?"

Even though it's torture to be around him, to constantly have my guard up, a part of me craves that look he gives me, the way he watches me, smiles at me.

"I told him, and it's made us enemies," I say.

Maggie makes a suspicious hum. "Sounds more like a friendly rivalry to me, and we both know how you love a challenge."

Busted. "But things are so tense between us. It's unbearable."

"Well, sounds like you have two choices. Either keep hating him or take him to bed and get it out of your system."

"Mags!" I groan. "That's not helping me."

Maggie sighs. "When was the last time you were with a guy?"

"July." Wyatt.

"And before that?"

"You know," I say, because I see where this is going. Yes, it's been almost a year since I broke things off with Hugh, and yes, hot sex with a handsome stranger did wonders for me three months ago. But I don't need another night with sexy Wyatt Morgan to wash the last of Hugh away. He's gone from my life. I'm focusing on the future.

"Sex with Wyatt is a dead end," I say. "He's not looking for a relationship and neither am I."

"So go blow off some steam with him instead," she says. "You don't need to have sex with him to enjoy yourself, right?"

"Oh, Mags," I say with a giggle. "I miss you."

"I miss you like crazy. Now are you going out or not? Inquiring minds want to know."

But she needn't have asked. I already decided.

I DRESS in jeans and my most comfortable boots but keep on my over-sized pink cashmere sweater. I don't want Wyatt to think I went to too much trouble. After refreshing my mascara and adding a shade of dusty raspberry to my lips, I tuck into my long down coat and bundle my scarf up to my nose.

I should have just walked out the door as I had been because getting a drink doesn't count as any kind of special occasion. It's just one drink.

But it's one drink with Wyatt.

Sourdough Gil's is on the other side of main street but within walking distance, which I decide is a good idea, even though the temperature has dropped to below freezing. It'll burn off some of this jittery sense that I'm somehow making a huge mistake.

Outside, the crisp night air stings my cheeks like a slap. I tug my scarf higher around my face. My breath warms the cocoon.

Will Wyatt be surprised to see me? What if he's already left?

I purposely didn't text him with my plans because there's still a chance I'll chicken out. Being near Wyatt Morgan somewhere dark that serves alcohol is a bad idea. I shouldn't be near him at all.

But I meant what I said to Maggie about wanting to enjoy myself just a little. Haven't I earned it after these last two weeks?

My blood heats as I walk, but the cold snakes around my shins and freezes my temples. My earlobes start to throb. And just like that, I'm back in my hotel room with Wyatt's lips on my ear, sucking softly while his fingers stroked and teased me. *Come here and let me make this awful ache go away, sweetheart,* he said.

I've never wanted something so badly. *Please,* I begged.

With one smooth motion, Wyatt rolled me to his chest and drove inside me, filling me so perfectly. Two thrusts later and I was coming, my fingers gripping his shoulders.

I lost count of how many times he made me come in that room. Four? Five?

In the middle of the next block stands a building illuminated by large bulbs around the sign and music sounding from inside the walls. My belly does a cartwheel as I slide past the parked cars and climb the steps.

Last chance to turn around.

The door opens and an older couple exits. I step aside and let them pass. Before the door closes, a cloud of warmth and the steady din of conversation arouses my senses.

Can I help that it smells good in there? That I'm craving company? One drink, and then I'll go.

With one last breath for bravery, I slip inside the bar.

To my left is a red leather L-shaped bench packed with a handful of people holding cocktails or pints of beer, a coffee table in front of them with coasters and empties. Along the left wall is the bar, lit from above and the back, where an impressive array of alcohol stands in rows. Half the red leather stools facing the glossed wood bar top are full and a bartender is buzzing back and forth, pouring, shaking, taking money, laughing with his customers. Along the right side are a series of cubby-like spaces with the red leather benches and coffee table setup. In the back right corner is a small stage where a band is setting up to play, and tucked into the back left corner stands a handful of tall bar tables with stools and an array of games: a pool table, dart boards, and a shelf full of what looks like stacks of board games.

The décor definitely matches the town and its outdoorsy roots. I count four stuffed animal heads mounted on the wall—elk, bear, deer, and a rabbit with antlers, the infamous and fake jackalope. A wooden canoe hangs from the ceiling and an ancient pair of snowshoes criss-crossed above the back hallway leads to the restrooms.

If it's this noisy during Slack, summer and Christmas must be nuts.

"Hey there, gorgeous, can I buy you a drink?" someone says. A man has approached from my right. He's got short, sandy blonde hair that's long in the back, thick sideburns, and a matching mustache. His hazel eyes sparkle, as if we're sharing a joke.

I give him a polite smile. "No, thanks, I'm meeting someone."

He scans the bar, then turns back to me with an amused smirk. "Well, looks like he ain't here. What do you say? There's no sense in wasting a perfectly good night."

I'm about to tell Sideburns off when a voice cuts through the music and chatter.

"Hey, you made it," Wyatt says, smiling in that way that makes my belly flip over.

"Yeah, thanks for the invite," I say as Sideburns saunters back to his friends, who are jeering at him for getting shot down.

Wyatt gives Sideburns a curious look, but it passes. He leads me to the last booth on the right, his land on my lower back. I ignore the shivers his touch sends down the backs of my thighs.

We round a partition. Three people are seated on the red leather benches, one woman and two guys. On the coffee table in front of them are several empty glasses and a bowl of mixed nuts.

"Guys, this is Brooke," Wyatt says, his hand disappearing from my back.

A chorus of "Hey Brooke" sounds back at me as I unzip my coat and hang it with my scarf on a nearby hook.

"I'm Tanner," a tall guy with scruffy black hair and green eyes says as he scoots over to give me more space to sit.

The woman across the table smiles at me. "Naomi." She has dark, straight hair cut just above her shoulders, with a blue streak down the middle of one side.

"Stan," the man sitting with his arm over her shoulder says with a grin.

"Nice to meet you all," I say.

Wyatt's dressed down in a dark gray fleece hoody and dark jeans. I'm not sure if it's the low light or the color of his hoody, but it makes his lashes even darker against his steel blue eyes.

"Want to order at the bar?" he asks, leaning closer to my ear.

"Sure," I say, and follow him to an empty space in the stools.

The bartender drifts over. "What can I get you?" he asks me with a sharp nod.

"Do you have Ballentine's?"

He raises an appreciative eyebrow. "Rocks or neat?"

"Rocks," I answer.

The bartender nods at Wyatt. "Johnny Walker Gold. Neat."

"Ballentine's, huh?" Wyatt asks as the bartender gets to work.

"It's a good one to start out with. It's a little on the sweet side." Ugh. Why did I say that? I sound like a total snob.

"How many drinks are you planning to enjoy tonight, Ms. Henderson?" Wyatt asks in a teasing tone that makes me laugh, and wow, does it feel good. Like maybe we can actually be in the same space and not want to strangle each other.

"Just one."

The bartender taps down our drinks. Because of Wyatt's stunt at the bakery, I'm ready this time and slide my card across the polished wood.

"Add it to my tab," Wyatt tells the bartender.

I wheel on Wyatt. "No, I'm paying this time."

The bartender is busy building a cocktail but keeps one eye on us.

Wyatt gives me a scrutinizing once-over. "All right." He nods at the bartender, who steps over to run my card.

I want to yelp for joy. Progress! But just as fast, Maggie's words return to my mind, though I can't really tell whose side she's on: make my girly parts happy and sleep with Wyatt, or listen to my brain and push him away. Then there's my shy little heart, but I can't read what she's saying.

The bartender returns with my card and our whiskeys. I lift my glass and tap it to Wyatt's. He nods and I take a sip. It's smooth with those vanilla tones and slightly smoky finish and oh so good.

"So," I say, setting my glass down. "After what happened in Ike's office, I'm surprised you wanted me here tonight."

He gives me a pensive look that shifts slowly into a smile. "You were right."

I watch him, waiting for signs that he's messing with me. "About what?"

He shrugs. "About my story being weak."

I cross my arms. "I see."

He winks. "Just don't let it go to your head."

Before I can reply, a guitar chord rings out from the lead singer in the corner. "Good evening," he says into the microphone. "How's everyone doing tonight?

A welcoming cheer rises up from the dance floor facing the stage, where Wyatt's friends and several other patrons are hooting at the three men getting ready to play.

"Hey, that's the guy who was in your office the day I showed up," I say as the memory surfaces. He's not as tall as Wyatt, but they have the same eyes and same boyishly cute nose. While they're both muscular, Wyatt's leaner.

"My brother, Caleb," Wyatt says with a broad smile.

"Oh. The firefighter I talked to," I say as questions tumble through my mind.

"Yep. This is his side gig."

The band starts to play and immediately the bar fills with music. It's a mix of rock and folk and they're pretty good, but it's loud.

"Let's dance," Wyatt says in my ear.

"Now?" I ask, cradling my glass.

Before I can continue my protest, Wyatt sets down our drinks and tugs me to the dance floor.

11

WYATT

I'm not a guy who impresses women with my dance skills, but hey, I *am* an opportunist. Plus, it's dark and dancing gives me an excuse to touch her.

We bump into Naomi and Stan. Nearby, my sister Annika is dancing with her sidekick Grady, and Caleb's girl, Lori, who comes down from Missoula on weekends Caleb isn't on shift.

When I first moved home, it was weird to hang out with my siblings in a bar, watching them flirt or drink, but it's normal now. Though being connected to a third of the people here tonight reminds me of how small this town is.

And how I can't wait to get away. In Los Angeles, I can live the way I want. Stay out late whenever I want. Bring a girl home if and when I want.

Maybe if I bring home enough of them, I can forget about Brooke.

The song ends and we stand there, panting. A sheen of sweat coats Brooke's forehead, but it only adds to her glow. A new song starts and Naomi, Stan, Brooke and I start jumping around again. It feels good to use my muscles, to give into the freedom of it. Brooke dances by wiggling her hips and doing some wavy thing with her arms, her face lit up, as if she doesn't care how she looks. It's a little surprising and a lot fascinating. I grab her hand and spin her. Instead of fighting me, she sashays effortlessly away from me, then back, placing her other hand on my shoulder. Our hips connect. I place my hand against the small of her back to keep her close as our bodies move together. My cock throbs to life inside my jeans. Brooke's eyes sharpen and she gently pushes me away, shimmying her ass just so in those tight jeans she's wearing. Is she doing it to drive me crazy? Or is this a solo performance and I just get to watch?

Ideas spark in my mind. What I'd give to watch a different kind of solo performance. Watch her eyes clench and her mouth open as she takes herself over the edge. Then it would be my turn.

We dance together for several more songs, with me pulling her close every chance I get and her gently pushing me away. I can't help but try to get her near me. Just to feel her tight little body, graze my fingertips down her arm or interlace my fingers with her slender ones.

I swore to myself that I wouldn't let my dick do the thinking. She's trying to steal my ticket out of Penny Creek. I can't get distracted by thoughts of scooping her into my arms and pinning her against the side of my rig so I can kiss her and caress all her soft places. I'm sure she would protest about the cold night air. But I'd be all the heat she'd ever need.

The next song is a slow, sensual number. It's not something Caleb's band usually plays. When I give him a curious look, he gives me a sly grin.

Behind Brooke's back, I give him the finger.

"What's wrong?" Brooke asks.

"Nothing," I say, and pull her close.

I expect her to resist, but she floats easily into my arms. Her breath is warm against my neck and her breasts press into my chest, making me hard all over again.

Brooke shifts slightly. "Can't you turn that thing off?" she says with a soft laugh.

"Sorry, it sort of has a mind of its own tonight."

"Just tonight?" she says in a teasing tone.

I laugh, and it feels so good to be able to let down my guard a little. "Okay, not just tonight."

I rock with her wrapped inside my embrace and try to savor her scent and the warmth of her frame against mine.

"I'm trying to ignore you, Brooke, but it's just not working."

She draws a slow breath, her shoulders expanding and relaxing inside my embrace. I want more of this, holding her, touching her.

"I'm having a hard time, too, if that's any consolation," she says, wrapping her arms tighter around me.

The need I've been suppressing all night ruptures, surging through me like a flood. I stop moving so I can cradle her face and gaze into her eyes that are reflecting back the same need. Before she can stop me, I lower my lips to hers.

A flutter breaks loose in my chest, pattering all the way up my throat. I realize it's my heart beating out of control. Our lips embrace once, twice, each time squeezing a little tighter. Her lips taste like vanilla and are as smooth as cream. I lick just inside her upper lip, then nip her there. She trembles against me, her fingers tightening on my waist. The music fades away and all that's left is her soft breaths and the thunder of my pulse. I don't care that I'm in the middle of the dance floor or that half the town will be gossiping about this kiss for the rest of my natural life. I may only get this one kiss with her, and I'm not about to cut it short for anything.

She kisses me back, her lips lingering in a sweet embrace that sends bolts of electricity over my skin. I caress the smooth skin behind her ears with my thumbs. She releases a soft sigh and her body arches slightly into me. I continue stroking her behind her ear while my tongue tastes and my lips embrace hers.

Gently, she pushes me back, her eyes fluttering open. "What are you doing to me?" she whispers as her expression turns desperate.

I caress the side of her soft face. "Kissing you. And I'm not one bit sorry about it."

I lean down and kiss her again. Her fingers close around a handful of my shirt as I slip my tongue between her lips to swirl gently. Our lips and tongues dance playfully, and my skin erupts with hot needles.

She's just as perfect as that first time, only it's better somehow, maybe because I haven't stopped thinking about the way she kisses, or the way she leans in for more.

The song ends and a fast one takes its place. The sudden change seems to break the spell between us, because Brooke opens her eyes again, looking dazed.

"Do you want to sit down?" I ask, not sure if I should cry in gratitude that she let me kiss her or scream in frustration that Caleb changed the tempo.

She nods, and I lead her through the dozen gyrating bodies to our booth. "I'll grab our drinks," I say once I've settled her on the bench, then dash to the bar where our drinks are waiting. The bartender slides over and replaces Brooke's, which had melted, then gives me a knowing nod.

I spin and hurry back to the table, but Brooke isn't there. I do a quick scan—she's not on the dance floor and her coat is still hanging on the peg. Then I see movement past the windows outside.

After setting down our drinks, I slip through the door. Light from Sourdough's spills onto the sidewalk, illuminating her troubled face.

"You okay?" I ask.

"Yeah," she says. "Just needed some air."

"I thought you hated the cold?" I ask, crossing my arms so I won't be tempted to pull her against me and kiss her again.

She smiles. "I do. It feels nice right now though. I got...a little overheated in there."

I chuckle and gaze up at the stars. "I think we both did."

"I shouldn't have kissed you," she says, her gaze darting away.

"But you did, Brooke," I say, stepping closer. The edge in my voice gets her attention because her gaze snaps to mine. "Don't put this on me. You wanted it as much as I did."

After swallowing, she levels her gaze at me. "I didn't come out tonight just to be with you," she says, releasing a firm breath. "I was looking for a distraction, maybe. At this same time last year, I broke things off with my fiancé."

My heart locks up for an instant. "You were engaged?"

"Yeah," she says, leaning back against the building to stare up at the night sky. "Crazy, right?"

I shake my head to banish the image of Brooke married to someone else. "It's only crazy that he fucked it up," I say. If I was lucky enough to have someone like Brooke agree to wear my ring, I'd never let her go.

"We went to this costume party. When he disappeared for a while, I didn't think anything of it. I mean, we each had friends there, and Hugh doesn't dance." She pauses to inhale a breath and I have to force myself to keep the distance she's put between us. "The next day there were pictures from the party on social media. There was one of him on a couch with these two girls. He was kissing one of them while the other one had her hands on his crotch."

I wince. "Fuck, Brooke, I'm so sorry."

"He said nothing happened, that I was overreacting."

He should have been with her, not sneaking off to make out with some random girls. "You had every right to be upset."

"Right?" she says. "He still blamed me, though."

I gaze into her troubled eyes.

"He said it was my fault. That if I wasn't so focused on my work all the time we could be having more fun."

"Okay, let's get something straight," I say, my voice taking on that edge again. "Him cheating on you is not your fault." Why the hell didn't he support her? What a tool. "This guy obviously didn't care about you, Brooke."

"I get that now," she says, her spine straightening. "In a weird way, I'm glad I saw those pictures. It saved me from what would have been a huge mistake."

It also would have kept her from being with me last summer. My stomach does a slow, sickening roll. I force in a slow breath, but the terrible feeling persists.

Unable to stop myself, I wrap her in my arms, savoring her small body tucked into my embrace. I'm relieved when she relaxes against me.

"Those pictures were sort of icing on an already doomed cake, though," she says into my chest. "I had a killer job offer that fall. It would have meant moving to San Francisco. I was thrilled...I mean, San Francisco! Plus, it came with a promotion. But he refused. Even though his company has an office there."

She steps back and the loss of contact with her warmth sends an achy throb through my insides.

"Hey, a threesome with two random chicks is hard to beat," I say.

To my relief, she laughs. "Not funny, Wyatt."

I give her tummy a playful poke. "Then why are you laughing?"

She tilts her head and gazes at me, the laughter fading from her face. "I turned down the job the day of the party. I thought he'd be happy, but he took the news like he expected it. There was never a question that we'd move. He was never willing to support me like that."

"I'm sorry," I say, taking her slender hand in mine. What I wouldn't give to feel her soft touch on my body. To hold her until she forgets all about this asshole.

"That's why I'm not going to let anything get in my way this time," she says.

The full picture of what she's going through becomes clear. "I understand."

She gives me a sharp look. "You do?"

The image of palm trees arching over a blue ocean flashes through my mind. "Yeah."

She slides her hand from mine and exhales a long breath. "I know you're applying for the job at the L.A. Times."

My throat tightens. "Oh?" I manage.

"I overheard you and Ike talking. I didn't mean to, I..." She hugs herself tightly. "I wish I could turn it off, but I hear things better than most people."

My hard exhale creates a tiny vapor cloud that vanishes instantly. If only my feelings for her would evaporate as easily. "It's okay."

"It is so far from okay," she says, her eyes flashing. "Only one of us can get it."

My ribs contract from the knot rapidly twisting inside me. "I know."

She exhales a ragged sigh. "Wyatt."

I shove my hands in my pockets and gaze up at the sparkling stars. The almost full moon has a ring around it, giving it an eerie glow. "I'm not trying to hold you back from your dream, Brooke." Or am I? If I get the job in L.A., her dream is as good as crushed.

"I'm going home," she says.

For someone who makes a living coming up with savvy, charming words, feeling like I have none is an unwelcome surprise. "I'll…walk you to your car."

"I came on foot."

"Then I'll drive you," I say, my voice tight.

She releases a long sigh. "I'm okay, really. I think I'd like to clear my head."

"You can clear it when you're safely inside your place. I'm not letting you walk home at this hour alone."

She groans. "Penny Creek is totally safe, Wyatt."

This hits me low in the gut because Penny Creek has its dangers just like anywhere. "I can either walk with you, or drive you. Pick."

"Fine," she says, drawing the word into a groan. "Walk."

After returning inside for our coats, I slap a twenty on the table for a tip. My friends are still dancing and Caleb's eyes are clenched shut as he belts out the chorus. Seeing him so happy gives me a welcome dose of satisfaction. He and Lori had so much to overcome. It was a hard road, but he fought for her. Their lives are far from perfect— she's still in school hundreds of miles away and he's raising a kid. But they're making it work.

I wish things were different with Brooke, but we're rivals. Why can't she see that?

Outside, I help Brooke into her coat then tuck into mine while she wraps her scarf around her neck and slides on her mittens.

We set off and it takes everything I have not to take her hand. I want her to know that I appreciate what she shared with me tonight, but inside, I'm like a caged animal trying to claw myself free.

"How did you become such a whiskey connoisseur?" I ask to fill the silence.

She smiles. "My dad."

"Tell me about him," I say.

Her face practically glows. It hooks my heart in its most sensitive place. For all of my dad's faults, I still miss him.

"He's a writer too."

"A journalist?"

She shakes her head. "No. He's writing a book. A coming-of-age story."

"Wow, that's cool," I say. "Who's his publisher?"

She pinches her lips together. "He's not represented. Yet." We stop at a red light. "He's also a high school English teacher."

"So his teaching supports his writing," I say. It's one of the biggest reasons I didn't pursue creative writing—it's so hard to make a living writing fiction. Plus, books are really fucking long. I like working under a daily deadline and the quick satisfaction of the daily news life.

"I wish he'd retire so he could write more, but he says the kids need him too much."

"He sounds dedicated," I say. "Kind of like someone else I know."

"Yeah," she replies softly. The light turns and we cross the street. The lights and noise of main street fade as we enter a neighborhood of single-story houses, some moderate, some in need of repair. This is the part of town where the real residents live. The grocery store clerks and teachers and plumbers. The bigger, fancier homes are located along the river, up one of the canyons, or up north at the edge of one of the many lakes.

We reach Brooke's block and turn left, passing a run-down car parked on the street and a house with a porch in the middle of a remodel.

At Mrs. Genesee's driveway, Brooke turns to me. "Goodnight, Wyatt."

Before I can reply, she turns and slips down the path to her cottage.

1 2

WYATT

The next morning, after I drag Leah out of bed for a grueling workout, then send her off for litter pickup with the ERC crew, I'm back home alone splitting wood under a gentle sun. The work is just what I need right now. Keeping my body moving helps my mind clear, helps me focus.

What Brooke shared with me last night tumbles over and over through my mind. I thought maybe I'd see her at the pool this morning, but Leah and I had the lanes to ourselves.

Fuck, what I wouldn't give to touch Brooke, to undress her slowly and kiss her, to hear those soft, pleading cries. But she's made it clear she's not going to let anything get in her way of her goals. Though I understand her focus, it doesn't erase the ache.

Why did she let me kiss her last night? If anything, it's only made my craving for her intensify, which is nuts. I need to forget about that kiss and how badly I want her.

Car tires crunch the sandy driveway. I get a quick fantasy that it's Brooke, that she somehow knows I'm alone for the next two hours. Not that it would be enough, but it would at least be a start. Maybe after that, I could think straight.

I sink the axe and walk around the house and meet Tanner, who's holding my wool hat and my debit card.

"Oh shoot," I say. "I forgot all about that."

He hands over both. I slip my debit card into my wallet, and stuff it and the hat into my back pockets.

"Yeah, you seemed in a bit of a rush to get out of there."

He's smirking at me, but I don't take his bait.

I nod at the house. "You want coffee?"

"Sure," he says.

I wipe my brow with the back of my wrist and lead us inside.

The pot is empty, so I brew using the stovetop espresso maker, the one reserved for company.

While I'm busy at the stove, Tanner leans his tall frame against the wall. "Everyone's talking about that kiss."

I shrug. "Big surprise."

"I've never seen you do something like that."

"Yeah, I'm not sure what came over me."

He snorts. "You were a goner the minute she came in the door."

The espresso pot starts bubbling. I turn the burner off and grab two mugs. "I was a goner the minute she entered the Valley."

"You walked her home," he says as I pour the rich espresso into the two mugs.

"And then I *went* home," I say, adding boiling water from the teakettle.

I hand him his mug and we walk back outside to sit on the porch. The fall bite in the air prickles my cheeks, but it's rich with the scents of pine and sun-warmed earth.

"Aren't you competing for the same job?" Tanner says as we settle on the porch step.

I lift my face to the sunshine and close my eyes. "Yeah." I sigh. "It's complicated."

"You don't think she'd try and, oh, I don't know…manipulate things at the paper?"

I rest the bottom edge of my coffee mug on my thigh. "What do you mean?"

"You told me she made you rewrite your piece." He takes a sip. "Nice work, by the way."

I lift my mug in a salute, though it feels hollow now that I've come to terms with my blind spot. "Thanks."

"She wouldn't try to whitewash your stories while amping up hers, so she looks like a crackerjack and you look like an uninspired schmuck?"

I grimace. "I don't think so. I mean, she's ambitious, but her scruples are airtight."

Tanner nods, sips his coffee. "That's good to hear."

A hawk soars above the trees. I sip my coffee and watch it spin in lazy circles, then float over a distant ridge. A tiny niggle of doubt creeps into my mind about Brooke. Is it possible that she wants this bad enough to try something like what Tanner's suggesting?

"I didn't actually come out here to pry into your love life," Tanner says, setting his coffee down.

Prickles erupt on the back of my neck. "That sounds ominous."

"Vonnie's struggling in my class."

I give him a look. "Vonnie the straight-A student?"

"Believe me, I'm as surprised as you are."

I cradle my half-empty cup of coffee that's quickly turning tepid in the chilly air. First Leah, now Vonnie? What the fuck is going on? "Struggling how?"

Tanner shrugs. "She's missing two essays and seems...well...disinterested, I guess."

My gut jolts into my diaphragm, souring the coffee I drank. "Huh."

"I didn't catch the missing work until this morning, when I was entering grades from the first quarter." He gulps from his cup. "Maybe she just forgot to turn them in?"

"That's probably it," I reply, though doubt quickly sets in. Vonnie doesn't forget something as important to her as turning in assignments on time. There's also the part about her seeming disinterested, which is definitely not like her.

After we shoot the shit for a while longer, Tanner drains the last of his coffee and stands, stretching his lanky frame. "Well, I better get back to my grading. I can give Vonnie a few days to turn in those essays. Normally I don't take late work, but this isn't like her."

We fist bump and I walk him to his car. "Thanks for bringing my stuff over."

He climbs into his Tahoe. "Welcome. We still on for tomorrow?"

My Sunday hockey game. Two hours of testosterone and sweat. "Yep."

He starts his car and gives me a two-finger salute. "Thanks for the coffee."

I tap the side of his door as he pulls away.

NOT SEEING Brooke all weekend slowly drives me crazy. I type out a dozen texts, then erase them. I resist the urge to drive by her place, see if she's there, make sure the cats don't have her surrounded. How is she spending her time? Is she out sightseeing? Our fall colors are gorgeous. She could be hiking, or taking a drive. Or is she pecking furiously away at her laptop, writing the story of the century that will land her the job?

An image of her welcoming trick-or-treaters from her doorstep pops into my thoughts. She's smiling at the kids and admiring their costumes as they grab candy from the bowl in her hands. Inside, her cottage is warm from the fire burning in the fireplace. Would greeting trick-or-treaters be the kind of colleagues do together?

No. Because in between doorbell rings I'd be going crazy with the need to kiss her.

My fingers clench and my heart races. How am I going to settle for being her coworker when can't stop thinking about all the dirty ways I want to make her come?

On Sunday afternoon, I come in from stacking wood to find Vonnie at the kitchen table doing homework, earbuds stuffed in her ears. I slip into the kitchen and crank out a grilled cheese sandwich then set it in front of her.

Her gaze lifts to mine and she removes one of the earbuds. "How'd you know I was starving?"

I cross my arms. "Call it a hunch."

She takes a bite and gazes back at her work.

"How's it coming?" I ask.

"Last problem, so…good," she says, snapping her book shut with a look of relief. "Calculus hurts my brain."

I pour us both a glass of ice water and carry them back to the table. After carefully moving a sleeping Gideon from the chair, I take his place next to Vonnie. "How are the rest of your classes going?"

She takes another bite and gives me an anxious glance. "Okay."

"Your English teacher says you've got a few missing assignments."

She sets her sandwich down and sighs. "The book we're reading is pointless."

"What's the book?"

"Catcher in the Rye."

I read every syllabus, so I know this was last month's book. Because of this timing, I conclude that the missing essays are very likely tied to it. "Why is it pointless?"

She sighs. "Well, Holden hates his life, right? So he goes on a walk-about to feel sorry for himself. Whenever we read it in class I feel like someone's drilling a hole in my skull."

"A lot of people think that book is a masterpiece."

"I'm definitely not one of them."

I slide a paper from under a textbook with the assignment details. "Is this the essay prompt?"

The most ambiguous encounter in the book is Holden's night at Mr. Antolini's apartment. What do you make of Mr. Antolini's actions? Was he making a pass at Holden? What is the significance of his actions, and how do they relate to his role as someone trying to prevent Holden from "taking a fall"?

I watch Vonnie's face. "That's a pretty juicy topic. Do you have an opinion?"

"Touching him like that was weird," she says, doodling on the edge of her paper.

I rack my brain for the details of the book. "You mean, when Holden was asleep and Mr. Antolini stroked his head?"

"Yeah."

"You think he made a pass at Holden?"

She gives a one-shoulder shrug, the universal teenage non-answer.

"When you were younger, before I went to bed I'd come check on you," I say softly.

She tears off a corner of sandwich and nibbles on it . "That's different. You're my brother."

"Maybe Mr. Antolini cared for Holden like a son."

"Maybe," she says, and takes a sip of water. "I'll get the essays done. I just...wish I could write about something else."

I resist the urge to remind her that she likely could have hashed out an alternative if the paper wasn't already a month late.

"Let me know if you need help," I say, then grab her empty plate and head for the kitchen.

A WEEK LATER, I'm in town finishing up an interview with a state park ranger about the herd of elk that have come down for the winter and remember that Vonnie needs a poster board for a health class project. I drive to the drug store that also doubles as an art and office supply depot. It's next door to a natural grocery store inside Penny Creek's only mall. I decide that after I get Vonnie's poster board, I'll pop into the grocery store for the chocolate covered almonds the twins love. They're twice as expensive as the prepackaged ones at the IGA, but Leah says these ones are made with sustainably farmed chocolate that gives back to the rainforest.

Inside the cramped, stuffy drug store that smells of cinnamon incense, I pace the aisles, looking for what Vonnie needs, when I hear a voice that stops me cold.

"Hmm, it's close, but I need a flat brush," the voice says.

Chills run down my spine.

"I can special order it," a man's voice replies. "I'll just get your information down. Should be here Friday, will that be all right?"

"Yes, thank you."

I grab the poster board, but my feet are rooted to the spot.

Hazel's muffled chatter with the clerk filters down the aisles, then the bell door chimes. She's gone, and I missed her.

Why the hell did I chicken out?

I purchase the poster and head for the exit, wondering why I didn't buy the almonds first. Now I have to lug the awkward poster board to the grocery store.

When I step through the entrance, Hazel Gunn is pushing a cart ahead of me. Her white-blonde hair is braided down her back. She's wearing a pastel pink down jacket and baggy jeans with a pair of worn leather hiking boots.

I spin on my heel and run into Brooke.

"Oh, uh, hey, sorry," I stammer, trying not to stare. She's wearing a soft sweater with a deep V and of all things, a skirt. My pulse gives a little jolt.

She's grabbed my arms to steady herself, but she lets go when Hazel hurries over.

"It *is* you!" Hazel says. To my surprise, she pulls me into a hug.

Back then, Hazel felt frail. Today, she feels strong, her arms giving me an impressive squeeze. The relief that she's fought back in order to be strong fills me with a feeling I don't quite understand. Pride doesn't fit. Admiration?

"Brooke, this is Hazel," I say and step back so they can shake hands.

"It's a pleasure to meet you," Brooke says, then flashes me a look. "I didn't know you and Wyatt were friends."

Hazel seems oblivious to the edge in Brooke's tone. "Yes," she says, her round face rosy. "We go way back."

"It's good to see you, Hazel," I say. "You're here until the end of the year, right?"

"How did you..." Hazel says with a smile that makes her eyes sparkle. "Oh, of course. I forgot you work at the paper."

"Brooke's a journalist too," I say, though I don't know why.

"How's the artist cabin?" Brooke asks.

"Cozy," Hazel says simply. "It has a lovely view of Dove Peak."

"It must be nice to come home," Brooke says.

I can hear the eagerness in Brooke's voice and have to resist the urge to stomp on her foot. *Leave Hazel alone*, I want to say.

A conflicted look passes through Hazel's eyes. "Yes, it is," she says.

"How are your folks?" I ask Hazel.

Her smile returns. "They're great. Still loving the California sunshine."

My gut leaps over my diaphragm.

"How's Peter?" she asks, her lips tightening. "Is he still here too?"

I don't correct her assumption that I've been in Penny Creek all this time. That I didn't also find my way out only to be sucked back in. "No, he's an E.R. doctor in Bend."

Her eyes light up. "Oh, that's wonderful. He was always so dedicated to helping people."

My gut gives another hard tug. *Is that why he refused to accept your way of handling what happened? Because he couldn't help you?*

Hazel gives me a sad smile. "Tell him I said hello."

"I will," I lie.

"It was nice to meet you, Brooke," Hazel says softly.

"It was great meeting you," Brooke replies. She gives me a sharp, side-eyed glance. One might think she's jealous. Interesting.

"I'm sure we'll see each other around," Hazel says warmly, then turns and pushes her cart down the aisle.

I stand frozen, watching her go. Brooke's eyes are practically lasers on Hazel's back. Once she's out of sight, Brooke faces me. "You didn't tell me you two were so close."

"It's not really your business, is it?" I say. Okay, so maybe I'm baiting her. Serves her right for wearing a skirt.

Her mouth drops open. "Oh," she says. "Well if you aren't going to help me set up an interview, I'll do it myself."

Before I can grab her arm to stop her, Brooke scoops up a grocery basket and dashes down the aisle after Hazel.

13

BROOKE

I chase after Hazel, trying to put my questions about her and Wyatt out of my mind. The way her face lit up when she called his name made it clear they were more than just classmates. But Wyatt didn't seem to reflect the same joy at seeing her. More like apprehension. Is it because of an old wound he's trying to hide?

"Hazel," I say as I catch up to her. On the way I've added a bag of organic blue corn chips to my basket so my trailing after her looks casual. I had only stopped by for more tea—the IGA's idea of English Breakfast tastes like dirty socks.

Hazel turns, surprised. "Oh, hello again."

"Hi," I say. There's a reason why Hazel hasn't wanted to talk to journalists, so I have to tread carefully. "I saw on Cavendish Gallery's door that you're doing an evening reception next month."

"Yes, Donna has been a big supporter. It's the least I can do since I'm in town."

"You have so many fans here," I say. "What's that like?"

Hazel pauses, her face emanating that same soft glow. She has a peaceful way about her. I can't quite put my finger on why I think that.

"At first, it was very strange," she says. "I was getting these long letters from people who had bought one of my paintings. The first time I was recognized on the street I couldn't believe it. Little old me? Signing an autograph?" She giggles, which softens her features even more, making her look like a teenage girl joking around with her friends.

We turn and follow the freezer section against the back wall.

"Are you a patron of the arts?" Hazel asks.

"Yes," I say. "Though I don't own very much of it."

She gives me a dismissive wave. "That's not important. You're a journalist, right? So you're a creative too."

I grab a box of gluten-free frozen toaster waffles to keep up the pretense that I'm shopping. I hope they don't taste like glue. "Yeah."

"Do you have fans? Readers who follow your work?"

"The only time I hear from readers is when they want to complain or correct me," I say with a laugh. I blink at the rows of ice cream containers, stunned by the plethora of dairy-free and organic options. For such a small town, there seems to be an inordinate number of specialty foods. But maybe this store caters to the wealthy fussy types who fly in for the weekend.

Hazel adds several loaves of frozen bread to her cart. "I'm sure plenty of people enjoy what you write, though," she says. "Have you been at the Gazette long?"

"About three weeks," I reply as we turn down the pasta aisle.

Hazel's pale blue eyes widen. "Oh my. How's it going?"

"Okay," I say with a sigh. "Penny Creek is a small town. It's hard for an outsider like me to break in."

"But you have Wyatt. He'll help you," Hazel says with a kind smile.

I try to read between the lines. Does she have feelings for him? I shouldn't care, but the idea of it makes my stomach jerk into my diaphragm.

"He's been great," I lie. Even though we've established a kind of détente, he torments me. He doesn't even have to say anything—it happens anytime he's near me, like minutes ago when we crashed into each other. I start to feel warm and jittery. Almost like I might be sick.

Hazel reads the label on a jar of sauce, then adds two of them to her cart.

"I think it's really special that you've come back to Penny Creek," I say.

A pensive look passes through her features, but then it clears.

"You have so many fans here, and I'm sure they'd want to know more about your work and your process." I inhale a deep breath. "Would you be willing to talk with me about it for the paper?"

Hazel's eyes tighten and her body stills.

"We could meet at your cabin. You could show me your studio and that view you told me about. It would be a lovely thing to share with your fans, this little glimpse of your world now that you're working in this same landscape that shaped you into an artist."

"I don't give interviews," she replies in a stiff voice.

"I know," I say in my warmest tone. "But this wouldn't be anything fussy. It's just a conversation. Your fans would love it. It could be like a way to give back to them for all of their support."

I manage to hold back my cringe. I hate myself for basically guilting her into this. But damn it, I need this story. Internet searches of Hazel's life have produced slim results. So far my biggest story for the Gazette has been the house fire that became an arson investigation, but that ended a week ago with a confession from the kid. Hardly enticing enough to garner an increase in subscriptions. But an exclusive interview of a shy and celebrated artist? It's at least a step in the right direction.

"Oh, well, all right then," she says, trying for a smile but it doesn't quite reach her eyes.

"It'll be fun, I promise," I say, and silently swear to make it so.

Her eyes lose their tense edge but her hands seem to be gripping the shopping cart handle.

"Would Friday be all right? In the afternoon?"

"Yes," Hazel says with a soft nod. "I can make that work. I usually stop for a break around three."

"Perfect," I say as a satisfied glow starts to pulse inside my chest. "I'll come by then."

"Okay," Hazel says, flashing me a brave smile.

We continue down the aisle. I need to part in order to grab my tea, so I say goodbye to Hazel and stroll to the wall of tea and naturopathic remedies. I snatch two boxes of English Breakfast and hurry to the checkout.

Then I drive to Cavendish Gallery and step inside. A woman dressed in a long cardigan in a gorgeous burnt orange color, low boots, and form-fitting black pants greets me, her heels clicking on the shiny hardwood floor.

"Let me know if there's anything you need," she says in a warm, sophisticated tone. "We also offer espresso or tea. Would you like something?"

"That's so nice of you," I say. "I would love some tea."

The deep lines around her bright brown eyes crinkle with her easy smile. She turns to the back of the gallery. I use the time she's busy to peruse the wall of Hazel's watercolor paintings. The first one is large, at least five feet wide, and features a stunning landscape of rolling hills dotted with aspen groves. The colors are soft and peaceful. Her brush strokes are feminine, playful. I can almost feel her joyful mood. I'm not much of an art buff, but I can clearly understand the appeal of her work.

"I'm Donna Hart," the woman says as she offers me a china cup of what smells like green tea.

I introduce myself and we share a soft handshake.

"I see you're enjoying Hazel's latest collection," Donna says with an appreciative smile at the wall.

I take a sip of my tea and want to practically weep in appreciation. So few people know how to brew it to its grassy, rich perfection without the bitterness. "I just ran into her, actually."

Donna's eyebrows arch. "Do you know her?"

I set the cup back on its saucer. "No, but we have a mutual friend," I say. "Wyatt Morgan." But "friends" isn't even close to what Wyatt and I are right now. It's like we're trying to hate each other, but it's not working. It's also not making it any easier to resist him. More like the opposite.

Donna nods, but her eyes have narrowed like she's thinking something through.

"I'm a journalist too. I'm at the Gazette for a few months on a temporary assignment."

If the woman regrets the generous welcome she's given me now that she knows I'm not buying a painting, she hides it well.

I turn my attention back to Hazel's paintings. Donna turns as well, and we share a silent moment of reverence. I notice there's no price tag on Hazel's work, but I know from my research that the sizable one I'm staring at would cost more than my car.

"I'd like to write up something about you and your gallery, maybe lean on your long-term relationship with Hazel and your support of her work." I'm betting Donna was one of the first art patrons to give Hazel a chance.

Donna's face brightens. "I'd be happy to assist in any way I can."

I gaze at the smaller painting to the left of the large one. Thick, black clouds hover over a valley, one side thick with pine trees, the other a carpet of wildflowers, the colors muted by the storm yet still rich. Everything about the painting is simple, yet it's that same sense of peace it brings that's so remarkable. As if all is as it should be, storm included.

Will I ever feel that way about Wyatt? There are giant storm clouds on our horizon, but nothing about them feels peaceful.

Donna and I set up a time for an interview, and then I thank her for the tea and slip from the gallery.

Back in Wyatt's office, I collapse into his chair and type up my notes, but the same niggling question keeps rising to the top: were Wyatt and Hazel once together? Wyatt spewed his coffee in the editorial meeting when he heard her name. Did Hazel once break Wyatt's heart? And does he still have feelings for her?

I open a browser window on my laptop and try to find any records from Rogue Valley High that would reveal Wyatt and Hazel's past. Did they work on the high school newspaper together? Swim together? I click on the few articles I find, but the connection eludes me. According to the Rogue Valley High's yearbook, Hazel was active in the cross-country ski club, youth group, and the art club. Wyatt didn't partake in any of those activities, but I'm guessing that's because of swimming. He won several medals at state, then at Junior Nationals his junior year, then got a scholarship to Oregon State. I follow the link trail, my curiosity getting the better of me. I follow along as he wins more medals, but then see a headline that stops me cold: "Olympic Hopeful Quits Relay Team."

I open the article, dated six years ago and written by a sports reporter for the Oregonian.

"Two weeks after the roster for the 400 Relay on the US Olympic Swimming Team was finalized, third leg and U.S. National Freestyle medalist Wyatt Morgan abruptly left the team, citing personal reasons. Morgan couldn't be reached for comment but teammates were in shock. 'He's wanted this so badly,' relay anchor Rob Bridger said. 'I can't believe he just walked away.'"

I sit back and stare at the article, an uncomfortable twinge sparking in my gut.

According to reports from the Olympics in Rio, the relay team didn't medal. A coach speculated that not having enough time to incorporate a new member of the relay before the event was the cause.

I don't have to pull up a calendar to know that the timing fits: Wyatt left the Olympic team to take over responsibilities here with his family.

The memory of my self-righteous speech about sacrifices outside Sourdough Gil's gives my stomach an uncomfortable jolt. Why didn't Wyatt stop me? Here I was thinking he would never understand, and all along, he's one of the few people in my life who does?

Though I know it's shitty, a steady rise of anger fills my insides.

He's had plenty of opportunities to tell me about sacrificing his dream for his family. Why has he kept it from me?

I stand and gaze out the window, over the bare streets below to the distant mountains. This doesn't change my conviction that sleeping with Wyatt would be a horrible idea. But he wasn't bullshitting me when he said, "I understand." The doubt I had that night is gone.

He *does* understand. He gets that part of me because he's been there. My breath hitches, but I gulp a soothing breath and force the emotion back.

Since our kiss at Sourdough Gill's, we've fallen into a kind of respectful rivalry. It's helped to keep my feelings at bay, but now...

I groan. If only I had known these things about him. That he and Hazel shared some kind of intimacy that still affects him. That he abandoned his dream to take care of his family.

But would I have chosen differently that night at the bar? I imagine him walking me inside my cottage and picking up where we left off on the dance floor. The longing to feel his lips on my body rises up so fast I have to steady myself against the wall.

A door slams somewhere in the building, snapping me back to Wyatt's office. I shake off images of Wyatt stripping me out of my clothes on the way to my bedroom and settle back in his chair.

I call my contact at the Denver DMV for a favor and learn that Hazel got her license at age sixteen, then renewed it in San Luis Obispo at age seventeen, in August. If she moved in the spring, why did she wait so long to update her license? But this gives me at least a ballpark starting point. After graduating San Luis High, she attended Laguna College of Art and Design. She sold her first painting as a sophomore at a school showing, then her career took off. She now has paintings in a dozen galleries across the U.S. and she's won several awards.

I pick up my phone and tap Maggie's number. If anyone would know about art, it's her.

"Can you hang on a sec?" she asks in a half-whisper.

I do, overhearing her cheerful goodbye to a customer.

"Okay, I'm back," she says.

"How's business?" I ask.

"The closer we are to the holidays, the better. I had a woman in here earlier shopping for lingerie for her wedding night, and the guy who just left is planning a babymoon over Thanksgiving."

"That's so romantic," I say. *Down, ovaries.*

"I'm sending you a little present," Maggie says. "They just came in and I'm so excited."

"You didn't have to do that," I say, sliding off my shoes so I can sit crisscross in Wyatt's chair.

"It was the least I could do after you sent me that hoody. I've been wearing it all week."

Next to the IGA is a little gift shop I've sort of fallen in love with. Inside, they sell just about every funky, quirky Idaho-themed kitsch imaginable. Stuffed Jackalopes, salt and pepper shakers shaped like Idaho spuds topped with a pat of butter, and of course, t-shirts and sweatshirts with the "Famous Potatoes" logo: a pair of potatoes wearing sunglasses. I knew Maggie would get a kick out of them, so sent her a red hoody. "I bought one in blue," I say. "So when I get home we can be twinsies at yoga. Maybe it'll impress that guy in row three you're always lusting after."

Maggie laughs. "Just because he's hot doesn't mean I'm lusting! Now, you know I love to hear from you in the middle of my workday, but what's up?"

I easily detect the change in subject away from Hot Guy in Row Three and make a note to circle back. Maggie has been single for over a year after she discovered her steady in one of her dressing rooms trying on women's underwear. This after several of her nicest pairs had gone missing from her dresser.

"Do you know Hazel Gunn, the watercolor artist?" I ask.

"She had a show in Denver last year," Maggie says. "I heard that every one of her paintings sold out beforehand."

"Was Hazel there?"

"I think so, which is why I remember it. She's kind of a recluse. Doesn't make appearances often."

"I met her today."

Maggie gasped. "Is she as sweet as she looks in her bio picture?"

"Yeah, I got a very 'kind soul' sort of vibe from her."

"The rumor is she had some kind of breakdown during her freshman year at art school. But a year later, she's winning awards, so maybe it's not true."

"What was the breakdown related to?" I ask, tucking my left foot further under my right thigh.

"No idea. It's probably made up."

"She did seem, I don't know…a little fragile, maybe."

"Maybe her art balances her out."

I think about this for a moment. "She seemed happy, just not super confident."

"What's she doing in Penny Creek?"

"There's a pretty substantial art appreciation crowd here, and the Guild offered her their Artist in Residence opportunity this year. This is also where she grew up."

"Are you running a story?"

"Bingo," I reply. "I'm trying to piece together her timeline and why it's taken her so long to return to Penny Creek. There's a gallery in town that's supported her work since the beginning, and hosted plenty of shows for her, but Hazel has never attended."

"Well, if she's choosing between Denver or L.A. and Penny Creek, can you blame her?"

"I guess not," I say with a sigh.

"What, you think she avoided coming back?" Maggie asks. "She's there now. And not just for a showing. For six weeks."

"I know, but why now? Why has she waited?"

"Sounds like you have your angle," Maggie says. "Call me tonight, okay? I want an update on Mr. Tempting."

My stomach flips, and because I'm hungry, it's painful. "I'll save you the suspense," I reply with a tight huff. "He kissed me at the bar that night."

Maggie gasped. "And?"

"And then I told him about Hugh and how I wasn't going to let anyone keep me from getting that job at the Times."

"Oh, Brooksie. Why didn't you tell him that after you let him tie you to your bedpost?"

The empty place inside me clenches. "Very funny."

"Well, at least you've made your case," Maggie replies.

"Yeah," I say. So why was it making me feel miserable? Especially now that I knew he understood my resistance. "The funny thing is, we're trying to be friends now."

Maggie's voice hitches in surprise. "Really? Wow. How's that working?"

"Oh, um, it's good," I say, but it's more to convince myself than Maggie.

"Hmm," Maggie replies.

"I think he may have a history with Hazel," I say, my voice lowering, though there's no reason to hide my curiosity. Is there?

"Ooh, the plot thickens," Maggie replies conspiratorially. "You mean like back in high school?"

"They were the same year. He said they knew each other, but when I met her today, he happened to be there too. You should have seen the hug she gave him."

"Well, high school was a long time ago."

"It's not that I'm jealous, or anything," I say quickly.

"Mmmhmm," Maggie says knowingly.

I groan. "It's more that...well...Wyatt lied to me. They are obviously closer than just classmates."

"All kinds of crazy stuff happens in high school. Maybe he'd rather not revisit it."

"Maybe. But he still hid it from me."

"I get it that's your hot button, but maybe hold your venom until you know the whole story."

"That's just it," I say with a sigh. "I feel like I'm never going to get the whole story."

"Yeah, right," Maggie says. "Nothing gets past Brooke Henderson."

This makes me smile, but I wonder if I've discovered a mystery I can't crack.

14

WYATT

That morning, I run the team through a brutal practice—we have a big meet coming up—while thinking about my upcoming meeting, which involves me getting on a horse.

After practice, I step outside and call to the twins who are waiting for me as usual. The crisp morning air tickles the back of my throat with icy needles.

"Why don't you at least give us the keys so we can wait in the rig? It's freezing," Leah says as she pushes off the wall.

"You two are too much of a flight risk," I joke as she and Vonnie fall in next to me as we walk to the Suburban. When I back out of the parking spot, a burst of color moves past my rearview mirror. I slam on the brakes just as a car horn sounds.

A woman gets out of the car and strides toward me. In a flash, I recognize her: a pissed-off Brooke dressed in black leggings and a red down coat.

"You almost T-boned me!" she says, her eyes flashing.

I meet her at the rear bumper. "Maybe you should slow down."

Her mouth tightens. "Well, if your pool didn't have such ridiculously early hours, I wouldn't need to drive so fast."

I start to laugh, which is the wrong move because her expression turns furious.

"It's not funny!" she says.

I have to resist the urge to cup her gorgeous face and kiss away her anger. In the pale morning light, her blue eyes match the color of the sky and her lips are the same shade of pink bathing the peaks behind her.

But I can't kiss her—colleagues don't kiss in the middle of the parking lot.

"I'm sorry I scared you," I say.

She gives me a tense huff.

The Suburban door behind me opens and I suddenly have company. Shit. Just what I need.

"It's her," Vonnie says to Leah.

Brooke raises her eyebrows at me.

"Uh, Brooke, these are my sisters, Leah and Vonnie."

"You guys kissed at the bar," Leah says.

Brooke's eyes widen.

I give Leah a stern look.

"What?" she says to me. "You pry into my life enough."

Touché. "It's in my job description to look out for you," I say.

"Whatever," Leah grumbles.

Vonnie steps forward. "Would you be willing to be a guest speaker in my AP English class?"

"Von, Brooke doesn't have time to be your show and tell, she's got—"

"I'd be honored," Brooke interrupts, sending me a defiant cock of her eyebrows.

"Awesome, gimme your number," Vonnie replies, whipping out her phone to type it in, then gives me a sly glance before saying to Brooke, "It's great to meet you. Wyatt never brings his dates over, so—"

I reach around Vonnie to clamp a hand over her mouth. "I think we'll be going now," I say, attempting to drag her backwards.

Beneath my hand, Vonnie is trying to protest.

We get to the door and I open it, then playfully push my sisters back into the backseat.

Brooke's surprised look has morphed into an amused smirk. "What are you up to today?"

I open my door. "I'm actually doing something you suggested," I say over the sound of my sisters fighting about something.

"Oh?" she asks, her mouth twitching with a tiny smile.

"I'm going to meet a new source for my CJ story." Apparently, I'll have to ride a horse to do it. Something I'm not looking forward to.

Her eyes brighten. "See? I'm full of all kinds of good ideas."

I step closer. "How about I return the favor with one of mine?" Yeah, this is flirting, and colleagues don't flirt, but the way she's smiling at me is throwing everything thing out the window.

"Why do I get the feeling this is going to be inappropriate?" she asks.

I take another step closer, drinking in the flecks of gold in her eyes. "Do you want it to be?"

She rolls her eyes and steps back, but I caught the look on her face she tried to hide.

I watch her go, my pulse thumping south so hard it hurts. "Have a good swim," I say.

Without turning back, she gives me a little wave.

It takes effort to climb into the Suburban with a raging hard on. By the time I get situated behind the wheel, in my rearview, Brooke is halfway to the pool door, her ponytail swinging and her tight little ass as tempting as ever.

I clench my eyes tight and release a groan. How much longer can I take this?

AN HOUR LATER, I pull into the parking area where Noah Tucker is tacking up a horse at the side of his dust-coated trailer. His tall frame moves easily among the animals. I park and step from the rig with the things I packed for our ride. Noah grew up with horses and agreed to escort me to CJ's winter grazing area so I can meet up with his sheep-herders, a group of Basque cowboys who so far have eluded me.

"Mornin'," I call out, my warm breath making white clouds in the chilly air.

He looks up from his saddle adjustments. "You bring coffee?" he asks with a grin.

"Of course," I say, lifting the thermos. "And fresh fritters."

"Good, cuz I wouldda sent you packing if you hadn't."

I laugh and approach the trailer. Though we weren't friends back in high school, as adults Noah and I have discovered a mutual respect. A few years ago, I helped him find a witness to a crime, and since then we've kept an open communication when possible. He tipped me off when they found Jonah Rundell's bones, which thankfully meant I got to write that story.

"You sure you remember how to do this?" Noah asks, ducking under the reins and accepting the cup of coffee I've poured him in the lid of the thermos.

"I guess we'll find out," I reply. When I was a kid, my dad traded building some guy's porch for an aging horse because Annika wanted one, but she was too little to ride alone, so I'd put her in front of me and we'd ride bareback up and down Cold Springs Road.

Noah flips up the side of the saddle to fiddle with the cinch under the horse, giving it a hard yank before securing it. "I got some news this morning that you probably don't know."

"Oh?" I ask.

Noah's horse stomps one of his back feet and swishes his tail. "Remember those bones that turned up last month?" he says, lengthening one of the stirrups. "The Youth Pastor's?"

Though his voice is neutral, it still feels like an accusation. "Sure do," I say and paste on a smile.

Noah unties my horse's reins and clicks his tongue to get her to back up. "Well, the expert at the university sent us a report. We're going through it today."

A tremor tingles through my belly. "Did they find something?" I ask, taking the reins from Noah.

"Not sure yet."

My heart patters into my throat. This is a warning—the closest he can come to telling me there's more to this story than a lost hiker.

Noah mounts then fixes me with a narrow gaze. "Word's going to get out once we start asking questions. I know I can count on you to be a straight shooter."

"You have my word," I say after a hard swallow.

"And I also know you'll do your own digging." He adjusts his cowboy hat. "Keep me in the loop."

"Done," I say, and hoist myself onto my horse. If Noah notices my lack of grace, he doesn't comment.

We set off up a double track, our horses plodding left, right, left, the saddles squeaking.

"What does your pop think about you helping a Morgan?" I ask. Noah's dad, Bill Tucker, and my dad have a long history, most of which I don't understand. Bill seems to have a special place in his cold heart for my younger brother Caleb that borders on harassment, especially when he was younger. Caleb didn't help things by being a hellraiser.

Noah gives a soft grunt. "Do you always ask such personal questions so early in the morning?"

I laugh. "It's an occupational hazard."

We cross a wide, shallow creek, the horses' hooves clattering against the stones.

When we're side by side again, Noah says, "My dad and your dad may have had their differences, but I'd rather keep an open mind."

I think about the risk he's taking, defying his father for me. From what I've experienced with Bill, that's not an easy task.

He gives me a wry grin. "Plus, you're going to repay me with any intel you gain from today."

"I'll do my best," I say with a laugh.

We ride on, side by side now on a double track cut into the faded, brown grass. I try to move with the horse's smooth gait, but my legs have long forgotten how to ride a horse. My ass is already getting sore. I'm not about to complain though.

Noah's revelation about Rundell's bones and what it means rattles around in my head. I wish I could tell Brooke about it. Why didn't I ask her to come with me today? We could fumble with our horsemanship together. Her feisty reaction to me in the parking lot fills my mind. When she's fired up like that I can't help but want to kiss her. It was like that the first time I talked to her.

Come on, tell me your name, I said while caressing down her arm.

You don't need my name for this, she replied, and pulled me to kiss her.

It's clear she doesn't like to get up early. Well, something must have been different that morning we were together, because she was up before the sun, ready for another round.

Fuck. It's nearly impossible to ride with a rod of steel in your pants, but looks like I'll be doing it anyway.

I liked that little smile on her lips when she heard I was doing something she suggested. It made me feel...I don't know...eager to please her, which is crazy. Normally I don't take orders from anyone, but somehow this felt different. Like we're a team.

How can we be a team? We both want the same job and there's only one of us who can win.

But damn I loved seeing that spark in her eyes when I teased her. I'm sick of avoiding her. Sick of having to come into our four o'clock meeting late so I don't have to sit next to her. I want to kiss her and touch her and bury myself deep inside her. And I know she wants it too.

Why do I get the feeling it's going to be inappropriate?

Do you want it to be?

I grimace at the pale blue sky. We're stuck and I don't know how to fix it and it's eating me up inside.

We ride up a gentle rise through a band of pine trees, the icy air tasting of dust. Ahead are the rolling hills of the north country in faded yellows and browns; behind me, the granite Sawtooths poke into the pale blue sky like daggers.

"There they are," Noah says, nodding to the cluster of white dots nestled into the sage in a wide draw between two broad hills. "Let's ride to the ridge above. They'll be up there."

True enough. As we crest the bald ridge, I spot two cowboys, one down in the scrub, gazing our way from his horse, and the other on the south side of the flock, one eye on the sheep and one on us. According to what CJ was forced to disclose for his defense, Marko Zuniga and his cousin Salbatore are in charge of the flock.

"They're legal, right?" I ask. "I don't want to cause some kind of immigration scandal."

Noah adjusts his cowboy hat. "They're legal, but I wouldn't doubt they've got an uncle or grandparent stashed somewhere who doesn't have papers."

"Morning," I say to the cowboy as we draw closer.

The tanned man with black hair, who is probably in his thirties but looks fifty, nods, his dark eyes full of suspicion.

"Salbatore Zuniga?" Noah asks, adjusting his hat.

"Yes," the man says with a hint of an accent.

Noah dismounts, and I follow suit, so relieved to hit the ground that I could kiss it. Noah takes my horse's reins, freeing me to approach.

"I'm Wyatt Morgan, from the Mountain Gazette," I say, then indicate Noah with a nod. "This is Officer Noah Tucker. I'd like to talk with you about those murdered lambs last summer and how they ended up in wolf territory," I say. Beating around the bush is for pussies. Maybe I should take this approach with Brooke. Just burst into the office and kiss her until she changes her mind.

Salbatore frowns, his distrusting gaze shifting from me to Noah. "I don't have to talk to you."

"You know that the woman he tried to set up is a graduate student, right? She's about as capable of kidnapping a lamb, on foot no doubt, as I am of winning the rodeo."

Salbatore's horse shifts on his feet but Salbatore moves with him, as if they are one being. "Maybe she had help," he fires back with glaring eyes.

"When was the last time you had a pay raise?" I ask.

His gaze darkens. "CJ's family is good to me and my family. He gave Marko a job, got his wife work as a seamstress."

"Yet you live in a shack," I say.

"We live free, under the skies," he replies as he calmly scans the flock, his hands stacked on his saddle horn. "It is enough."

"Is it enough when it's twenty below and your kids can't get warm?"

He turns away with a disgusted grunt. "You cannot possibly understand."

"What if there was a way to make things better for you and your family?" I ask.

He turns his horse to face me. "By poking your nose in our business? No, that would not make things better."

"Where does CJ keep the arsenic?"

Salbatore shakes his head in defiance. "I think it is time for you to go."

"I hope for your sake that CJ didn't put you up to killing those lambs," I say. "Because there's no doubt in my mind he'd be willing to sell your hide to save his."

Salbatore's eyes flash with unease, but then he waves the back of his hand at me, as if I'm a pesky fly he's trying to deter.

I step forward and extend my card. "Push is going to come to shove when he goes to trial. Call me when you need someone to hear your side of the story."

Salbatore is still gazing at the sheep, his face expressionless. Finally, he glances at the card, then into my eyes, as if trying to read my soul. Then he takes the card and slides it into his shirt pocket.

15

BROOKE

After seeing how carefully Hazel chose her groceries, I decide not to show up with food and choose a bouquet of roses and a box of my favorite herbal tea instead. Maybe it's overkill, and maybe it's going to make her suspicious, but I can't help myself. And showing up with something in my hands will hopefully make them stop shaking.

I shouldn't be nervous. After all, I live for these moments—that feeling like I'm on the edge of something meaningful. Something that's exclusively mine to share with the world.

Hazel's cabin is located west of town, on land donated long ago to the art guild. I follow Buck Creek road past an abandoned sheep corral to a Y where a creek trickles out of the hills, then around a broad ridge. A dusty blue minivan with California plates is parked outside the single-story wood structure with a tiny porch and a view of the meadow and distant White Cloud Mountains.

I'm no artist, but I'm definitely inspired. What is it like for Hazel?

When I step outside, a breeze rattles the leaves on the aspen trees growing along the creek. The cold air tastes of the coppery water and faintly of the dust my tires kicked up. A thin column of smoke rises from the cabin's chimney into the blue sky dotted with puffy clouds that cast shadows over the broad valley. A tingle races down my spine —maybe because of the stark beauty, or maybe because of what I'm about to attempt.

During my swim I tried to shove back the feeling that coming here is somehow betraying Wyatt. That makes no sense, but that look of apprehension in his eyes won't fade from my thoughts. If he's not willing to use his connection with Hazel—whatever it is—to land a scoop like this, I'm certainly not going to be shy. I shouldn't care what he thinks, but a growing part of me does. This morning, when he teased me, I should have shot him down, reinforced the distance between us. But these past few weeks he hasn't even looked at me. I've missed it. I've missed his playfulness, his sultry little smirk that makes my insides clench, those dirty words that make my blood heat.

I grit my teeth as I walk up to the cottage. Of course it has to be me enforcing the friend zone. This morning is proof that he can't stop himself.

And a growing part of me doesn't want him to.

My soft knock on the door brings Hazel to it almost immediately, as if she was waiting behind the door. She's wearing a tie-dyed sweat-shirt, faded, baggy jeans, and wool slippers. Her white-blonde hair is tied back in messy twin buns.

Her eyes widen when she sees the flowers. "You didn't have to do that."

I smile. "I have a feeling you don't buy them for yourself."

She gives me a confused look, as if she's surprised I've guessed this. "That's true." She buries her nose into the cluster of tight petals and inhales a slow, deep breath. She's not wearing any makeup, which in this moment makes her seem even younger. "Mmm, they're lovely. Thank you."

"I brought you some tea, too," I say as she welcomes me inside.

Her look changes to a shy smile. "Are you trying to butter me up?"

I laugh and it feels good, like maybe I've broken through to her a little bit already.

"Not at all," I reply. "I appreciate you talking with me today, and I'm kind of a tea snob, so I figured I'd better bring some."

Hazel laughs again, making her round face shine. "Then I'll make us a pot," she says, then busies herself with finding a vase for the roses and filling the kettle.

From where I'm standing in the middle of the main room, I take in the cozy space. To the left is the tiny kitchen and to the right are two rooms separated by a bathroom. One must be the studio space, the other, the bedroom. A wood stove sits in the back corner, wood gently crackling from inside the thick iron oven, with a loveseat and matching chair facing a huge window with the same valley view I ogled at from the driveway. Evidence of her passion is everywhere in the cabin. A collection of paint tubes on a side table. A Fed Ex box opened on the floor with several sizes of brushes inside. A paint-spattered portable speaker on the coffee table.

Hazel exits the tiny kitchen with two mugs of tea. She's smiling, but her eyes have a guarded edge about them. "I wish we could sit outside, but I'm afraid it's too cold. Is that okay?"

"Wherever you're comfortable," I reply. "Do you want to show me your studio first?"

She shakes her head. "I don't allow anyone to see a work before it's done."

"Oh," I reply quickly. "I didn't mean that I wanted a sneak peek at anything. I just thought you'd like to share your space. Where the magic happens."

She laughs softly, which makes her eyes twinkle. "Magic, hmm? I don't know about that."

I give her what I hope is a reassuring smile. "But you don't have to share anything you're not comfortable with. How's that sound?"

Hazel gives a satisfied nod, then moves to the couch. She sets the mugs down on the weathered-looking coffee table and perches on the edge of the couch cushions. I take the chair and pull my phone and notepad from my purse. Is it my imagination or does Hazel stiffen?

"I don't have to record this if you don't want me to," I say. "I can just jot some notes?"

"Yes, if that's okay," Hazel replies.

"No problem," I say, and slide my phone back into my purse.

I click on my pen and add the date, location, time, and Hazel's name at the top of a new page in my notepad, then set it aside and pick up my tea.

Hazel's dunking her tea bag, her eyes fixed on her task. I can see the tendons in her fingers working beneath her pale skin. A thin, pink line on her wrist catches my eye but I look away before she can notice.

"How are you settling in so far?" I ask as questions about that scar unspool in my mind. Quicky, I shut them down. It isn't my business, though it does bring on a feeling of empathy. Had Hazel hurt herself in the past? Or did some kind of accident make that scar?

Hazel's gaze jumps to meet mine. "Good. This is the most incredible time of year here, with the leaves changing and those big, expressive clouds. I've missed the wildflowers, but somehow I prefer the more muted colors and the softer sunlight."

"The views must be quite different from coastal California," I say, then take a tentative sip of my tea.

"Oh yes," she says.

"Most of your paintings are of mountain landscapes," I say, remembering the collection on the wall of Cavendish Gallery. "Why not switch to oceans and beaches?"

Hazel gazes out the window. "I guess I'm just a mountain girl."

The question I want to ask is burning the tip of my tongue, but I bite it back. We're not there yet.

"When did you first start painting?" I ask, cradling my tea.

"I actually didn't really want to paint until we moved to California. Before that I was really into photography, some sketching."

I set my tea down and pick up my notebook. "Do you know what inspired you to try watercolor?"

Her sudden smile lights up her face. "My art teacher my senior year. Mrs. Kerr. I think I was missing home, and though I'd taken lots of photographs of these mountains, it didn't feel close enough."

I jot down her teacher's name. "You needed to recreate them," I say.

Her eyes widen. "Yes! That's exactly it. How did you know?"

I shrug. "It's easy to see from your work how much this landscape is a part of you. Being away from it must have been hard."

The joy fades from her face. She doesn't reply.

I so want to push her for answers, but again...caution. "You won an award that year, and the following year attended Laguna College of Art and Design. What was that like, to be surrounded by other artists, and such dedicated teachers?"

"It was strange at first, actually," Hazel says. "I had gone from art being just something I did for fun to really focusing on it."

"That sounds like a big transition," I say, reaching for my tea again.

Hazel gives a somber nod. "It was. At the time, I didn't know what I was doing. I wasn't sure I wanted to be an artist. I...didn't think I was good enough."

I give her an encouraging smile. "Plenty of people thought you were."

She shrugs. "It still took a while for me to—" Her face takes on a pensive expression. "—commit, I guess is the word."

"What else would you have studied?" I ask, setting down my tea.

Her soft laugh is musical, almost playful. "Exactly," she says. "I couldn't stop if I tried. Back then, though, I thought I wanted to be a teacher or a nurse or something."

"Why a teacher?" I ask.

"I love kids," she says simply. "I used to beg my parents to have a baby so I could help raise it."

My skin prickles. I used to beg my mom for the same thing, back before I knew the reason why they didn't have more children.

"Have you ever thought of painting people into your landscapes?" I can picture kids playing on a playground, or at a beach.

She shakes her head. "I tried, in the beginning. It was part of my training. But I always come back to these mountains."

I grip my mug with both hands. "It must be very satisfying to return here after so many years," I say.

Her eyes still have that wistful gleam to them. "Yes. It's just as beautiful as I remember."

"Being back means you no longer have to rely on or photographs, or your memory."

"That's true. I've hardly stopped painting since I arrived. Every minute it seems like there's something new that I want to capture."

"That's exciting," I say, because hell yes, I've felt this too. That undeniable urge to create.

"Why do you think these mountains inspire you so much?"

Hazel tilts her head in thought. "So many of my good memories are here. Ice skating on the ponds in the winter. Hiking in the summer with my parents. Pressing wildflowers with my mom. The sound of the aspen leaves quivering. Snowstorms and cross-country skiing. Fishing with my dad."

I release a slow breath. Here it is. "Why haven't you been back until now?"

Hazel's smile fades. She rocks to her feet and steps to the window, her back to me. The sudden movement catches me off guard, but I sit as still as possible.

"Is there a reason?" I ask.

"I...worried it wouldn't be the same," she says softly.

My heartbeat taps into my throat. "The same how?"

Her shoulders rise and fall in a deep breath. "I thought maybe...it wouldn't be as beautiful as I remembered. That all these years I'd created something that wasn't true."

I let this settle inside my chest for a moment. "That must have been very difficult for you to face," I say.

She hugs herself. "It was...terrifying."

I don't want to cause her anguish, yet my story brain is eating this up.

"How does it feel now?" I ask.

She turns to me with a brave smile. "Good."

"So you were wrong to be afraid, then?"

Her face tightens. "No, I was never wrong about that."

I've touched a nerve—it's clear from the look on her face. *Careful.* "So, what finally motivated you to take that risk?"

She releases a breath that ends in a soft laugh. "Promise me this won't be in the paper?"

My heart stutters. "Sure," I say with effort. The trust she's opened between us feels intimate and I'm doing my best to treat it gently, but I don't like keeping secrets.

"My therapist."

"Oh," I say.

Hazel gives me a hesitant smile. "It's okay. I'm not crazy or anything."

"Of course not," I say quickly.

"At least not any more than the rest of us," Hazel adds.

"I've known some crazy people," I say. That she's maybe not as fragile as I thought fills me with relief. "So I can vouch for that."

"Would you like to take a walk?" Hazel asks. "I could use some fresh air."

A few minutes later we're walking a dirt path along the creek. The clouds to the south have thickened to a gunmetal gray and the air has a bite to it.

"It's supposed to snow in town tomorrow," Hazel says over the sound of the rushing water.

"I heard that, yeah," I say as I brush past sage and the faded stalks of lupine and mule's ear.

"Are you a skier?" she asks.

I shrug even though she's ahead of me and can't see it. "Kind of?" I reply. "I mean, I grew up doing it, and it's fun in the right conditions."

"Ah. A fair-weather skier, huh?"

I laugh. "You got it. I hate being cold. So those people who are out there in like, twenty below are nuts."

"But you're from Colorado," she says, looking back at me. "It's cold there."

"That's why I'm hoping to leave."

"Oh?" Hazel replies. "Where will you go?"

"Los Angeles," I reply as a surge of hope fills my chest.

Hazel turns to send a puzzled look my way. "Really? Wow. It's so… big there."

I laugh. "That's sort of the point."

We start walking again and pass a grove of aspens tucked against the hillside that slopes to a broad ridge. The golden leaves flash in the breeze like coins. Hazel stops to gaze at them.

"That's very exciting for you," she says, then inhales a slow breath, taking a measured scan of the valley and surrounding mountains. Cloud shadows move languidly across the broad planes of the ridges while the creek water trickles past our feet.

She turns. "But I think a place like that would suck the soul right out of me."

A chill races down my spine, though I don't understand why. I don't need peace and quiet and beautiful views. I'm a writer. I need action, drama, intrigue.

"You're cold, aren't you?" Hazel asks with a smile. "Why don't we head back?"

I lead the way this time and savor the view of Hazel's little cabin framed by the vast hillsides and distant craggy peaks. She's right. It is beautiful here, and peaceful. Pretty much the opposite of L.A.

Once we're back at her cabin, I grab my purse and take one last look at Hazel's space before she walks me out.

She stands in the driveway with her hands clasped in front of her. "Say hi to Wyatt for me."

My belly flutters. Is there something wistful in her gaze? "I will."

"He might seem like a tough guy, but inside he's very kind."

I cover my curiosity with a smile, but it feels tight. "Yes, I can sort of see that."

"He was a very good friend to me when I needed it," she adds.

There's that word again: *friends*. I'm beginning to think Wyatt and I will never get to that place. Seeing him at the pool parking lot the other morning was the first time he's smiled at me since the night at the bar. I miss that smile, the way he looks at me.

My stomach clenches with an intense ache. Damn it, why can't this be easier?

"I hope you have enough to write about," Hazel says.

I reel in my tumultuous thoughts. "I do," I reply as I open my door.

Though I have just as many questions as answers, I have what I need for now. "Thank you again."

She nods, and I settle into my seat. As I pull away, she waves.

An uncomfortable sensation takes over as I drive down the gravel road. I realize it's envy—I'm wanting a piece of Wyatt's caring, complex side that he apparently showed Hazel.

I yank the wheel to the right and stomp on the brakes. A cloud of dust envelops my car as I grip the wheel and try to calm my breathing. But my heart squeezes so tight in my chest I wonder if Maggie's right and I'm suffering from some medical condition.

I shake this ridiculous notion from my head and stare at the distant mountains. There's nothing wrong with my heart. At least, nothing a doctor can cure.

16

BROOKE

I know something's up the minute I enter the newsroom—the pulse feels different. Rushed. I scan the room but it's empty. I burst into Wyatt's office. His coat is hanging on its hook but he's not here. Then I race to Ike's door.

Wyatt and Ike stop their conversation mid-sentence when I step inside.

"Hey," I say, trying to keep my voice casual despite my pulse hammering against my chest. Something's going on.

"Nice of you to join us," Wyatt says.

"I've been texting you for the last hour," Ike says, crossing his arms.

I cringe at my carelessness. After my little tantrum on the side of the road, I drove to a nearby picnic area and dictated my thoughts from Hazel's interview, which drained my battery.

"Sorry," I say.

Ike nods for me to close the door, which is odd because we're the only ones in the office right now. But I do, then take a seat next to Wyatt. A current of energy tingles through me but I do my best to ignore it.

"Has something happened?" I ask, eyeing both of them.

Ike's normal poker face is tense. He nods to Wyatt. "You want to tell her?"

Wyatt's rigid posture and tight eyes say no. He shifts in his seat, then huffs a giant sigh. "Last month some kids stumbled on a bunch of bones. Turns out they belonged to a guy who disappeared from here seven years ago. Everyone thought he ran off with some widow. When his bones turned up, police changed the story. Said he likely got lost while out setting up an activity for his youth group the next day and froze to death."

"I know that story," I say.

Wyatt side-eyes me warily.

"My dad actually remembered it. So I looked it up. You wrote it."

"I did," Wyatt says with a nod. He glides his thumbnail up and down the top of the metal armrest of his chair. "The police just released the forensics report. They're going to investigate."

I suck in a breath.

Ike taps his whiteboard pen on his desk. "The guy was a youth pastor. Been here for a couple of years. People are going to want answers."

"What are we going to write?" I ask, because, duh, this is tomorrow's story.

Ike and Wyatt exchange a glance.

"Wait, you're *not* going to write about it?" I ask.

"Hell yes, we will," Ike says, tapping the whiteboard pen on his desk again, almost as if he wants to emphasize this. "I want you two to work on it together."

Next to me, Wyatt swallows hard.

"It's too big of a scoop for one person," Ike continues. "Especially if they discover foul play."

A fire starts to burn in my belly as provocative headlines flit through my mind. An ongoing story about a developing investigation? Subscription rates are going to skyrocket. I resist the urge to pump my fists and shout "Yes!"

"Wyatt here's got a source inside the police," Ike says. "And you have experience stringing together a series."

"I'm perfectly capable of handling this," Wyatt says.

Ike gives him a stern glance. "This has nothing to do with your capabilities. It's about giving folks the best story we can write."

"And you think it'll be better with her?" Wyatt asks.

"Excuse me?" I ask.

Ike gives us both a "calm down" gesture with his palm, then shoots me a steady glance. "I know it will."

Abruptly, Wyatt stands. "All righty then."

"Get Brooke up to speed on what we know so far," Ike says, leaning back in his chair. He checks his watch. "You've got one hour. If you need more time, I can hold it for another forty-five minutes but not a minute later."

"Got it," Wyatt says, and strides from the room.

I'm scrambling after him when Ike calls me back. "I appreciate your perspective on this, Brooke."

"What do you mean?" I ask from the doorway, torn between wanting to catch up with Wyatt before he ghosts me, and parsing Ike's wisdom.

Ike grimaces, then crosses his arms. "This is a small town. It's easy to overlook things when you've lived here awhile. I need you to see through all that."

"I'll do my best, sir," I say, not exactly sure what I'm agreeing to.

He gives me a nod, and I turn to chase after Wyatt.

I find him in his office, typing at his desk.

"Were you even going to wait for me?" I ask, setting my satchel on the chair facing him.

"Sounds like you have other priorities," he says.

"Look, I'm sorry I wasn't here sooner. My phone died and the cord in my car sucks."

He just shakes his head.

"You heard Ike. He wants us to do this together."

"I heard him fine."

I should be mad that he's being stubborn, but his wounded tone tugs at my heart. Does he feel like Ike doesn't believe in him? Oh boy, do I know that one, and it sucks.

"Okay, how can I help?" I ask, mentally rolling up my sleeves.

Wyatt glances up from his computer to scrutinize me, like he's trying to decide if he can trust me.

"There's not much of a story yet," Wyatt says, turning back to his screen. "All we have are the forensics report and a statement from the police."

"Can't we get more?"

"By the deadline? No," Wyatt says, crossing his arms.

I start to pace. "What about this guy's past? We could interview people who knew him. Parents of the kids he worked with, or we could research his job history."

"We don't have time, Brooke."

There's an edge to his voice, but Ike's plea returns to my mind. I owe it to the paper and the readers to give them the best we can create. "Will you let me try?"

He scrubs his face with his hands, then pushes to his feet. "Go ahead," he says, and shoves a piece of paper across the table at me.

"What's this?" I ask.

"Pastor Fredrickson's office line at the church."

I snatch it up. "See? Was that so hard?"

He glares at me.

I miss you, I want to say. *I miss the way you look at me, the little thrill in my belly whenever you say my name,* but I clench my fists instead.

"I can tell you're not excited about working with me," I say. "But you need to get with the program. Ike's right. We're better together."

Wyatt shuts his eyes for a moment, that tiny muscle in his jaw flexing. "It means we'll have to spend time together, Brooke. A story like this could take on a life of its own."

I blink. "Yeah, I know."

His slate blue eyes darken, like a storm about to break. It's powerful enough that I have the urge to take a step back.

"Oh," I say, and swallow the hard lump in my throat. *So, the friends thing isn't working so well for you either, is it?* I want to ask.

I clasp my hands to keep them from trembling. "We'll just have to make it work."

He shakes his head with a derisive grunt. "I've written a first draft already. Look it over, call the pastor if you want. Maybe he'll give you something for the ending."

I blink at him in shock. "You're turning your story over to me?"

"It's our story now, remember?" he asks, striding to the hook on the back of the door and snatching up his coat.

"Wait, where are you going?" I ask.

He slides into the sleeves and zips the coat up to his neck. "I...have to meet with someone."

"Right now?"

We lock eyes. I wait for him to share more, but his lips are pressed tight.

"Okay, sure," I say, letting my hands fall to my thighs.

"I'll be back by the deadline," Wyatt says, then hurries down the hallway.

The exterior door to the office thumps shut a moment later. I slump into Wyatt's chair and groan at the ceiling. I replay our conversation and my mixed-up feelings. I hate that he's put up such wall, yet I also can't blame him because I'm the one who made him build it.

We need to write this story together. Somehow.

But how can I work with him if he's running off without telling me where he's going? However, my worries go deeper than that. He's right. A story like this will require the two of us spending time together, collaborating, making decisions, sharing ideas. How can I do that while keeping my head on straight?

I shove my feelings aside. Right now, I have a deadline to meet.

Though I had come back to the office to type up my story about Hazel Gunn, it's not urgent, so I switch gears and focus on what Wyatt has written so far.

Reading something of his that's unpolished feels intimate, like he trusts me. Though if that's true, why didn't he tell me where he was going just now?

It's our story now, remember?

I tinker with the story, moving phrases, tightening his sentences. It's a solid approach. He's laying the groundwork for more with a recap of Jonas Rundell's disappearance, plus a review of how the bones were found last month. The final two paragraphs give only the hint of what we've learned about the forensics findings—that he had a skull fracture—and a quote from Officer Noah Tucker. "There's two options. Either he injured himself that day, possibly in a fall, or someone else did him harm." The story ends with the obvious, "Rogue Valley police plan to pursue the case. If anyone has information that may be pertinent, please call..." followed by the department's phone number.

I tap my fingernail on the edge of the keyboard, thinking. Though there's only precious little time remaining to add to the story, I grab the scrap of paper with Pastor Fredrickson's number. A thrill races through me as I use Wyatt's desk phone to dial it.

A female voice answers. I introduce myself and ask for Pastor Fredrickson.

"Well, I can ask," the woman replies, sounding worried. "He's just getting out of our senior bible study group. May I tell him what this is about?"

"Youth Pastor Rundell," I reply, gripping the phone. "It's a bit urgent. I'm under deadline."

"I see. Hold please and I'll be right back."

While I wait, I swivel Wyatt's chair, using my heels as anchors.

The woman returns. "I'll patch you through now."

I sit up in my chair as a man's deep baritone comes onto the line. "How may I help you, Ms. Henderson?"

"Thanks for taking my call," I say, swiveling in my chair to grab my notebook without yanking the phone off the desk.

"It's no problem. Though I don't know what else I can tell you about Jonas. I was new here when he disappeared."

This detail resonates in my memory—it was in the original story that ran when Rundell disappeared. "Have the police contacted you yet? About the forensics report?"

"Yes, they have. It's such a tragedy. It was bad enough that we thought he had been suffering out there with no one to help him, and now the possibility that someone could have done him harm..."

Pastor Fredrickson releases a heavy sigh. "I pray the police get to the bottom of it."

I jot this down as it's ideal for the story, then ask, "Youth Pastor Rundell was out setting up some kind of geocaching activity for the kids that day. Is that something he did often?"

"Oh yes. He was always coming up with activities. Pool parties in the summer, cookouts. In the winter they played hockey, went cross country skiing."

"Was he well liked?"

"He was very devoted to the kids and helping them find the path of God."

I realize this doesn't exactly answer my question, but I can hardly expect a pastor to talk smack about his colleague. "Is there anyone you can think of that would want to hurt him?"

Pastor Fredrickson sighs again. "I've already told this to the police."

"Since they aren't always eager to share, would you mind telling me too?" I ask, crossing my fingers.

"Very well," Pastor Fredrickson says. "It's a simple answer: no. Never, at least in the eight months I knew him, did I experience him being anything but kind. He even went the extra mile with some of his youth, meeting with them to discuss their faith, addressing their doubts and fears."

I scribble down a few of his words while my mind races ahead. "Isn't that what youth pastors normally do?" I ask. When I was in middle school, one of my friends invited me to a Bible study group. She promised ice cream, so I went. But it was really a way for the pastor, a college-aged girl with soulful brown eyes to discuss how I needed to be "saved." Though I balked, her commitment was clear.

"Yes, of course," Pastor Fredrickson says. "But he took an interest in their lives. He was very involved."

I jot this down, though I'm not sure it's relevant.

"Are there people in Penny Creek who are against religion?"

He gives a chuckle. "Not that I've seen. We have our fair share of atheists, that's for sure, but I've never felt unwelcome. Quite the opposite, actually."

"That day he disappeared," I say, adding more notes, "a storm had been forecasted. Wouldn't Pastor Rundell have called off his geocaching activity? I mean, all his clues or whatever would be buried under the snow."

"That's hard to say," Pastor Fredrickson replies slowly. "We *are* mountain people, after all. We rarely cancel plans for a few inches of snow. The ski area runs the ski lifts in gale force winds. And even in twenty below temperatures, the kids are out on the ponds, skating."

I suppress a shudder. "When Pastor Rundell disappeared, and it was rumored that he'd run off with a rich widow, were you surprised?"

"Oh my, yes," the pastor says with a light chuckle. "I never believed it for a minute."

I take a moment to process this. "Could he have had a girlfriend, like, in secret? Maybe the rich widow?"

Pastor Fredrickson sighs. "Like I said, I didn't know him that well, so I suppose that means anything is possible."

By the time Wyatt returns ten minutes before deadline, I have the pastor's quotes added and I've cut it down to the size Ike needs for the space he's reserved.

"Do you want to read it?" I ask Wyatt. His eyes have lost their furrowed look, but now they're distant.

"Did the pastor talk to you?" he asks.

"Yeah. I got a few good quotes about how dedicated he was."

A tiny muscle in Wyatt's jaw twitches.

"Do you, um, have anything to add?" I ask, nodding at his computer screen. I stand as he comes around to take my place. He sits down and leans forward, skimming down the story.

"Looks good," he says, then taps a key. "I'm sending it."

"You didn't even read it," I protest.

"I'm sure it's good," he says, standing.

I put my hands on my hips. "Are you going to tell me what the heck is going on?"

17

WYATT

"Nothing's going on," I reply.

She looks like a human firecracker right now, with her hands gripping her hips and her eyes dark and intense. A pulse of heat shoots through me. Being near her like this is dangerous because fuck it, I'm done trying to play friends. I want her and trying to deny it is slowly killing me.

"Bullshit," she says. "You race out of here an hour before the deadline for the biggest story of the year. We have to work together, not keep secrets from each other."

Secrets.

I rub the back of my neck. She's right. How am I going to keep mine safe without lying? "I'm sorry. I...had to meet with a source."

"A source for what?"

I sigh. "It's actually something you encouraged me to do, and...it's working."

She gives me a puzzled look.

"Someone inside CJ Parks' operation agreed to talk to me. I need to protect him. He's got a lot to lose."

"Does he know who poisoned the lambs?" she asks.

I draw my lips tight. "He hasn't come out and said it, but I think he will. He wants a guarantee that his family will be safe. Noah Tucker's on standby, ready to pass his involvement up the chain."

"That's incredible, Wyatt!" she says. "Why didn't you just tell me?"

Her genuine enthusiasm triggers a feeling of guilt. Why *didn't* I just tell her? Am I afraid she's going to try to steal this story from me? I wince. Fuck, that's an ugly thought.

"There wasn't time," I say because it's true. "Ike gave me the tip right before the news about the forensics from the University came in and I was afraid my source was going to bolt." And I didn't feel exactly safe, meeting him at a BLM campsite just north of town, tucked into the cottonwoods. But if he confesses to helping CJ plant those poisoned lambs, the risk is going to be worth it.

She watches me with admiration. "Wow, we're following two huge stories right now. This is amazing, Wyatt!"

While I want to share her excitement, caution flags are flying in the back of my brain. I still have Hazel's secret to protect, and if CJ finds out I've flipped his employee to rat on him, all hell could break loose.

"When do you think you'll have intel?" she asks.

I shake my head. "Not sure. Could be a few days."

"Okay, well, what's our next move on the Rundell story? Do you want to split up the interviews?" Brooke asks. "I already talked with Pastor Fredrickson. I could follow up with the rest of the staff. We also need to look into his past. Maybe he made enemies."

I steady myself with a deep breath. "Easy, there. We need to be cautious."

"Well, sure," she says slowly, "but that doesn't mean we can't ask questions."

A painful prickle erupts on the back of my neck. "It's just...this is a small town, and people might get upset if we hint at the idea of foul play." While this is true, digging deep into this case might uncover things that would be better left buried.

"Sure, I get it, it's delicate, but Wyatt, what if we can help crack the case?"

"That's what you want, isn't it?" I say, my voice tightening as an emotion I can't place—or control—surges through me. "A big story would look good on that resume, right?"

Her face twists in confusion.

"You want to use other people's suffering to win another award?"

"What?" she says. "Wyatt, hold on. Just because—"

But the look in her eyes says I hit home. "These are people's lives, Brooke. Not opportunities for you to climb the corporate ladder."

She takes a step back, blinking hard.

The right thing to do would be to ask Ike to take me off this beat. But that would mean being in the dark, and I can't risk that.

"That's what you think?" she asks, her cheeks reddening. "That I'd go for the jugular, screw the consequences?"

"Well, yeah, the thought crossed my mind," I say as Tanner's warning about Brook intentionally sandbagging me pops into my mind.

"You know me better than that," she says, her gaze fierce.

"Actually, I don't," I say. "I tried and you shot me down, remember?"

"Yes, I remember, okay?" she says, her eyes filling with a look I can't read.

I turn away from her and huff a hard breath. "Before we can work together on this story, I need to know I can trust you."

"Trust me? And you're the one who thinks I'm ruthless enough to destroy people's lives for a promotion."

"Damn it, Brooke," I say. "These are my people. My friends and neighbors. People who watched me grow up. Families I know and care about. And now I have to think about one of them causing this guy harm."

She leans her hip against my desk and exhales a hard breath. "When I helped expose that plastic surgeon in Denver, and those patients finally got justice…it wasn't about any award, or a job. Those people were finally able to start healing. Getting their life back. Knowing what really happened to this guy might give someone that same chance to move on."

"What if they've already moved on, and dredging up the past is only going to hurt them more?"

She cocks her head and seems to think this over. "If we're lucky enough to get that close to the truth, we'll make that decision very carefully."

"This is so fucked up," I say, my veins pulsing with an energy that's going to burst out of me unless I do something—climb a mountain or run until my legs give out.

"Why do I get the feeling you're trying to protect this guy?" she asks. "Did you know him or something?"

I put up my hand. "I'm definitely not protecting him. And no, I didn't know him. Some of my friends were in his youth group, but I was never into that stuff. I was too busy with swimming."

"Okay," she says, her voice softening. "It's going to work out, Wyatt. We'll tackle all of this together."

I resist the urge to groan. I'm not worried about the damn work-load. Frustration has been building up for weeks—from not being able to get near her without something dying inside me, from worrying about my sisters flunking out, from the very real possibility of losing the Times job to Brooke.

The only way I've stayed sane is by avoiding her. That plan is now effectively dead.

"Let me take over at the church," I say, unable to look at her. "They might be more likely to share information about a prior employee with someone they know," I say, playing off her thinking that a solid plan will soothe me. But I need a different plan. One that will keep me from wanting to touch her *and* that protects the one secret I can't share.

"Okay," Brooke says, her eyes now focused, charged.

Her trust in me is like a kick to the gut because she's just agreed to my terms while I'm the hypocrite breaking them by hiding something. It makes me feel like shit, but I don't have another option right now.

"And I'll stay in close contact with Noah," I add. "In an ongoing investigation, he won't be able to tell me much, but I know I can get access to the old police reports. He might share tips, especially if I give him a witness in the CJ Parks case he can use to impress the feds."

"Good," Brooke says. "I'll dig into Rundell's life before he came to Penny Creek, find out where he worked and lived. Maybe someone knows something."

"Good idea," I say.

"How about his old neighbors or friends in Penny Creek?" Brooke asks, tapping her lower lip, then lifting her inquisitive gaze to mine. "We can tackle that together?"

I pause as it sinks in that if I wasn't trying to hide something from her, I could actually enjoy this. Collaborating, brainstorming, our ideas bouncing back and forth and leading to something bigger, better. A fantasy of the two of us hashing out ideas in bed between kisses flashes through my mind.

Ike leans into the room. "Story looks great, you two. Let's meet in the morning. I'm betting our phones are going to be ringing."

Brooke and I eye each other, but the spell we seemed to be under has broken. "Sounds good," I say, and curse because I need to get home. The twins have been begging me all week to make lasagna and I promised them we'd do so tonight.

Ike tucks his wool hat on. "Stay safe tonight. We're supposed to get six inches."

I glance out the window to the street where big white flakes swirl in the cone of light made by the streetlights. When I glance back to the room, Brooke's slipping through the doorway, her laptop under her arm.

A sense of relief fills me, but it's edged with remorse because I lied out of the same mouth that questioned her trust.

"How'd it go with Salbatore?" Ike asks after the main door shuts behind Brooke.

"Okay," I reply. "I think as soon as we can promise him protection, he'll talk."

Ike nods. "My contact at the Department of Labor's getting back to me tomorrow about the violations going on out there. Hang in there, this is good work, Wyatt."

Even though I don't have time, Rundell's church is on the way home, so I pull into the parking lot. To my surprise, Brooke's ancient VW Bug is here.

My stomach bottoms out somewhere below my knees.

Squinting through the flakes of falling snow, I race to the rear door. When I knock, nobody comes. After a quick check of my phone for the time, I curse. I don't have time for this, but I need to be the one to pry into Rundell's history here.

I try the knob—it's open.

"Hello?" I call into the dark hallway.

An older gentleman with a trim beard comes to the door, looking flustered. "May I help you?"

Down the hallway, light spills into the space from an open door. "Are you Pastor Fredrickson? I'm Wyatt Morgan from the Mountain Gazette. Would you—"

The man cuts me off. "Another one of you? Heavens." With a sigh, he adds, "Come in."

I follow him in toward the front of the church to an entryway and a small office nook in front of a side door. In a heated conversation with the secretary is Brooke.

Brooke spins around. "Wyatt," she says in surprise.

"What are you doing here?" I ask.

"I'm getting Pastor Rundell's Youth Group records."

My heart thuds hard against my chest. She's what?

The secretary, a middle-aged woman with shoulder length hair and red bifocals, pushes back from her chair to level Brooke with a steely gaze. "Actually, no, you're not."

The pastor focuses on Brooke, his eyes widening. "What do you want with his records?"

I flash Brooke a firm gaze to back off. "We're just looking for...any connections," I interrupt. Damn it. Why didn't Brooke just go home?

"The kids Pastor Rundell worked with would all be adults now," Brooke says. "Maybe one of them saw or overheard something back then."

While this is excellent logic, if she gets a hold of his roster...

Pastor Fredrickson sighs heavily, which seems to drain some of the tension in his shoulders. "I suppose. But wouldn't they have come forward already?"

"Maybe," I say, trying to keep the edge from my voice.

Pastor Fredrickson nods at the secretary, who shakes her head in displeasure. "Very well. But we'll need some time for this."

I give the pastor my card. Now that I have this under control, relief floods me.

"Thank you for talking with us," I say to the pastor and secretary.

"Of course," Pastor Fredrickson replies, looking troubled.

I catch Brooke's eye and nod toward the door. She gives me an anxious glance, then hitches her purse against her shoulder and hurries from the room.

Outside, I catch up with her, nearly slipping in the snow. "What the hell, Brooke! I told you I'd handle this."

"I'm sorry," she says, wincing. She pulls her fur-lined hood over her head. "I didn't mean to...overstep."

I exhale a shaky breath. I hate that I'm trying to hide something from her but fuck! I don't have a choice. "Did you not trust me to do my part?"

"I do," she says, wincing. "I just...saw the two cars and thought I'd try to catch them. I'm sorry! Sometimes I have a hard time turning things off."

She blinks up at the falling snow, then at me.

"I know the feeling," I say. A long moment passes, our eyes locked while my heart pumps out of control. Why is she looking at me like this?

"I won't do it again," she says.

I relax another notch.

"I...liked working with you today," she says.

I give her a tentative smile. "I liked it too."

Several flakes land on her long lashes, and before I can stop myself, I brush them away.

A look of yearning tightens her features. "Why didn't you tell me about the Olympics?"

The air leaves my lungs. "How did you find out?" I ask, then laugh. "Right. It was probably pretty easy."

"Yep."

I shove my hands into my pockets. "I don't know...because it's hard?"

She reaches for the edge of my coat and pulls me to her.

The surprise of kissing her after telling myself not to for weeks pulses through me like a shock wave. I taste the snow on her lips and inhale the spicy-sugar scent of her skin. I tug at her lower lip as a shiver rattles through me. Her tongue darts playfully. I flick mine against hers and she parts her lips, inviting me inside. I taste her hungrily, my tongue swirling deep into her mouth. She makes a soft sigh and reaches for my waist, her fingers gripping the fabric of my coat.

Wet flakes land on my cheeks but I barely register them because heat is exploding at the base of my spine, sending ripples of energy through me. I cup the back of her neck and slide my fingers into her silky hair, pulling her closer, but we're wearing too many clothes for me to feel her body. It's as if she's irritated by this too because she utters a little groan.

"You were right," she says.

"About what, sweetheart?"

Her eyes grow desperate. "About that ache getting worse."

I caress her face as all my cravings break loose. "I tried to warn you."

"You did," she says, and glides her fingers beneath my shirt. Her touch sends goosebumps down my arms.

I kiss her again. Beneath my coat, her chilled fingers caress up my chest, making me shiver. I tug her closer, which presses my now-painfully erect cock against her firm belly. She arches into me.

"You need me to make that awful ache all better, don't you?" I ask. I'm beginning to get some very dirty ideas involving the back-seat of the Suburban when she breaks away to fix me with an intense gaze.

"Come over," she says, her voice a frantic whisper.

Reality crashes down with my very unsexy to-do list. "I can't," I say, then wince. What the fuck did I just say?

"I don't expect you to stay," she says, grazing her thumbs over my nipples.

"Fuck, are you sure?" My cock gives another throb. I think of all the reasons I need to say no, but they melt away the instant she kisses me again.

"Yes, I'm sure."

18

BROOKE

I drive with shaking fingers the short distance to my place.

What the hell am I doing?

I think about calling Maggie for an intervention, but there's no time. And I'm not sure I want to hear her voice because it might shatter the blissful bubble I'm in right now. All I know is that Wyatt's the gasoline and I'm the spark and the craving to light the house on fire is killing me. There is no escaping this. I know we're rivals. But that was before I learned about what kind of person he is. About the sacrifices he's made. About how much he cares for his family and friends, for the people in this town. Yes, we're still competing for the same job. Yes, we're in the middle of a controversial story, but somehow, these conflicts only make me want him more.

I must be crazy because none of it makes sense. But how could I not want to kiss him when he looked at me like that? With snow in his hair and the intense look in his eyes? Like he needed me too?

I park in the alley and Wyatt glides in behind me, his headlights already off. It makes me feel even more jittery, as if we're breaking some kind of law. Maybe what we're about to do isn't illegal, but it does break several rules. I list them in my head as I tuck my keys into my purse. Number one: don't go back for seconds. Number two: don't get involved with a coworker. Number three: don't get distracted from my goal.

But if anything, Wyatt is helping me reach my goal—this story could be a huge break, not just for me, but for both of us, and I realize how much I want that. I want this to be something we accomplish together.

I release a shaky sigh and step onto the dark street. Wyatt is there, reaching for my hand. He pulls me to my feet and shuts my door quietly, then leans in to kiss me. His lips are tender, hungry. I'm pressed against the side of my car with no escape, but I don't want one. I only need his mouth on mine and his hands in my hair. I kiss him back while pulling him closer. The firm ridge of his erection grinds against my hip bone as our bodies connect. I release a whimper of anticipation.

Wyatt must have heard it because he threads his fingers with mine and leads me around the side of my cottage. At the front, I fumble with my keys until he gently takes them from me and unlocks the door. As soon as the door closes, he kisses me again. I drop my purse to the floor and he unzips my coat, then slides it off my shoulders. I kick off my boots and he tugs off his coat. We meet again, still in the middle of the living room, his lips on mine.

"I'm going to do such dirty things to you, Brooke," he says as he kisses to the place behind my ear. "Things I've been wanting to do to you since you walked into my office."

"You hated me then," I say as my pulse pounds in my ears.

He takes the edge of my earlobe in his teeth and the combination of his wet mouth and the firmness of his grip makes my thighs quiver.

"You rock my world then walk out of my life," he says, kissing down my neck while unbuttoning my shirt. "And then you march back in looking like an all-you-can-eat buffet."

"I almost didn't take this job," I say, tugging his shirt up.

"Then I'm going to make doubly sure you're happy you did," he says in that growly purr.

He shuffles me so the backs of my thighs press against the armrest of the couch, then kisses the side of my neck. Shivers race down my spine. I tilt my neck to encourage him, lost in the sensations pulsing through me.

He caresses down my shoulders, sliding my bra straps down. The motion is slow but deliberate, peeling the fabric over my breasts until I'm bare. He glides his fingertips over my erect nipples, making me startle. I arch to his touch while hot blood pulses to the empty place between my thighs, the place that's craving him so badly it aches.

"Do you, um, have a condom?" I say, wishing I didn't have to break the mood with something so unsexy, but it's better to get it over with.

"Yes, and it happens to have your name on it."

I shift so I can see his eyes. "It does?"

He laughs. "Naw. Are you still on birth control?"

"Yes," I reply.

He winks at me. "I'm glad we've had this chat, now take off your pants," he demands, kissing the place behind my ear.

"So bossy," I manage, popping the button of my slacks.

"Get used to it, sweetheart."

He steps back to watch me slip off my pants, his eyes burning with hunger.

"Oh, Brooke," he whispers, caressing over my hip where the lacy thong arches with my curves. He glides his fingertips under the thin scrap and traces it to my backside.

"Did you wear these for me?" he asks while nibbling down to my shoulder.

"No, I wore them for me," I say. Though why today of all days I chose the fancy new set from Maggie is a curiosity for another time.

"Because it makes you feel sexy?" he asks. He's caressing my bare ass with both hands, massaging and kneading in a way that's making my core clench.

"Yes," I gasp.

"I like that," he whispers as he gently widens my thighs. With light strokes, he caresses over my panties. "But it's going to make me think very naughty thoughts about you in the office."

"Maybe that's the point," I say.

He gives an appreciative groan when he feels how wet I am.

I run my fingers through his hair and urge him up so I can kiss him, devouring him with my mouth. His tongue flicks and darts with mine while he slides his fingers under the fabric.

"I think we should make a point of working after hours so I can fuck you on my desk. Or against the wall. Your choice."

I suck in a gasp as he delves my folds, his firm touch igniting my skin.

"Both," I manage, practically breathless because I'm already imagining him swiping the surface of his desk clean so he can lay me down and slide deep inside me.

"Such a dirty girl," Wyatt says while spinning me around.

He places my hands on the armrest, which makes me bend forward slightly, then unzips his pants and tugs them off. He comes back, pressing his chest against my back. His bare cock slides between my thighs. It's so hard and warm, the contact sending a fervent yearning down my thighs.

Wyatt grabs my hip with one hand and slides his fingers beneath my panties with the other. He starts to move in little thrusts, his firm hips pinning me against the couch while the friction between my legs starts to drive me insane.

I arch my back to get him closer, so consumed with my need to feel him inside me that words flit away faster than I can grasp them.

It's as if he can read my mind because he slides my panties off, pausing to stroke me from behind, his fingers so slick and my body so eager that I have to pull myself back from the edge.

"Let me make you come," he says, nibbling at my ear.

"Only if you're inside me," I reply, shameless but I don't care. There's only one way I want this first time to end.

"You're going to ruin me, princess," he says. Then he kisses his way up, sucking on my flesh almost to the point of pain as he does, but it releases another pulse of desire that only makes my craving stronger.

He tears open a condom wrapper and seconds later he's pressed against me again with his lips on my shoulder and his thick length right where I need it.

"You've wanted this all along, haven't you?" he asks, kissing the place behind my ear.

"Yes," I gasp, my thighs trembling.

With one hand on my hip and the other guiding his cock, he thrusts inside me.

I cry out as every nerve ending fires, sending a bolt of delicious pleasure through my core. Wyatt drives into me again, filling me all the way this time.

"Fuck," he groans, sliding his hand to grip my shoulder. I arch back to him, wanting him deeper.

He thrusts again, deep and so sensual. Perfect. I utter some kind of sound but not even I can make sense of it. We move together, each thrust making me gasp, with him holding me firmly and my body braced to receive him. It's so deliciously sweet yet carnal, like we're locked in some ancient dance.

We rock together, moving faster as I get closer and closer to that blissful edge, the boundary between that growing ache and release.

"Wyatt," I say, my voice a soft whimper.

"I'm right here, baby," he replies, sliding his hand into my hair and bending over me to kiss the place behind my ear.

It's exactly what I need to go tumbling over the edge. The desperate yearning expands inside me like a band stretched to the breaking point. Wyatt thrusts again, full and deep.

Everything releases in a blissful rush. I cry out as waves of pleasure pulse through me, shattering everything loose. Wyatt milks every last drop of pleasure from me until I slowly return to the room, panting.

"Fuck, that was beautiful," Wyatt says.

I'm so spent I can't move, but I needn't have worried because he scoops me up and settles us on the couch with me straddling him and his cock poised at my entrance.

"I want to watch your beautiful face when I come," he says, and lowers my hips so that he sinks inside me.

It's this that almost breaks me, that draws all my emotions to the surface. How can he say something like this to me and expect me not to want more from him?

Cupping the back of my neck, he pulls me toward him for a sensual, deep kiss while rocking his hips in time with my rhythm. His pace accelerates, then he breaks away to grip my hips with both hands, pumping me faster, harder. With a soft groan he urges me against him hard once, twice, pulsing deep inside me.

He gathers me close, our chests rising and falling in tandem, our skin warm. I wrap my arms gently around his middle and rest my head on his shoulder. We stay like that for another minute, just breathing. He strokes my hair and rubs my back until he finally leans into the couch with a sigh.

"All better now?" he asks with a sly grin.

I lean in and kiss him once, slowly, our lips lingering. "Yes."

He caresses my face and gives me a pained look. "I wish I could stay."

I try to smile but something inside me catches. I push through it by leaning down to kiss him again. His lips press softly against mine, and the sensation of how gentle it is compared to how aggressive we just were draws me even deeper into the trance I've been in all night.

He tucks a lock of hair behind my ear and smiles, then helps me off of him.

After a quick trip to the bathroom, he returns and starts tugging on his clothes. Though it makes no sense because I'm just going to shower, I get dressed too, quickly so I can walk him out.

We leave the cottage, holding hands. Outside it's still snowing, and a chill races through me, but I'm not cold.

Wyatt leads me over the snowy ground to the alley. At the side of his Suburban, he pulls me into a long hug. Then I step back and savor the way he looks standing under the streetlight, his hands deep into his pockets while the snow falls softly all around him, his eyes boring into me with an intensity that makes me shiver.

"Bye for now," he says.

"Bye," I say, then watch him climb into his car and start the engine. He pulls away from the curb and slowly disappears into the night, leaving me wondering what the hell I've gotten myself into.

19

WYATT

When I get home, I'm surprised to see the table set and Vonnie pulling the foil off the top of a pan of lasagna. I had texted them before I got to Brooke's that I was "running late" and to start cooking without me.

"Smells good, guys," I say as I slide off my shoes and hurry into the kitchen.

"See?" Leah says with a grin that makes her tiny nose piercing sparkle. "We're not completely helpless."

"Aw, I knew that," I say, going to the sink to wash up.

"Why are you so happy?" Leah asks, narrowing her eyes at me while biting down on a carrot stick.

I try to turn off the bulb glowing at ten megawatts inside me but it just keeps pouring out no matter how hard I try. "I'm just fired up you made dinner."

Leah and Vonnie exchange a look.

Leah takes an exaggerated sniff of the air. "You smell funny."

"It's a new shampoo," I say evasively. "Let's eat."

I manage to avoid the third degree until that night, when I'm in the garage waxing Leah's skis while she double checks all of her other gear—trying on her boots, checking that her shovel handle isn't bent, changing out the batteries in her avalanche beacon. Since realizing that she preferred all the free skiing she did with her team on the mountain when they *weren't* racing or training, Leah's turned all of her energy toward big mountain skiing—going into the backcountry, searching out cliffs to huck, and steep lines to ride. With the ski area on Cowboy Mountain opening soon, Leah's become a single ray of focus. If only she applied this much attention to her schoolwork, she'd have a PhD by now.

"So where were you really tonight?" Leah asks as she flakes out a nine-millimeter rope at her feet.

"None of your business," I reply, sliding the wax scraper down the underside of her left ski.

"How's Brooke?" she asks.

My pulse thumps against my temples. The high from being with Brooke has faded, and in its place is a heaviness I can't shake. I either need to tell Brooke about Hazel's secret, or break things off, and the idea of breaking things off makes me want to jump off a cliff.

I test the edge of her ski with my thumbnail—sharp as a razor. "She's good."

"Is she going home for Thanksgiving?"

"No idea," I say and release the ski from the vice.

"You should invite her," Leah says, stuffing the coiled rope into her day pack. "Nobody should be alone on Thanksgiving."

I eye her, trying to read if there's some little-sister evilness going on, but her look is thoughtful, kind.

"I'll ask, okay?"

Leah nods. "Okay."

To my surprise, who should be in my neighboring lane the next morning but Brooke. She has her back to me and is tucking her hair into her cap, giving me a split second to admire the graceful curve of her spine and her narrow, sculpted shoulders. The memory of gripping her there while slowly sliding inside her hits me like a flood. I clench my fists to fight the urge to dive into her lane and maul her with kisses.

"What's with the early start today?" I tease, then jump in. Icy chills race over my skin from the frigid water, but I relish the sensation. Cold water makes me swim faster.

"I…um, couldn't sleep," she says, chewing on a corner of her lip.

I grab the lane line to steady myself as this sinks in. "Me neither." Partly because of how good it felt to be with her again, and partly because the secret I'm keeping from her is burning a hole inside my chest.

With a sigh, she lowers her goggles. "I'm hoping this will help," she says, then pushes off the wall.

I add my cap and goggles, wait for the second hand on the giant clock propped up in the corner to reach the top, then kick off. The cold water bathes my hot face as my muscles come alive. It takes several laps to find my rhythm, and the red blur that is Brooke passing in her lane next to me doesn't make it any easier.

After my warmup, I decide to swim sprints because my mind is too scattered for distance. Brooke comes into the wall and stands to grab a drink from her water bottle, her chest heaving.

"Are we going to his old house today?" she asks.

It takes me half a second to switch from imagining all the other places I'd like to explore in her cottage to remembering that we're supposed to be writing a story together.

Right. Rundell. My gut jiggles uncomfortably. "Sure. But I have something to take care of before I can meet up."

She nods. "That's actually perfect because I have some snow to shovel."

"Fair enough," I say, thinking ahead to what I'm going to say to Hazel. "I'm doing sets of ten fifties on the minute, you want in?"

"Hell yeah," she says, not looking at me. She snaps her water bottle lid shut and gets ready.

Both of us eye the black second hand as it swings up to the top. Then we both burst off the wall.

I'm faster, but not by as much as one might think given our difference in size. She's right off my left flank as we race, her arms and legs moving furiously. At the wall, I flip and, underwater, catch a glimpse of her tucking and pushing off. Kicking furiously for the end of the pool, I find myself digging deeper than I normally would on a Wednesday workout, which is stupid, because of course I'll beat her. And I do, by four seconds.

At the wall, we pause, sucking fast breaths while we wait for the clock, then push off again. Each time I can sense the way she's churning up the pool, trying to catch me. Even though there's no way she could. We do three sets, and by the end, she hasn't given up a millisecond and seems to be as sprightly as ever, whereas my lungs ache from sucking so much wind and my quads are on the verge of cramping.

"You giving up yet?" she says, her sweet lips curling into a smile. "Because I could do this all day."

I laugh. "While that's a tempting offer, I have forty kids to coach and two teenagers to feed and escort to school."

"All right," she says in a playful tone. "I'll let you off easy this time."

"What if I don't want you to let me off easy? Like, ever."

She scoffs, but behind it is a secret little smile. She pushes off the wall, the spray from her powerful kick misting my face.

By the time swim club practice is over an hour later, my quads have turned noodly, but fuck, it feels good. Like I earned something.

Why am I so freaking happy about getting my ass kicked by a girl?

My happy bubble bursts when I push through the pool door to scoop up the twins and hear shouts.

Ten feet away are two figures, locked in some kind of scuffle. Someone screams. I know that scream—Vonnie. I start running.

Though I'm sprinting at top speed, what happens in the next several seconds might as well be in slow motion.

Two swimmers from my team are fighting; one shoving the other against the hood of a truck. It's Jackson and a new kid named Isiah. Leah and Vonnie are both shouting at them, their back to me. Jackson slugs Isiah just as one of my sisters tries to get between them.

"No!" I shout, but my voice pours into a void.

"Vonnie!" Leah shrieks, and dives for the crumpling figure.

I hit the ground and scoop up my sister. "Vonnie," I say, breathing hard.

Both boys have stopped fighting.

"Oh, jeez, is she okay?" Isiah says, crouching down.

She curls into me, holding the side of her head and wincing.

"You asshole!" Leah shouts and pounces on Jackson.

"Leah!" I bark, but she starts pounding on Jackson's chest while he stands there looking shocked. Isiah tries to stop her but she waves him off. Blood trickles down from Isiah's nose.

"I'm sorry!" Jackson says, trying to block Leah's blows. "I didn't mean to, I..."

The pool manager arrives. "What the heck is going on out here?"

"Can you get Leah off Jackson, please?" I ask him, then turn my attention to Vonnie.

"Where does it hurt?" I ask her over the din of the pool manager trying to separate Leah and Jackson and Leah arguing with him.

"My head," Vonnie says.

"Let me look," I say, and comb back her hair from her temple. No blood, but she winces when I touch it.

I flash three fingers in front of her eyes. "How many fingers do you see?"

She squints. "Three."

"Who's the President?"

"Joe Biden, you moron."

"Who's your favorite brother?"

"Caleb."

I let my mouth drop open in dramatic disbelief. "Seriously?"

She gives me a weak smile. "He made me an auntie. Have kids and I'll reconsider your status."

I laugh. "I think you're going to be fine. Can you stand up?"

She nods, and I help her to her feet. Leah is now standing to the side, her eyes blazing. Jackson is explaining something to the pool manager, his voice rising.

"How's that feel?" I ask Vonnie.

"Okay," she says through a grimace.

Leah lunges for Vonnie and wraps her in a hug. The two embrace each other tight. Leah whispers something into Vonnie's ear.

Now that I know she's okay, anger hot like a blow torch kicks on. "Leah, take Vonnie to the truck and then go get an ice pack," I say, and dig my keys from my pocket.

Leah steps back from Vonnie and snatches my keys. With one arm around Vonnie, she leads her toward our Suburban.

"You want to bring them back inside?" the pool manager says from his stance between both boys.

I nod. "Yeah, can you call both of their parents? Get a meeting with them for after school."

"No problem," he says. I walk with them back toward the pool and make sure they both follow the manager to his office.

Then I hurry to the Suburban and climb inside.

"Did you guys see what happened?" I ask my sisters. "Why were they fighting?"

I can't see Vonnie's face behind the ice pack.

"Jackson's been bugging Von," Leah says.

"Ever since I turned Jackson down to go to homecoming, he's been a dick," Vonnie adds. "Isiah told him to back off."

"I'm sorry," I say, then glance at Leah. "Why didn't either one of you tell me?"

Vonnie leans into Leah, who puts her arm around her and stares out the window.

When we get home, I make doubly sure Vonnie is okay. I offer to let her stay home but she refuses—she's got some big project due and a test in History she says she can't miss. Maybe it's overkill, but I call the school nurse and tell her what happened, ask her to check in with Vonnie during the day.

There's an undercurrent of things unsaid as the three of us go about getting ready for school and work, but everything's so rushed and truthfully, I need the day to think over how I'm going to talk to Vonnie some more about what happened.

But when I pull into the school drop-off line, before Vonnie can scoot out of the rig after Leah, I tap her hand. A slight bruise is growing at her temple, but it's not too swollen. Her deck coat's hood probably softened the blow.

"Feeling okay?" I ask.

"I'm fine," she says, rolling her eyes.

I cover her hand with mine. "I want to talk to you later about Jackson, okay?"

"Are you really going to leave us?" she asks.

I blink. "I'm applying for a job, yeah, but I won't leave before spring break. And Annika and Caleb are still here."

She twitches her lips, then in a flash, slides out of the truck.

I watch her duck past a group of boys throwing snowballs and disappear into the throng of students heading inside. My chest tightens with an ache I don't know how to quell. I should have been there for Vonnie. Have I been too preoccupied—with my goal to leave Penny Creek, with fighting my feelings for Brooke—to notice she's being harassed?

First Leah skips school, and now Vonnie's been hurt.

As much as I try to rationalize that the twins are old enough to take care of themselves, I can't help but beat myself up. Here I was thinking they can't wait to get rid of me, but instead they think I'm abandoning them.

Fuck.

A honk from the car behind me startles me from my heavy thoughts. I cruise ahead in line to the exit. On the holder affixed to the dashboard, my phone lights up with a series of texts.

The first one is from Annika: *Whoa, Rundell died of a head injury?*

The second one is from Tanner: *You've got a typo on page 3. Nice story BTW*

My fingers tighten around the steering wheel. Somehow, I'd lost track that I've been handed the scoop of the century.

Then, my phone rings. It's Ike.

"CJ's lawyer just filed testimony indicating that his sheepherders killed those lambs."

"The fuck?"

"It's time to reel this fish in."

Of course this has to come down now, when my plate is already full. "Got it."

I'm at the exit, I'm glancing both ways before turning when a new text arrives, this one from Brooke: *I'm at the Growly Bear if you want to meet up?*

Prickles dance down my spine. The longing to see her so I can kiss her and make her laugh floods through me so fast I have to grip the wheel and force a series of breaths into my lungs.

But instead of turning toward downtown, I head in the opposite direction, toward Hazel Gunn's cabin.

20

WYATT

A thin column of woodsmoke curls into the sky from Hazel's chimney, which is good news because it means she's up. They don't plow Hazel's road, so the drive has taken me a little bit longer. Her cabin looks like something out of a postcard, the dark wood contrasting with the pure white snow and the backdrop of soft white hills rising to mountains obscured by low clouds.

I'm halfway to her door when it opens.

"Goodness, what time is it?" Hazel asks, blinking at me through the lightly falling snow.

"Too early for visitors?" I ask, adjusting the newspaper tucked under my arm.

"Oh no. I'm up early." She glances at the sky. "The snow makes everything so quiet. I've been working."

I shuffle through the snow and climb the steps. "Okay if I come in?"

She must sense my serious tone, because her smile fades. "What's wrong?"

I slide the newspaper from under my arm and show her the headline: "Youth Pastor's Death Under Investigation."

Her face takes on a stricken, faraway look that puts me on edge. I don't want to force her to dredge up the past, but I'm the only one who can look out for her.

We enter the small space. It's warm from the fire, the orange flames flicking behind the glass of the wood stove in the far corner. Through the big window opposite is a sweeping view of the broad valley, rolling foothills, and if it wasn't snowing, mountains.

"Do you want some coffee or something?" I ask as the fire cracks.

She nods. "Sure, but I'll get it."

"Let me," I say, and steer her to the couch.

"Oh," Hazel says, her eyes anxious. "All right then."

I place the newspaper on her coffee table and step to the cramped kitchen. There's already a pot brewed so I find two mugs and fill them.

"Cream? Sugar?" I call out.

"Cream," she says, so I spin to the fridge, my fingers clumsy. I pour a dash of cream into her mug and stir with a spoon, using the seconds ticking by to organize my thoughts. When I return to the living room, Hazel is sitting on the edge of the couch, staring at the fire.

"When his bones were found in September, I felt this giant weight lift off my shoulders. Isn't that terrible?" she says as she takes the mug and cradles it.

I sit next to her on the couch, the springs squeaking beneath me. Opposite me is a worn easy chair with a blanket thrown over the back. Evidence of Hazel's early morning painting session is easy to spot: a pale blue paint smear on her forehead, pastel colors crammed under her fingernails, her tennis shoes splattered with yellows and greens.

"You knew you were safe, Hazel," I say. "There's nothing terrible about feeling that way."

"But, Wyatt, is it really true?" she asks, cradling her mug. "He was injured. Does that mean...someone may have hurt him?"

"We don't know yet." I stare into my coffee. "The police are going to open everything up."

Hazel sighs and her eyes gently close.

"I went to try and get the records of the youth group from the church last night so I could protect you. I got the feeling the police had already been there."

"Oh."

I balance my coffee on my knee while the fire pops and the snow falls outside. "Did you ever tell your parents?"

She tucks her lips together, then exhales a tight breath. "No," she says.

A tightness strangles my throat. "Hazel, why?" I force out.

"I couldn't!" she says, her voice rising. "My dad was an usher. My mom taught Sunday School."

"But they're your parents."

She sets her coffee down on the table and runs her palms down her thighs, like she's wiping away bad memories. "It would have broken them."

I force my jaw to quit clenching. "So instead, it broke you."

She's rubbing over her knees and rocking slightly, her hair falling forward to shield her face. "They knew something was wrong. Especially after...what happened."

"You mean you ending up in the emergency room?" I'll never forget seeing her in that gown, her wrist wrapped in gauze. I wasn't supposed to be there, but hell if I was going to stay away.

"Wait, is that why your parents tried to keep me from seeing you? They thought I was the cause?"

"No," she says, tucking her hair back into place. "But they didn't want other kids to know. So we moved. They put me on medication. I started a new school."

"And your parents still don't know," I say for confirmation.

She shakes her head.

I stand to give the sudden twitch in my muscles something do to. "Fuck, Hazel. If anyone hurt my daughter like that, I'd kill him." With a jolt in my stomach, I remember cradling Vonnie this morning and suffering through those terrifying moments when I didn't know if she was okay. I'm not lying—if anyone hurt my sisters the way Rundell hurt Hazel, there'd be no stopping me.

And here I am thinking of leaving them. Of sending them off into the world without me to protect them. What kind of selfish asshole am I?

"That's why I knew I couldn't tell them," Hazel says, her eyes begging for understanding. "My dad would have lost it. And it would have ruined their faith completely. They adored Jonah. You should have seen how upset they were when he disappeared. We came back from a camping trip and it was all over the news."

I stop my pacing and rub the back of my neck. "Jeez, that must have been hard for you."

She hugs herself. "I was struggling at school. I was so alone, and so scared. I had nightmares that he was coming to find me."

I exhale a long breath. "Why didn't you call me?"

She inhales a firm breath and seems to straighten. "Because I didn't want to burden you any more than I already had."

"Come on, it wasn't a burden."

"Wasn't it though? You and Pete fought about it. I know you did."

I wince.

"See?" she says. "I knew I needed to rescue myself. I wanted to stop feeling like a victim."

I give her a sympathetic smile. "I'm glad you got help, but I could have been there too."

"That's nice to know, Wyatt," she says, her eyes glistening. "I never really had a chance to thank you for saving me and being my friend as everything fell apart."

"Why did you choose me that night, Hazel?"

Her worried features ease and her eyes shine. "Because you were the only person who listened."

The night Hazel ended up in my truck, I came out from practice and opened my door to find her curled into the corner of the cab. She said she just ran, then saw my truck.

A log in the woodstove shifts, making a soft thunk. I walk to the window. "I guess I just wonder why you told me and not Pete."

She joins me at the window, the brightness of the white landscape making her round face shine. "I loved him. I should have told him. But I was too scared."

"Of Pete?"

She turns slightly, hugging herself. "Of him seeing me differently. I know it's hard to understand, but I was so…ashamed."

"But you didn't do anything wrong. What happened isn't your fault."

"I understand that now, but then?" She shakes her head. "It's been a long road getting there, Wyatt."

A flush of heat prickles the back of my neck. "I just wonder…if anyone else knew. Or found out."

Hazel exhales a shaky breath and there's a hitch in her voice when she replies, "Do you think someone wanted to hurt him, because of me?"

"The thought crossed my mind, yeah."

"That's horrible," Hazel says in a fearful voice. "Is this why you came? To warn me?"

I put my hands on my hips. "The police are going to find out you were in his youth group. They might pay you a visit. It might be time to tell them the truth."

"But my parents," she says, sinking onto the edge of the coffee table. "They're going to be so upset. I don't know if I can do it, Wyatt."

I settle in next to her and put my arm around her shoulders. "I'm not saying it's going to be easy, but they'd want to know, Hazel. They love you more than their faith. They can't support you if they don't know what you're going through."

Hazel puts her face in her hands. "I thought I was safe. I thought all of this was behind me."

"You are safe," I say and kiss the side of her head. "I'm here, remember?"

She tucks into me and wraps an arm around my waist. "I'm glad I came back if it means I get to keep you as a friend. I don't know what I'd do without your help."

"I'll always be here for you," I say, rubbing her arm.

I hold her while the fire snaps behind us. Outside, it's stopped snowing, but a haze of low clouds obscures the mountains, creating a flat-light landscape of pure white. "There's something else I have to tell you. And it's not meant to put pressure on you or make you decide. I'll always protect you, okay?"

She gives me a wary glance.

"There's someone I care about, Hazel. And I can't keep her in my life and keep your secret. I have to choose."

"Is it Brooke?" she asks.

I squint at her, surprised.

"You're not the only one who's perceptive," she says with a twinkle in her eye.

I release a sigh. Has it been that obvious?

Her tone softens. "You love her, don't you?"

The question hits me like a kick to the sternum. Emotions fly by me so fast I'm like a spaceship in hyperdrive. Stars and planets stream past me at lightning speeds. My heart pounds and my belly hollows.

I clench my eyes shut. Fuck. I do love her.

"I don't want this to keep you from being with her, Wyatt," she says as a tear trails down her cheek. "From loving someone. Don't make the same mistake I did. Choose her."

My breath rattles in my chest. I don't know how I'm going to do this. I can't possibly be in love, not now. Not with Brooke of all people.

But of course I'm in love with Brooke. Nobody else makes me feel this way. She's the first thought in my mind when I wake up and the last one when I close my eyes at night. Seeing her makes my heart jump. I love teasing her, challenging her, holding her, and fuck do I love satisfying her. But most of all, I love just being near her. I want to take her to bed every night and wake up with her in my arms. I want to plan my day with her, know everything about her, be there for her.

I love her, but how am I going to tell her?

21

BROOKE

I give up on Wyatt and take the last of my tea back to his office. This morning at the pool, something felt different, and I don't think it was just about last night. So why is he blowing me off?

When I arrive at the Gazette, Pastor Fredrickson passes me on the way out, looking distraught in a cheap gray suit. Ike greets me in the middle of the entryway, holding several sheets of paper.

"Where the hell is Wyatt?"

"I saw him earlier," I say, unable to take my eyes off the papers in Ike's hand. Though I spent the evening digging into Jonah Rundell's life, according to my contact at the Denver DMV, Rundell never got so much as a parking ticket. I was able to sweet talk the police precinct clerk in Laramie to share a copy of the meth lab bust that recovered Rundell's Jeep Cherokee. If the cops leaned on the meth heads for intel about the theft, or tried to get information about Rundell's death, it's not in the report. So I'm no closer to the truth about what happened to him. Maybe the answer is in Ike's hands.

"Here," Ike says in frustration while thrusting the papers at me. "Samantha called in sick today and there's a semi jackknifed across the highway with two cars in the river."

"You need me to go cover it?" I ask, hoping he'll say no.

He grabs his coat from his office. "No, stick with the Rundell story. I'll go."

The urge to scurry away to look at the papers is making me hyperventilate.

"And hey, the church secretary called to get up in my ass about poking around in their business." He puts on his coat and zips it, then crams a wool hat onto his head. "When Wyatt gets in, text me. We need to meet."

As soon as he pushes through the door, I dash into Wyatt's office, then settle in his chair and leaf through the papers. On top are four pages of names formatted into a spreadsheet: first name, last name, birth date, and columns for various other details like "permission slip signed" and "volunteer hours." Based on the birthdates, I conclude that it's a roster of the kids Youth Pastor Rundell worked with. The second set of pages is a copy of Rundell's resume for when he applied for the youth pastor position.

It lists a reference from a previous job at a church in Billings, Montana. Ideas run away in my mind faster than I can reel them in, none of them pretty.

Maybe his death was a horrible accident. But my gut is telling me something different.

Before my rampant imagination can run away any further, I get on the phone to the church in Billings. When the secretary puts me on hold, I indulge in a brief fantasy of having my own secretary one day. Someone to answer my calls, keep me on schedule, bring me perfectly steeped tea so all I have to worry about is writing. Then the fantasy shifts to Wyatt padding into my den, my mug of English Breakfast doctored with milk and honey in his hands. He's shirtless and barefoot, his hair mussed from the night before. He says good morning as he hands me the mug, then plants a soft kiss on my lips.

"This is Pastor Olson," a rich, firm voice says into the phone.

I push back the craving that's tugging at my insides and introduce myself and what I'm looking for. But the quiet desperation to make this wisp of a dream reality doesn't go away. Maybe when Wyatt comes back and I can yell at him for ghosting me this morning, it will.

"I'm afraid I don't have much to tell you," Pastor Olson says with a sigh. "He took over the program and built great rapport with the kids and families."

"Why'd he leave? Looks like he was only there for two years."

"I must admit this is a bit...delicate," Pastor Olson says, his voice lowering. "And it seems all very silly now."

I bite my tongue to keep from begging him to continue.

"He was almost too good at his job," Pastor Olson says with a nervous chuckle. "Some of the girls developed a bit of what I guess you'd call a kind of...following. He was young, just out of seminary school, and I suppose, handsome. I don't think he truly appreciated the power he had."

"So you fired him?" I ask.

"No, no, he was wonderful with the kids, he just needed mentoring," the pastor says in a kind voice, the sort of voice I imagine him using to receive my confession. *Forgive me, Father, for I have been thinking very impure thoughts about a certain coworker. And his cock. I think about his cock almost constantly.*

Stop, I tell myself with a hard sigh, then glance at the clock on my computer. Where the hell is he?

"I helped Jonah see what was happening," the pastor says, pulling me back to the conversation. "And when he realized it, he was beside himself. It really humbled him. I think he decided it would be best to start fresh somewhere new."

Prickles erupt on the back of my neck. "Did you ever suspect he had...inappropriate relations with any of the kids?"

Pastor Olson draws a breath through his teeth. "No."

I lean back in Wyatt's chair, waiting for more, but the line is silent.

I steer the conversation back to other details about Jonah, but apparently, he was a model citizen: never late, never had disagreements with anyone, never caused any kind of trouble—aside from making teenaged girls swoon.

After we hang up, I swivel Wyatt's chair and gaze at the gently falling snow outside his window. A tightness pulls at my chest as the details of the conversation fall into place—Rundell may never have been caught in an inappropriate relationship, but encouraging teenaged girls to crush on him was close enough. Did Rundell run from something he did in Billings?

Then, I remember the list, and swivel back to scan it. In the middle of page one is a name that makes me pause.

Hazel Gunn.

I release a long, slow breath.

Questions pile up in my mind faster than I can sort them. A surge of energy pulses through me. I grab my coat and purse and stride for the door.

Outside, the flakes aren't falling as hard, but a wind has kicked up, sending tiny needles of snow into my eyes. I pull up my hood and hurry to my car. Another inch of snow has fallen since I arrived, but I quickly scrape it from my windshield and get on the road. Even though I have good tires, my car isn't meant for the snow and I slide into the street. Main Street has been plowed, but Buck Creek road looks like it was cleared earlier in the storm because several inches blanket the ground. When I get to Hazel's turn, there's a set of tire tracks leading up the road. My empty stomach does a slow roll. I don't have to wonder for long about who would be up here this early in the day during a storm, because when I round the wide bend, Wyatt's Suburban is parked in front of Hazel's cabin.

I slow to a stop next to the other cars and stare at the cabin. Do I really want to climb the steps, find out what's going on inside?

My shaky breaths make fog clouds inside my car. Somehow, I find the strength to open the door and follow Wyatt's footsteps to the porch.

When I knock, there's a soft cry of alarm. My gut tightens. What am I about to see?

Wyatt opens the door wearing a guarded look that quickly turns distressed. "Brooke," he says.

Behind him, Hazel is standing in her baggy jeans and an oversized fleece coat against the big window, a shaded silhouette against the snowy landscape.

I face Wyatt and swallow hard. "I didn't know you were here," I manage. My brain is telling me to burst inside and demand answers, but my heart is running for the hills.

Wyatt and Hazel exchange a look that shatters my heart.

I suppress the cry rising up my throat. "I'll...go," I say with difficulty.

"No, Brooke, wait," Wyatt says, sounding distraught. "This isn't what you think."

Hazel comes to the door, her eyes and nose red, like she's been crying.

My eyes widen. It's too much to take in. I bite my tongue to keep the pain inside. "How could you do this? Especially after..." But I can't finish the thought because obviously I let myself believe in the fantasy that Wyatt was different. That he cared about me.

"This is my fault," Hazel says, looking anguished. "Please, come inside and I'll try to explain."

I need to go. I need to get in my car and drive away as fast as I can. But Wyatt's wounded gaze has me rooted to the spot.

"Brooke," he says in that firm tone that sends shivers down my spine, "please come in."

"I'm betting it's related to the reason you came here," Hazel says, glancing at the list in my hands.

All my runaway emotions slow to a confusing halt. "What do you mean?"

Hazel steps back from the door to let me inside. A gust of warmth tinged with the scent of old wood envelops me. I send one last glance at Wyatt, who nods.

"All right," I say.

Inside, the three of us stand in uncomfortable silence for several seconds, then Hazel leads us to the couch. It's warm inside, but I don't want to take off my coat in case I change my mind and need to flee.

Wyatt takes the chair, leaving me to sit next to Hazel on the couch. He glances at Hazel, who is wearing a nervous expression. My belly clenches.

"I told you that Hazel and I knew each other in high school," Wyatt says. "She dated my older brother, Pete. So, we became friends."

Across from me on the couch, Hazel's fingers are clasped tight in her lap and she's rubbing her thumbs together, like she's nervous. "Something...happened to me back then," she says. "Something I've never talked about."

My pulse thumps into my throat.

"Something I...can't share." She glances at Wyatt with anxious eyes. "Or at least...I'm not sure how to."

"You don't have to talk about it," Wyatt says.

"No," she says, shaking her head. "I want to. I'm just...scared." She breaks away to press her lips together.

Wyatt moves to the edge of the coffee table and puts his hand on her knee. "It's okay, Hazel. We're here." He glances to me. "We'll do everything we can to help you."

My thoughts zing from side to side of my brain. I'm pretty sure I know where this is going, but I don't trust myself to speak, so I nod.

Hazel inhales a deep breath. "Maybe it's been wrong of me to keep it a secret," she says. "I certainly never meant it to hurt anyone." At this, she lifts her gaze to meet mine.

I focus on staying still.

"When I was eleven, Pastor Rundell started asking me to stay after meetings. He would bring me little gifts. Give me extra attention. A reward, he said. For being so special." She licks her lips and presses them together. "He said...God had a special plan for me."

The shock of what I'm hearing reverberates through me. I glance at Wyatt, who breaks from watching Hazel to give me a tight grimace.

"At first, I didn't understand that it was wrong. I liked the attention." She pauses to shake her head. "I didn't know anything about sex or any of that. My parents...aren't part of the cool club that talks to their kids about those things. It started with him taking pictures of me. Then he...touched me. But he kept saying it was like God's hands, loving my body. And it...felt good."

She breaks down, covering her face with her hands. "I was so stupid!"

"Hazel, no," I say, "you said it already. You were so young. You didn't know." I shove down the bitterness rising through me with a hard swallow. "You trusted him. He's the one at fault."

She wipes her eyes and blinks at me, then Wyatt. "As I got older he started asking me to do more. By then I had started realizing that it was wrong, but I didn't know how to stop it. One night, I didn't stay after like he asked. I ran." She shakes her head. "I didn't have a plan, or anywhere to go. But I saw Wyatt's truck outside the pool and the next thing I knew, I was inside."

"You told Wyatt," I say as all the pieces lock into place. The way he reacted in Ike's office that first morning when he heard Hazel's name. The way she hugged him outside the grocery store. How he's been hiding this from everyone to protect her.

Hazel nods. "But I begged him to keep it a secret. And he has." She gives him a sad smile. "All these years. Please don't hold it against him. He's been the only friend I could count on."

I lock eyes with Wyatt. He's wearing an expression that's both defiant and proud.

He reaches for my hand and I let him hold it. My emotions spin like a whirlpool as the warmth from his touch pulses through me.

"There's something else I need to tell you." Hazel dabs her eyes with her wrists and gives us both an anxious glance. "I don't think I was the only one."

I draw in a slow breath. "I think you're right."

22

WYATT

"Jonah Rundell was a sexual predator," I say to Ike after Brooke and I step inside his office.

Ike hasn't even had a chance to protest our barging in. He leans back in his chair and rubs his chin. "You're sure?"

I side-eye Brooke, who is standing straight as an arrow with her arms crossed and her lips pursed. After leaving Hazel's cabin, we both came straight here, so I haven't been able to read her. Has she forgiven me for hiding Hazel's past? Will she keep her secret safe?

And what am I going to do about the feelings that came up for Brooke? I need to tell her about them, but not now, in the middle of this.

"We have a source," I say, rocking on my toes.

"Is this source willing to go on the record?" Ike asks.

"No," Brooke answers.

Ike grimaces. "Then what the fuck does it matter?"

"I think there's a pattern we can show without her testimony," Brooke says. "Rundell left his last youth pastor position after his supervisor warned him he was letting the teenage girls in his group crush on him."

I give her a look. "This supervisor said that?"

Brooke nods. "He said Jonah had no idea and was beside himself with shame. Decided it was better to start over somewhere else."

"More like he feared he was about to get caught," Ike says with a grunt. "Any chance we can get someone from that congregation to go on the record?"

Brooke winces. "I didn't want to spook him, and now, with the police investigating Rundell's death, I doubt he's going to give up any more information."

"Damn," Ike says, then seems to ponder something. "Do the police know?"

"No," I say.

Ike heaves a giant sigh. "But you're going to tell them, right? This might influence the investigation."

"Yeah, I'll share it with Noah."

"Maybe there's someone else from this valley that he coerced," Ike says.

"We think that's a possibility. But we don't know who."

"You got that list of kids, right?" Ike says. "Use it."

We hash out a plan, and then Brooke and I hurry through the door. But standing in the middle of the newsroom, looking lost in a cowboy hat and jeans, is Salbatore Zuniga.

Brooke and I both come to a halt.

"Um, take the office," she says. "I'll can make phone calls from that cubby," she adds, pointing to Samantha's empty cubby along the far wall.

"Thanks," I say, and approach Salbatore.

"It is like you said," he says. "He fire us and say the police are coming."

He's nervous—evidenced by the way his English has tanked. "Why don't we talk in here?" I say in what I hope is a compassionate tone, and gesture to my office door just as Brooke dashes through it, sheets of paper in hand. Seeing her so focused gives my gut a little twist.

Salbatore takes a quick look around the busy space, his dark eyes tightening. "All right."

Once in my office, he sits in the chair and sets his hat across his thighs, but looks far from comfortable. He'd probably prefer to be in the saddle than my hard chair.

"Where's your family now?"

His lips tighten. "We have family in Jerome."

"So they're safe?" I ask.

He nods. "We left before the police come."

Shit. He's a fugitive? "I know it's frightening, but the police are going to be able to help you."

He stiffens.

"You can't hide from them forever." Though I'll bet he'd give them a good run. But I don't want that for his family.

"Senior Parks is blaming me. He say I'll go to prison." Salvatore's face twists like he's in pain. "I would never kill his lambs. It was him."

"Did you see him do it?"

"He ask me which two lambs are the weakest, so I tell him. Next day they are nowhere. And he's gone all day. In the middle of calving season." He shakes his head. "He is always there. Then he sells his best horse."

"He's trying to frame you, Salbatore, and unless you fight back, he's going to win."

Salbatore grimaces, his shoulders drawing in tight as he blinks hard at the ceiling. "I never want this. We come here for a better life. But he tries to destroy it."

"I think it's time we went to the police."

Salbatore scrubs his weathered face with one hand.

"I know someone there," I say. "He'll make sure you're taken care of."

"I don't know what to do," he says, tapping the brim of his hat with his fingertips.

I lean across my desk. "Let's start by telling your story."

An hour later I'm dropping off Salbatore with Noah at the police station when an unfamiliar ringtone sounds from my pocket.

Noah gives me a nod and escorts Salbatore away. I snatch up my phone and check the ID—it's the high school.

"This is Wyatt," I say while pushing through the police station's doors. The parking lot was plowed but what remains is a slick layer of compressed snow so I make sure to step carefully.

"Hello, Wyatt," a friendly female voice says. "This is Janice, the nurse at the high school."

"Is it Vonnie?" I ask, trying to hurry, but the ground is slicker than snot. Fuck, I should have taken her to the E.R. "Is she okay?"

"I'm concerned because she vomited during fifth period," Janice says in a soothing voice that does nothing to calm me. "Can you come pick her up?"

"I'll be there in three minutes," I say, and jump into the Suburban.

When I get there, I sprint from the curb and push through the big glass doors, then realize I don't know where to go. I've barely spent any time in this school because Vonnie never gets in trouble. Never forgets her lunch or a permission slip. I turn left and enter what looks like the office.

"May I help you?" a woman behind a square enclosure asks, glancing up from a laptop.

"Nurse's office," I say, my gaze bouncing off all the doors, looking for the right one.

"Sign in please, and then it's down that hall," the woman says, pointing first at the clipboard on the edge of the counter and then to somewhere behind me.

I scratch out my signature and rush into the hallway, my footsteps muffled by the carpet. Finally, at the end of the hall is a door with NURSE written in white. I turn the knob and inside, a woman in jeans and a blue cardigan sweater is perched at a white Formica desk. Behind her are two sick bays with dark green curtains drawn around them.

"Mr. Morgan?" the woman in jeans says.

"Yeah, where is she?"

"Wyatt?" Vonnie's voice calls from behind the first curtain.

I follow her voice to where she's lying on a plastic-covered mattress, her wavy blonde hair fanned out on a paper-lined pillow. A kidney shaped bowl is resting at her side. I'm relieved to see it's empty.

"Sorry, honey," I say, stroking her forehead. "I should have taken you to the doctor instead of letting you come to school."

She starts to cry. I sit sideways on the bed and pull her into a hug. I'm no expert on teenaged girl emotions, but tears from my sensible Vonnie are sending up red flags.

"Hey, it's okay," I say in a soothing voice.

"I'm sorry you had to come," Vonnie says. "I didn't mean to…"

"It's all right," I say, and kiss her on the top of her head. "Let's get you out of here, okay?"

She nods, then pushes back and wipes her eyes. I notice the bruise on her temple looks worse. Fuck, I'm a bad parent for letting this happen to her.

I help her stand, then scoop up her backpack and coat.

"Thank you," I say to the nurse.

She gives Vonnie a sympathetic smile. "Feel better, okay?"

At the E.R., the wait to see a doctor is thankfully not the normal eternity. The last time I was here, it was a Sunday night and Leah and I waited three hours. She'd wrecked on her skateboard and broken her wrist and several fingers. By the time she got seen, her hand had swollen to the size of a grapefruit.

We're led back to an examination room, and a forty-something with a gray-blonde ponytail and the build of an ultramarathoner comes in seconds after the assistant takes Vonnie's vitals. Even though she's not wearing a white coat, I know she's a doctor by the way she carries herself.

After introducing herself, she completes a brief physical exam. "Do you have a headache?" she asks Vonnie.

"Kind of," Vonnie says.

"On a scale of one to ten, how bad?"

"A three?" Vonnie answers as the doctor inspects the scalp area where she was hit.

"How many times have you vomited?" the doc asks.

"Just once," Vonnie says, grimacing.

"It's okay, Von," I say, squeezing her hand.

"Are you nauseous?" the doctor asks.

174

"Not...anymore," Vonnie replies.

The doctor finishes her exam and stands with her hands on her hips. She glances from Vonnie sitting on the bed to me, like a coach about to deliver the winning play. "I'm ordering a CT scan. The tech will be in shortly."

During the time Vonnie's gone I pace the room, worrying. I know Vonnie's going to be okay, and I know it's not directly my fault that she got hurt, but I can't help but feel responsible. Why didn't I bring her in sooner? Was I too focused on my life to see that she needed help?

To keep myself from going crazy, I grab my laptop and use my thighs as a desk to type up my first go at the Salbatore Zuniga story. My phone pings with a text but I ignore it. Whatever it is can wait.

By the time Vonnie returns, I've hammered out twelve hundred words. I'll need to proof it one last time before it's ready, but it's good. Really good, actually. I get a little itch to send it to Brooke, see what she thinks. Instead, I send it to Ike with a favor to fact check for me so I can take care of Vonnie, then snap my laptop lid shut and set it aside to help her out of the wheelchair.

The doctor arrives soon after, wearing a soft smile. "I see no intracranial swelling or indication of internal hemorrhaging."

"So she's okay?" I ask, my chest filling with a warm flush of hope.

"Yeah, she's going to be fine. Just got her bell rung." The doctor adjusts the stethoscope around her neck. "Try to stay out of any more brawls, okay?"

"Why'd she hurl?" I ask while sliding my laptop back into its case.

The doctor slides the sleeves of her thermal undershirt up to her elbows, revealing forearms so lean and veined I wonder how much she benches. "It's not unheard of. But if it starts up again, or her headache worsens, bring her back."

"Okay," I say as Vonnie disappears into the bathroom to change back into her clothes.

The doctor eyes me. "On her form, she ticked a couple of boxes that have me concerned."

"Oh?" I ask, briefly remembering the stack of papers Vonnie filled out while we were checking in. "What boxes?"

The doctor's lips tighten, then she tilts her head at me. "Signs of anxiety. Frequent stomachaches, or allergies. Sleep issues."

"Vonnie has sleep issues?"

"According to her."

"She's always been a little bit of a worrier. She asked me not to make her compete in swimming. And she gets kind of worked up about tests."

The doctor purses her lips. "A lot of kids have mild anxiety now and then, but good nutrition and exercise can help keep it under control."

"Well, Vonnie definitely gets those things," I say as my defensiveness kicks in.

"Has she suffered any trauma?" the doctor asks.

I blink my surprise. "Well, I guess, yeah, our dad died when she was eleven." I decide not to reveal my mom's breakdown and six-year battle with depression and substance abuse, or that she lives in Seaside, Oregon with our aunt Claire who we pay to take care of her, because it makes our family sound like a train wreck.

"It might be worth having her talk to someone. Make sure she's not still harboring feelings about it."

As much as I'm reluctant to open this door with Vonnie, maybe the doctor's right.

"Especially before she moves on to college, when it can be harder to cope without the family support always there."

This hits home because Vonnie's college choices are spread all over, and none are near L.A.

I'm thanking the doctor when Leah pushes into the room, her eyes tense. "Where is she? Is she okay?"

"She's fine, Lee," I say. I'm still processing the idea that Vonnie may have an anxiety disorder that I need to fix, so my voice comes out harsher than I intended.

"Where is she?" Leah asks.

"The bathroom. Hey, aren't you supposed to still be in school right now?" I check my phone for the time. My screen displays several missed texts and calls from Brooke. "How'd you even know we were here?"

She gives me a flat look. "She wasn't answering my texts, so I called to check on her, and the nurse said you'd brought her here," Leah replies. "Why didn't you come get me?"

Sometimes I forget that they're twins and as much as they fight, they share a deep connection.

"Because you're in the middle of seventh period right now and aren't you not supposed to have your phone on during school hours?"

The doctor gives me a wave and slips from the room.

The bathroom door opens and Leah hurries over to grab Vonnie in a hug. I let them have their twin reunion, but then I see Vonnie crying again and shuffle over. "Hey, it's okay," I say, rubbing Vonnie's back. "Come on, I'm going to take you home."

On the way to the Suburban, my phone rings. It's Brooke.

"Hey, sorry I've been out of pocket. Vonnie got sick at school and I had to take her to the E.R."

"Is she okay?" Brooke says.

"Yeah, she's going to be fine. It's sort of a long story. As soon as I drop them off, I can get back to the office." I open Vonnie's door and watch her climb in next to Leah, then shut them in. "How's the research going?"

"Wyatt, there's someone who used to be in Rundell's youth group that I think you need to know about."

From inside the rig, I hear Vonnie and Leah joking around about something. The sound of Vonnie's laugh sends another wave of relief through me. She's fine.

I realize Brooke is waiting for an answer. "Okay. Who?"

Brooke releases a hard breath. "Is Vonnie's real name Yvonne?" Her voice has an odd tightness to it that sends a cold snake of dread coiling around my spine.

I brace an arm against the hood. "Yeah, why?" My voice is shaking.

"Because her name is on this list."

23

WYATT

My heart drops into my stomach. "What?" I manage. I glance to the backseat where Leah is now showing Vonnie something on her phone.

"It doesn't look like she was part of it for long. Less than a year."

"When?"

"It was seven years ago. Started in summer and ended the following spring."

"Our dad died that spring," I say.

"Oh, Wyatt," Brooke says. "Just because she's on the list doesn't mean he did anything to her."

I nod. "Right. And she was only there for a short time."

"Exactly."

"But I'm going to need to ask her," I say, rubbing the back of my neck. "Before the police do."

She exhales. "I'm so sorry this is happening. I hope it's nothing."

I lean against the side of the hood and stare at the thin horsetail-shaped clouds riding across the blue sky. "I'm going to take the girls home. Think over what to do."

"Okay," she says. "Can I help?"

A magic wand would be fucking fantastic. "Maybe later?"

"I'll be here," she says.

I hang up and climb into the rig, then drive home on autopilot while my mind spins out of control.

Once we're home, I get Leah working on her chores, adding Vonnie's to her list. Meanwhile, I send Vonnie upstairs to rest. "You want to watch some TV in the rec room?"

She shakes her head. "No, I'm actually pretty tired."

The doctor's warning about Vonnie not getting enough sleep pops back into my head. "No studying, okay?"

She gives me a suspicious smile that turns my guts inside out. "Okay."

While Leah's outside dealing with the chickens, I dive into research mode. The first search I type—"how do you know if your kid has been sexually abused?"—brings up all kinds of symptoms. At the top are anxiety, sleep problems, depression.

Shit.

Something that's not on the symptom list is never having a boyfriend. When I've asked Vonnie about it, she's claimed she doesn't want to get serious about anyone. Which is totally valid. She's heading to college next year and wants to be a neonatal nurse someday.

But could it be a sign that she doesn't trust men because of something a pastor did when she was eleven?

Fuck. The enormity of my task blasts me like me like a bomb.

I tuck into my coat and boots and step outside. The cold air has that winter bite that tastes of snow and spruce. My nose starts to tingle as I descend to the driveway. I slide my phone from my pocket and call my brother Caleb. Even though he's younger, he's been through a lot and has been my parenting wingman these last six years.

"Hey, man," he says. "Saw your story this morning. It's crazy that—"

"Can you come over?" I ask, cutting him off.

"Now?" he asks. "Um, I'm on shift. Why? Is something wrong?"

"Not exactly," I say quickly to keep him from sounding the alarm. "I could just use someone to…bounce ideas off of."

"Huh. Well, you can come to the station. Or I can come over tomorrow."

I realize I need to call Annika too. She and the twins became even closer when Mom started to fall apart. Nowadays, she and Leah butt heads more often than not, but as far as I know, she and Vonnie talk regularly. "Is Annika watching Taylor tonight?"

"Yeah, why? You need her too?" He pauses. "Wow, must be quite the doozy. You wanna tell me what the hell's going on?"

"I think Vonnie may have been targeted by a predatory pastor."

The line goes silent for several seconds. "Okay, let's start this conversation over. When you say 'bounce ideas off of' what the fuck are you actually saying?"

"I don't know if it's true or not. I just found out that she was in Jonah Rundell's youth group. The guy I wrote that story about in today's paper, the one who may have died under suspicious circumstances." I try to contain the rush of emotion blasting through me so I can finish the rest. "And I know from another source that he...sexually abused girls."

Caleb utters a tortured growl. "Just hold on. You're saying this guy —" He inhales a shaky breath. "—this pastor...may have hurt Vonnie?"

Hearing him grapple with this too makes it all real. I clamp my hand over my mouth but the sob building in my throat breaks free.

"I don't know," I say in a shaky voice as the fear I've been stuffing down inside me shatters loose, my words tumbling with it. "She hurt her head today and the doctor said she was fine, but there was this form she filled out and she might have anxiety and it could be from something like this. Or it's from Dad dying or maybe Mom falling apart and fuck, Caleb, I don't know what to do."

"Okay," Caleb says, then sighs. "Okay," he says again, and just hearing his voice is enough to bring me back from the ledge.

"Fuck, I'm coming over," he says. "Just give me ten minutes. We'll figure this out. Call Annika too." A second later, the line clicks off.

I close my eyes and lean against the back of the Suburban.

There's someone else I want to call, but I'm scared by what it means. I do it anyway.

"Hey," she says, her voice filled with worry. "How are you doing? Did you find out anything about Vonnie?"

"Can you come over tonight?" I ask because I can't answer her questions right now.

"Are you sure you want me there?" she says, sounding surprised.

Fuck yes. For now and fucking always, damn it. "My sister and brother are coming so we can make a plan of how we want to talk to Vonnie, but after that..." I rub the back of my neck to keep from saying I need you because I can't go down that road right now. "It might be late."

"I don't mind," she says.

"Okay," I say, so relieved she said yes that my knees quiver. "I'll call you."

I'm still pacing up and down the driveway when Caleb pulls in. I jog after him and the minute he steps from the cab, he pulls me into a tight hug.

"It's gonna be okay, man," he says, slapping me on the back. "We'll work this out."

I exhale hard and let his strength pour into me. "Thanks for coming over."

"Hey, that's what being part of a crazy family is good for, right?"

I try to see the humor in this but my smile breaks and I have to hug myself and stare at the twilight to keep everything inside. I can't fall apart right now.

"You wanna tell me how this came up?" he asks.

I start with the fight outside the pool this morning, then tell him about sending Vonnie off to school. "I know all about concussions. The team takes it really seriously. Every kid has to sign an agreement to alert a coach if they hit their head or think someone may have a head injury. I should have known better," I say. "I fucked up."

"You checked her out, right? Who's the president, how many fingers?"

"Yeah, but later, she threw up."

"A single episode of vomiting is totally normal with a mild head injury. You're beating yourself up for no reason."

I lean against the side of the rig and try to let go of my guilt, but it persists. How can I not feel like I've let her down? "I interviewed someone today who admitted to being coerced by Rundell."

"Someone came forward?" he asks.

"Something like that, yeah," I reply, picturing Hazel's brave smile.

Caleb bends to scoop snow into his bare hands, then packs it into a tight ball. "Some of my friends were in that guy's group in high school. They were always doing stuff. Ski trips and hockey games and pool parties."

"Did you ever go to any of them?"

"Fuck no. I was about as welcome in church back then as the devil himself." Caleb throws the snowball at the large pine flanking the porch, making a white bullseye, then sends me a hard look. "Sounds like Vonnie was part of it, though?"

"She was on the list of kids in his program that we got from the church."

"Who's 'we'?" Caleb asks, his lips tightening.

"I'm working with another journalist on the story. Brooke Henderson from—"

"The one who was sent to bust your balls?" Recognition dawns on his face. "She's the one you kissed that night at Sourdough's, isn't she?"

I nod. "The list came in while I was...interviewing that source, and she put it together."

Caleb's eyes darken. He makes another snowball, packing it tight. "If this really happened, I don't want any outsider knowing about it. It's private and we'll deal with it as a family, and get Vonnie whatever help she needs."

"Getting the list was my idea," I say. "And Brooke's not an outsider."

Caleb fires off the snowball and it hits the same spot with a thud. "Since when?"

"Since the beginning," I say as my insides clench with a longing so intense I have to grit my teeth to keep the groan inside. "It just took me a while to figure that out."

A look of understanding flashes in his eyes.

Annika's Volvo turns down the driveway.

Once she's parked, she jumps out and hugs me. "Sorry I couldn't get here sooner. Claudia was at her knitting group." Her eyes turn worried when she steps back to look at me. She flashes a look at Caleb. "Okay. What's going on?"

"It's Vonnie," I say. "I'm not sure yet but I think that youth pastor I wrote about in the paper may have targeted her."

Annika's blue eyes turn frantic. "What do you mean by targeted?"

"He sexually assaulted someone else in the group for several years," I say.

Annika gasps. She wipes at her eyes. "Oh my God."

"According to church records, Vonnie was in the group for about a year," I add.

"How old was she when she was involved?"

"Eleven."

She rubs her forehead with shaking fingers. "Eleven? Wait a minute...you said you're not sure. Which means you don't really know."

I glance at Caleb but his eyes have gone stoic. "You're right. I don't." I share with her what I do know, and when I finish, Annika's lips are quivering and she's hugging herself tight.

"This is awful," she says.

"You were still at home when she was eleven. Do you remember anything about her then? Anything that changed about her?"

Annika shakes her head. "I was a senior in high school. Self-absorbed would be an understatement."

"You don't remember her going to youth group?" Caleb asks.

Annika shrugs. "Sometimes Mom asked me to drive them places, but I don't remember picking her up at a church. Was Leah part of it too?"

I shake my head. "Not according to the list, no."

"Wait a sec," I say as a detail rises through my mind's frantic mess. "Vonnie got sick during fifth period. That's her AP English class. Tanner has the paper delivered and they spend the first five minutes reading it."

"So you think Vonnie saw your story about Rundell and threw up?" Annika asks.

It fits. If I was Vonnie, and the person who hurt me long ago and who I thought was out of my life suddenly appears in a newspaper story, I'd be sick too.

"Look, guys, all this is wasting time," Caleb says, throwing another snowball. "We need to just go ask Vonnie."

"Have you said anything to her yet?" Annika asks.

"No," I reply. "I...knew I needed reinforcements."

Annika gives me a look of compassion. "Caleb's right. We need to just ask her."

The three of us walk inside just as Leah comes in from the back porch. She takes one look at us and her eyes go wide.

"I didn't do it," she says, putting up her hands. "I swear."

"We need to talk to Vonnie," I say. "Can you start dinner?"

She's still as a statue but her gaze darts to each of us. "What's going on?"

"There's just something we need to talk to her about," Annika says.

Leah narrows her eyes. "Then I'm coming too."

I shake my head. "It's...private, Lee."

"The hell?" she says, striding over. "Von and I don't have secrets."

A chill races down my spine. I glance at my sister and brother.

Caleb shrugs. "Let Vonnie choose," he says.

"Okay," I say with a sigh. We climb the stairs and walk in silence to Vonnie's door. I give a soft knock.

"Yeah?" Vonnie replies.

"It's me," I say. "Can I come in?"

"Sure," Vonnie says.

I open the door to see her sitting up in bed with a book facedown next to her. When she sees all of us file into the room, her calm expression turns wary. She locks eyes with Leah, who walks over to the bed and settles in next to her.

"What's going on?" Vonnie asks, looking to each of us. "Has someone died? Ohmigawd, someone's died, haven't they?"

I walk to the edge of her bed and sit, facing her. Annika goes to the other side and Caleb stands at the foot. I hope Vonnie doesn't feel trapped. I hope she feels welcomed, loved.

"We heard about your trip to the E.R. today," Caleb says.

Vonnie gives us a scoffing glance, the tension in her body deflating. "Jeez, that's what this is about? You guys are worried about me?" She rolls her eyes. "I'm fine. The doctor even said so."

"The doctor said some other things, though, Von." I watch her face as I add, "That survey you filled out. Some of those boxes you checked raises some concerns. She thinks you may be suffering from some anxiety."

"What?" Vonnie says. "No, I'm fine. Just…a little out of sorts, I guess. It's been kind of a crazy day." She attempts a laugh but it's so obviously fake. My gut clenches.

"Honey," Annika says, turning her gaze from me to Vonnie. "You know we love you no matter what, right? If you need to tell us something, we'll listen."

Vonnie swallows. "Look, I'll try not to obsess so much about tests and my college applications. I'll learn how to meditate or something."

The need to know the truth is gnawing my insides raw. "I'm working on a story right now about that pastor, Jonah Rundell."

Vonnie's eyes lock with mine and she takes a measured breath.

"We're doing some digging," I say, scrubbing my chin with my fingertips. "Trying to find out more about him and the people he associated with. Your name was on the list of kids in his youth group."

Leah's gaze flicks from mine to Vonnie's. I notice her fingers are threaded through Leah's.

"This isn't out in the open yet, but he had an inappropriate relationship with a girl in his group," I say.

Vonnie squeezes Leah's hand.

"Vonnie, I know this might not be easy to talk about," I say. "But did he—" The effort to keep my composure drains me and I have to clench my fists to stay in the moment. "—do anything that made you uncomfortable?"

Vonnie glances at Leah, her eyes filling with tears.

"It's okay," Leah says, stroking her hair.

185

Vonnie closes her eyes as a shaky breath rattles free.

"I think it's time we tell them," Leah says.

My heart stops.

Vonnie's eyes blink open. She breathes fast, her gaze flicking from mine to Annika's then Caleb's. She licks her lips.

Leah squeezes her hand again.

Finally, Vonnie seems to decide something, because she exhales hard. "My best friend Joy invited me to that group, even though we're not, like, religious or anything. She said they did all kinds of fun stuff." From the guarded look on her face, "fun" is the farthest thing from her mind right now.

"He was so nice, and he was always telling jokes and he would plan all these activities like game night and hockey parties and trips to the waterslide park." She looks down at her hands, which are both clasped in Leah's now, then back up at me. "He started...I don't know, saying stuff like God loves me and what a good girl I was. It felt...I don't know...good I guess? I mean, nobody had ever, like, singled me out before. I'm not pretty like Joy, or popular like Leah."

I want to interrupt her to tell her she's wrong. She's gorgeous and smart and perfect and I hate that she's ever looked down on herself. That she needed some sick bastard to prop her up.

"Oh, honey," Annika says softly, and rubs Vonnie's knee.

Vonnie presses her lips together then sighs. "One time he had this pool party at someone's house, and I had to leave early so I went to change, and he walked into the room. But he didn't seem weirded out by it. He told me this story about how happy God was that we had found each other. That God wanted him to show me how good his love could feel." Tears spill over Vonnie's lids and her shoulders shake. "He wanted...to take pictures of me, and...I let him. He made it sound like it was something special. That *I* was special. He had this way of looking at me that was...anyways...after that he said we needed to keep things a secret so the other girls wouldn't get jealous."

I lean over and scoop Vonnie into a tight embrace. She flings her arms around me and sighs. I rest my cheek against her silky head.

"This is connected to that English essay you were dealing with, isn't it?" I ask her, though I don't need to. I'm sure of it.

"I guess. It just...made it seem like it was happening again. But I couldn't write that. It was too...intense."

I kiss her on the forehead. "I'm sorry."

"It's okay," she replies, heaving a full breath. "I should have just told you." She glances at Leah. "But I couldn't without talking to Leah first."

"Did you ever tell Mom or Dad about this?" Caleb asks, crossing his arms.

Leah's eyes turn fierce as she gazes first at him, then me. "After Vonnie told me, I convinced her to tell Mom," she says, and swallows hard.

Vonnie and Leah clasp hands again before turning back to us looking scared.

Then Leah says, "And then that asshole disappeared."

24

WYATT

The room goes completely silent. My pulse thumps hard into my throat while all the thoughts swirling together in my mind mash into tangled mess.

"Okay, Vonnie," I say, as much to calm myself as to slow this whole thing down. "Whatever happened to him doesn't have anything to do with you."

"What if it was Dad?" she blurts, then pinches her lips shut.

Annika, Caleb, and I exchange an uncomfortable glance.

Annika touches Vonnie's hand. "You mean, what if Dad had something to do with him disappearing?"

"I don't know," Vonnie says, focused on her fingers entwined in her lap. "The weekend he went missing, we were gone with Mom," she says. "We went to Boise to watch Dylan's team play. Dad didn't come."

"But then, Dad died, and everything just got so…out of control," Leah says.

"Fuck," Caleb utters next to me. I give him a sideways glance, but he's focusing on a point above Vonnie's head, like he's lost in thought.

Caleb rakes his fingers through his hair. He was the last person to see Dad alive, but he doesn't talk about that day. All I know is what he told Search and Rescue—that he'd tried to convince Dad not to run the Rogue at that water level, but he went anyway. Without Caleb, who refused. I used to blame him for not trying harder to stop Dad, but that wasn't fair. It's not Caleb's job to convince a grown man to make better choices. And thank God he didn't go with Dad that day or he'd be dead too.

"The police are looking into Rundell's case, right?" Annika asks, looking to me for confirmation. "They'll figure this out." She rubs Vonnie's back. "But there's no way Dad had anything to do with this, okay? I want you to let that go."

Vonnie flashes us a look of relief, and nods.

Guilt washes through me. "I'm so sorry you've been holding onto this." I'm sure her anxiety and sleep issues are directly tied to this experience—both Rundell and her misplaced fear that Dad did something to him. I need to get her help so she can work through everything. The E.R. doctor's warning about college blares in my mind like a giant alarm. Fuck! How can I let her try to handle all of this alone next year?

Then I realize that Leah needs help too—this has affected her. Has she learned to cope the same way Dad did, by doing risky shit?

"I'm so glad you were able to share this with us, Von," I say. "That took a lot of courage. How are you feeling now?"

She releases a sigh and sends me a weak smile. "Tired," she says. "And...kind of hungry."

I smile and she smiles back. Her courage and tough spirit shine through, and it gives me hope. We have some work to do, but she's going to be okay.

"I'm calling a family dinner night," I say, rising and reaching for Vonnie's hand.

"Hell yeah," Caleb says, grinning.

"Want me to go get Taylor?" Annika asks.

"Yes, please!" Vonnie says, her eyes brightening.

As we migrate from Vonnie's bed, everyone takes turns hugging Vonnie and Leah. The heavy mood lifts and that sense of optimism and renewal strengthens. We're going to get through this. Together. A rush of gratitude pours into me. I'm so lucky to have my family.

After a simple dinner of spaghetti and homemade sauce I thaw from our stash in the freezer, Annika and Leah tackle dishes while Vonnie reads picture books to Taylor in front of the fire.

I'm wiping my hands on a dishtowel when I see Caleb standing by the front door, wearing a look I can't read. He nods toward the porch, then slips outside.

I slide into my coat and join him. The light from the windows bathes the snowy ground in pale yellow. With the clouds gone, the night air is frigid. I zip my coat to my chin, then pull a hat from my pocket and put it on.

Caleb's leaning against the back of the Suburban, his arms crossed. "I can't believe they've been keeping this a secret. Why didn't they tell someone?"

Above, stars shine in a black sky. "Put yourself in their shoes. When Dad died, we were all out of the house, right? Dad and Mom were their world then. And then Mom started falling apart."

"Do you think this might be why Mom got so bad?" Caleb says. "I mean, I wasn't even here, so there's not really anything I could have done, I guess, but I still feel this horrible guilt." He eyes me. "I can't imagine how Mom felt."

I stuff my hands in my pockets and draw an icy breath into my lungs. "Do you think we should call her?" I ask.

Caleb snaps his gaze to mine. "Why? So she can try to explain why she bailed on us? Justify what she did?"

I release a slow breath. "Maybe it'd help her."

Caleb shakes his head, his lips tight. "She chose her own sorrow instead of helping Vonnie." He pushes off the rig. "She's known about this for six fucking years, Wyatt. I get that shit gets hard. And yeah, Dad was gone, but she could have gotten help. She could have done something. Instead she just buried all of this. She abandoned them."

Caleb's right. A lot of things are starting to make sense, all of them heartbreaking.

Caleb grips his hair with both hands. "Fuck! I wish I would have known about this back then. I wish they would have let us help."

A car rumbles up Cold Springs Road, the sound muffled by the snow. "We're here now," I say, clenching my fists inside my pockets. "That has to count for something."

He eyes me. "It does, Wyatt. We're going to get through this."

From inside the house, the kitchen light turns off, plunging us deeper into shadow.

"What are you going to do about the story and the police and all that?" he asks.

"You mean as it relates to Vonnie?"

"Yeah."

"The police need to know he was a predator, but I don't need to tell them he targeted Vonnie."

"Right," Caleb says. "And even if they found out, she's a minor. They won't be able to release her name."

"I'm pretty sure there were others," I add, clenching my fists.

Caleb grimaces. "God, that's a sickening thought."

I nod. "But now that Rundell's death is under investigation, anyone who comes forward automatically becomes a suspect."

"So there's a chance nobody will. Meaning we may never know the truth about what happened to this asshole," Caleb says, then turns to me, his face tight.

"That's a very real possibility."

He crosses his arms and sighs. "Do you think this fuckwit touched Vonnie?"

"Does it matter?" I reply as prickles erupt on my skin. The way I feel right now, killing Rundell with my bare hands a hundred times over wouldn't ease the grief growing inside me. It's a good thing he's already dead.

"You're right," Caleb says. "I just hope she's going to be okay. You know how badly she wants to be a mom someday. I've always pictured her with some awesome guy and them having like five kids." His nostrils flare as emotion takes over his face. "I want that for her. I want her to have the life she deserves."

"She will," I say, fighting the hitch in my voice. "We'll make sure of it."

"They're both going to need help."

I gaze at the stars again, wishing they would grant me answers. "Yeah." I sigh. "I'll figure it out."

"Let me be a part of it," he says, his eyes fierce. "This is something all of us need to share."

I nod. "Okay, that actually feels really good."

"You've dealt with a lot," he adds.

I lock eyes with him. "We all have."

We clasp hands and he pulls me into a man hug, thumping my back. "I better get Tay home. Call me tomorrow."

He steps back and we share a short but reassuring glance. Then, we walk back into the house.

By the time I get the twins settled in bed, it's almost ten o'clock.

I stop by Vonnie's room. "I know this probably sounds like a weird thing to ask, but…I want to make sure it's okay with you," I say as my guts twist into a knot.

She gives me a puzzled look.

"That journalist, Brooke, and I…we've sort of been hanging out lately and…"

"Yeah, I know," Vonnie says with a grin. "You want her to come over, right?"

I laugh. Busted. "How did you know?"

She rolls her eyes. "Anyways, the answer is yes, big brother. Thank you for asking."

I smile and stroke her hair.

Her lower lip gives a little quiver, and I pull her into a hug. "It's going to be okay."

She sighs against me. "Okay."

I tuck her under the covers.

"Will you tell me a story?" she asks. "Like you used to do, when I was little?"

I smile. Back when I first took over as elder in chief, Vonnie sometimes had a hard time falling asleep, and I started making up these little meditation-type stories. A rush of remorse floods through me. Why hadn't I dug deeper to find out what was wrong? I had just assumed it was all the turmoil and grief of losing Dad coupled with Mom's slow decline. If only I'd taken the time to help her then.

"Of course," I say, pushing my sadness aside. Someday I'll deal with my own grief. For now, I need to be strong for my family. "You want the one about walking in the meadow? Or the beach?"

"The beach," she says with a contented sigh.

After Vonnie's drifted off to sleep, I text Brooke the green light, then pad down to the kitchen, using my pent-up energy to put everything in its place and pre-make coffee for the morning. I pour myself two fingers of whiskey, then shift the logs in the hearth, the heat from the coals warming my cheeks. My whiskey's half gone when a set of headlight beams splash against the walls. In a flash, I'm out the door. I meet Brooke in the middle of the driveway and pull her into a tight hug.

"Is everything okay with your sister?" she says, wrapping her arms around me.

"Rundell *did* target her," I say as a heavy weight drops through me. "We don't know how...extensively yet, though."

"Oh, Wyatt," Brooke says, stepping back so our eyes connect. She caresses my face. "I'm so sorry."

"Thank you," I say, and close my eyes to kiss her, a soft, tender kiss. The cold air has chilled her smooth lips, but the subtle mint of her lip gloss is candy-cane sweet.

She nuzzles into my shoulder. "How are you holding up?"

"Better now," I say.

Her eyelashes flutter against her pink cheeks as I kiss her again, my hunger growing. She makes a soft sigh and kisses me back, her tongue flicking gently against mine. I brush the side of her face, caressing with my thumb. She pulls me tighter, grasping the fabric of my shirt.

I break away and take her hand in mine. Then I lead her inside the quiet house. The dying fire glows red and orange in the hearth and casts its flickering light on the walls.

"Wow, for being such a big house it's really cozy," Brooke says as she slides off her shoes and unzips her coat.

"My dad built it," I say with a touch of pride.

"Really?" she takes in the living room, large dining room table, kitchen. "That's amazing. Nobody does stuff like that anymore."

"I'm afraid he was a dying breed." The words leave a bitter tingle on my tongue. I don't want to think about anyone dying right now.

She gives me a kind look.

"Another time, I'll give you the tour, but tonight, there's really only one room I'd like to show you."

She raises an eyebrow.

I extend my hand and she takes it.

25

BROOKE

An annoying sound wakes me out of a dream. I reach out, my arms flailing as I try to turn off the alarm, but someone else beats me to it. Wyatt. It dawns on me that I'm in his bed, in his family's house. But then he gently scoops me to him and the heavy tug of sleep carries me away. I barely register his soft voice when he says, "Stay as long as you want. We'll be back after practice," and gives me a kiss on my forehead.

I wake again to my own alarm but make sure to get up instead of snoozing. I'm not missing my swim this morning either. It'll help focus my thoughts. Maybe my heart will come along for the ride, because right now, she's up in the clouds somewhere.

My poor car slips a little on the icy roads, but I make it to the pool just in time to see Wyatt walk out with his sisters.

His eyes light up when he sees me. My tummy erupts with flutters. Vonnie and Leah continue past me, both turning their heads as they do, while Wyatt stops me with his million-dollar smile.

"Good morning," he says.

"Morning," I reply.

He stuffs his hands in his pockets. "I was sort of hoping you'd still be in bed when I got home."

I grin. "Maybe next time."

"I'd like that." He smiles back, his eyes sparkling in the early sunshine. "Thanks for coming last night," he says, then catches himself and rubs the back of his neck, and it's so cute that I laugh.

He chuckles, then reaches for my hand. He stares at it, caressing the back with his thumb. "When we get back to the office, can we talk? About the story and…my family?"

My belly flutters again, and with it comes a growing ache that tightens the base of my core. "Of course," I say.

"Good," he says, then draws a deep breath. "Have a good swim. I wish I was staying so you could kick my ass again," he adds with a wink.

"Anytime, cowboy," I reply.

He gives me one last smile, then jogs after his sisters.

After my swim, my focus thankfully feels sharper. On my way into the Growly Bear, I pass a delivery van dropping off a bound sheath of newspapers and get a little tingle of excitement. According to our marketing department, subscription rates are up eleven percent. All my efforts are paying off. The fantasy of a warm ocean breeze in my hair and sand between my toes fills my mind. What kind of stories will I cover in L.A? Probably a lot more gruesome stuff than a pastor's old bones or an illegal wolf extermination plot.

A strange chill prickles my skin, but the more I try to understand it, the more it fades. I grab a copy of today's edition to speed read while I wait for my turn at the register when the headline stops me cold: "Local Rancher Fingered in Conspiracy Plot."

I get so carried away reading Wyatt's clever story that I forget my purpose.

"Are you having your usual?" the woman behind the counter asks.

I blink at her. "What? Oh, um, yes please." How did she know what I want? I've only been here a handful of times. Or maybe more often. I guess I've lost track.

The woman rings me up and nods at the paper I've set down on the counter. "I can't believe that guy. Trying to get his poor sheepherder to do his dirty work." She turns to fill a cup with water, then adds my tea, her face tight with a look of disgust. "Shame on him."

Tea in hand, I drift to the door while reading the rest of the article. When did Wyatt have the time to write this given the day he had yesterday? I feel…well, I can't help it. I feel a little bit left out. But not in a jealous way. More like…I wish he'd shared what he'd learned from Salbatore with me, so we could hash it out together before the rest of the world got a hold of it. I know it's stupid to feel that way, and the resulting pang in my chest only makes me feel worse. Like I'm some needy, shallow girl with a bad case of FOMO.

I climb the stairs and head for Wyatt's office when my phone chimes from my purse. I dig it out and hurry to set down my tea on Wyatt's desk.

"Dad?"

"Way to go, tiger!" he says in his affectionate growl. "What a story." He rattles off the parts he liked, the suspenseful hook we planted at the end.

"Thanks, Dad," I say, the warmth in my belly spreading through me. "Aren't you in class right now?"

"I have a few more minutes before first period. I couldn't wait until this afternoon to call you. I see they've paired you with that Wyatt Morgan guy. I hope he's not holding you back."

My stomach does a flip, making me wince. "No, we're…collaborating. And it's good. A mysterious death is a big story. Ike didn't want either of us handling it alone."

"Is he treating you like an equal?" he asks.

I have to lean into the counter for support. "Yes, Dad."

"Good. Because nobody is going to get in your way, right? The sky's the limit," he says with admiration. "I'm proud of you."

"Thanks."

"I'd better go. You have some hot leads to chase down, I'm sure."

"Yeah, actually, we do," I say, my heart heavy for the victims Rundell drew into his sick orbit.

"Well, I'm excited to read whatever you dig up," my dad says.

We hang up and I go to the window with the last of my tea, my hands shaking. *Nobody is going to get in your way, right?* Back when I was offered the job in San Francisco, he was the first person I shared it with. And when I told him a week later that I had changed my mind, I'm sure he suspected I'd done so because of Hugh.

The door behind me opens and Wyatt strides in, Steno notebook tucked under his arm.

My stomach lurches into my diaphragm. *Nobody's going to get in your way.* But Wyatt's not in my way. I like him exactly where he is, even though this makes no sense.

"Nice story today," I say, dropping my empty cup into the trash.

"Thanks," he replies, setting down his notebook on the desk. "It came out pretty good considering I wrote it while waiting for Vonnie to come back from her CT scan."

I wince. "How is she?"

Wyatt sinks into the chair opposite the desk. "Okay, I guess?" He crosses his arms and releases a hard sigh. "I offered to let her skip practice and school but I think the routine is comforting for her. That and being with her friends."

"I wish this hadn't happened to her," I say.

A wave of grief passes through his eyes. He nods, then fixes me with a firm stare. "We can't put this in the paper."

"What do you mean?" I ask slowly.

"What happened to Vonnie."

"Wyatt, I would never dream of doing that to her," I say, stepping closer to him. "Why would you think that?"

"I'm sorry," he says with a slow breath that expands his entire chest wall. "I'm...not thinking straight right now."

"It's okay," I say. "You're going through a lot."

He nods.

"What about the police? Do you think they'll find out about Vonnie?" I ask, perching on the edge of Wyatt's desk.

"I don't know, but I have to tell Noah about Rundell's history as a predator," he says.

I cross my arms. "Are you sure, Wyatt?"

He huffs a hard breath at the ceiling. "Yeah. It could be a factor in their investigation. I just have to trust that if they start digging, they'll be discreet."

My stomach does a slow roll. I send Hazel a silent beat of strength. "Have you talked to Hazel today?"

He shakes his head. "I will, though. I want her to know that we'll do everything we can to support her."

Ike knocks on the door, then steps into the room. "We've got a couple of calls about this Rundell story," he says, holding out several yellow message slips. "You want to follow up?"

Wyatt springs from the chair to grab them. "Yeah, thanks."

Ike puts his hands on his hips and eyes us both. "What's your game plan today?"

Wyatt glances at me, then back at Ike. "We need to talk with Noah Tucker."

Ike raises his bushy eyebrows.

"He needs to know about Rundell's behavior," Wyatt says.

"And then we're going to write about it," I add.

"I thought your source refused to go on the record," Ike warns.

"Brooke got some compelling stuff from his boss in Billings," Wyatt says, giving me an admiring glance.

"Is it enough?" Ike asks.

"It'll be...delicate," I say, crossing my arms. "But yeah."

Ike whistles. "Okay."

"Okay?" Wyatt asks.

"Hell yes," Ike replies. "Though I better get some volunteers to man the phone lines tomorrow. It's gonna be a shitstorm here. What do you need from me?"

Brooke and I lock eyes. "A killer headline," Wyatt says. "Other than that, I think we're good."

Ike gives us both a nod, his eyes gleaming. "All right. Let's see what you two are made of."

Once he's gone, we hash out tasks: he'll meet with Noah Tucker while I tackle the Billings angle. He also needs to write a short follow-up piece about the CJ Parks case.

"To the Bear?" Wyatt asks, a smile creeping onto his face.

"Yes!" I reply. "I'm going to need a gallon of tea for this."

After we're settled at our table, I open my laptop and he flips to a blank page in his Steno notebook and starts scribbling. We work in companionable silence, me tapping softly at the keys as my ideas unfurl, him filling several pages, stopping now and then to rub his forehead and stare at his notes. I try not to get distracted by his blue-green eyes and the confident motion of his fingers as he writes.

When I lift my mug for a sip of my tea, I catch him watching, and smile. "What?"

His intense gaze locks on me, sending a prickle of heat over my skin. He reaches across the table to stroke my bottom lip with his thumb. "I so badly I want to kiss you right now."

"I wish I could kiss you, too," I say.

"Maybe we could...have an editorial meeting later," he says as he drops his thumb and picks up his pen again. "At your place."

I press my thighs together to keep them from quivering. "Maybe."

His face lights up. "I'll bring takeout. Do you like Mexican?"

"What makes you think I'm going to let you eat anything besides me?" I say in a low voice, giving him a look.

He laughs out loud—a joyful, rich sound that vibrates through me like a perfect chord. "Such naughty words, Brooke Henderson. Just for that I'm going to have to punish you." He raises an eyebrow. "Severely."

I grin. "Stop or I'm not going to be able to get any work done."

He smiles back, then folds his notebook closed and tucks it into his bag, then leans down to kiss me gently. "See you in a bit."

For the rest of the morning, I immerse myself in the story, relying heavily on the quotes from the pastor in Billings, being very deliberate in my language. The tone has to be perfect. I send it to Wyatt just as he texts me with: *lunch?*

I smile to myself as I pack up my laptop and hurry for the door.

At my cottage, Wyatt's Suburban is already parked. The minute I step from my Bug, he jumps out and approaches, grinning, a bag with two Styrofoam boxes stacked inside dangling from his fingertips.

He leans in for a kiss, and I slide my fingers around his waist to pull him closer.

"How was your meeting?" I ask, breathless as I step back.

A thoughtful look crosses his face. "Productive," he says, taking my hand and walking with me to the front door. "How's the Billings piece coming along?"

"Good, I sent it to you."

"I'm going to have to read it later," he says from behind me as I unlock my door. He leans down to kiss the place behind my ear, making me shiver. "I'm going to be kind of tied up for the next little while."

I step inside. To my surprise, Wyatt grabs me around the middle with one arm and carries me to the kitchen. I shriek and squirm, but his grip is firm, steady. He sets me down on the counter and unzips his coat, shrugging it off, then in a flash, unbuttons my pants and tugs them down.

"What are you doing?" I ask.

He kisses up my inner thigh. "Punishing you, remember?"

I glance at the windows lining the wall that face the street, the lower half covered by a thin, gauzy curtain. "What if someone sees?"

"Serves you right for baiting me," he says, tugging my panties aside to deliver a soft lick to my folds. "It took everything I had not to finger you under the table."

I gasp. "You wouldn't!"

He tugs my panties down, then parts my thighs and scoots me closer to the edge of the counter. "You're right, but I sure liked thinking about it."

His mouth lowers, and I grip the edge of the counter. "Wyatt," I whimper because my thighs are already trembling.

He flicks his tongue and strokes me, and I forget my fear of being watched. His warm mouth and skilled fingers bring me to the brink in minutes, and soon I'm grabbing his hair and crying out, my whole body vibrating. And then he's yanking open his belt and sliding down his pants. I watch him hungrily as I pant, my skin tingling with anticipation. He rolls on a condom and steps close, tugging me to him for an aggressive kiss as he enters me in one firm stroke.

"Fuck," he utters, pausing as his cock stretches me perfectly. I wrap my arms around his shoulders and arch my hips, begging for more. He closes his eyes and kisses me again as he starts to thrust, slow and deep, gripping my thighs. It's intense and so good. I hold him tight as he thrusts faster, harder, my release building so fast a tingle spreads through me, like I'm a spark about to explode.

"Yes, oh God," I moan, burying my face in his hair as my climax bursts. He thrusts deeper, and I cry out his name as I come, pulsing tight around him.

He comes with a firm grunt, his fingers digging into my thighs. He holds me there as we breathe, his heart thumping hard against my chest.

He kisses me once, tenderly, and caresses my face. "Come stay with me again tonight."

I gaze into his eyes, feeling like I'm falling into their deep blue pools. "Okay," I reply.

THE NEXT MORNING, true to Ike's prediction, the phones are ringing off the hook. Two women have come forward about Rundell. I offer to take the lead talking to them, with Wyatt there for backup. One woman tells us he took pictures of her, the other says he tried to, but she turned him down and never went back. Watching the faces of these women as they reveal their closely guarded secrets tears me apart, but their bravery spurs me on.

After I walk the second woman out, Wyatt and I reconvene in his office. He's perched on the edge of his windowsill, his plaid shirt-sleeves rolled to his elbows.

"Okay," I say. "Today we crank it up a notch, agreed?"

He nods, his eyes an intense gray blue. "Agreed. I'll check in with Noah. You get the first draft down. Then I can fill in what I get from the police."

Just before lunch, Wyatt returns, his face tense. "Rundell had a hidden file on the church's server."

I push back from my chair and walk to him. "Don't tell me...pictures?"

Wyatt nods stiffly.

"Did they find any of..." But I can't finish, the idea of it is too horrible.

"Noah couldn't say. He's getting the State Police involved. They have a task force for this exact thing. They have some kind of software that can track down images."

"Oh," I say. "That's intense."

His eyes tighten. "What if Vonnie's pictures are in the hands of some pedophile?"

I grab both of his shoulders. "You don't know that he shared them."

He nods, then huffs a hard breath. "You're right. How's the rest of the story coming?"

"I just ran through it again. Did you get anything from Noah we can print?"

He tosses his Steno on the desk and pulls a chair around so we can sit side by side. I slide on my glasses and scroll down to the spot I've reserved for his section.

He reads over my shoulder, and I can't help it, I give him a quick kiss. "It's going to be okay," I say.

He closes his eyes and rests his forehead against mine. "I'm so glad we're in this together."

I smile and caress his face. "We're a good team, aren't we?"

He gives me a weak smile. "Yeah."

That afternoon, for the first time in twelve years, the Gazette sell out of papers—all the pay boxes in town are empty, all the racks in the grocery stores and the restaurants are bare. Everywhere, people are talking about our story. I check in with the marketing department to check subscription rates and just like I'd hoped, we're up thirty percent since last week.

The next day, we get the good news that the files on the church's server don't match any of the sites connected to the illegal child pornography network, meaning Rundell didn't sell or share his pictures. We're in the middle of a heated discussion about how much of this to share in our story when Ike steps into Wyatt's office.

He extends a cell phone to Wyatt. "I've, ah, got someone on the line who wants to talk to you. You want to take it in my office?"

Wyatt's brow furrows. "No, I can take it in here."

Ike pauses a moment longer, then shrugs. "Okay." He hands Wyatt his cell phone, then ducks out of the room and closes the door behind him.

"This is Wyatt Morgan," Wyatt says into the phone, one hand planted on his hip. He listens for a moment, then a look of disbelief captures his features.

"Thank you, ma'am."

I chew my lip and wonder if I should leave to give him privacy.

"That's, uh, very kind of you," Wyatt continues.

Who is it? I mouth, but he's focused on whatever the person on the other end is saying.

"Wow, seriously?" Wyatt says, his face lighting up. "I...don't know what to say."

He lowers onto the edge of the desk, his fingers wrapping around the corner so tightly his skin is turning white.

Who the hell is he talking to? Some rabid fan?

"Thank you, ma'am," Wyatt says, then looks up at me. His face turns pale. He swallows as a look of panic fills his eyes. "Can I, uh, have some time to think it over?"

My gut drops into the floor.

Wyatt's mouth forms a thin line as he says goodbye and lowers the phone. "That was Trina Vargas at the L.A. Times," he says, his voice tight. "They offered me the job."

26

BROOKE

A low buzzing sounds in my ears and the room seems to spin. I grab the back of the chair for support. The brightness of the room hurts my eyes and there's an odd, coppery taste in my mouth. I realize it's blood—I must have bitten my cheek.

"Congratulations," I manage.

Wyatt's stunned expression shifts to worry. "I'm sorry."

Breathe. "Why are you sorry?" I swallow, but the blood in my spit makes my throat constrict like I might be sick.

Wyatt scrubs his face with his hands and rakes through his hair, making him look half-wild, and if I didn't just get the worst news of my life, I'd think it was handsome.

"Because you wanted this too," Wyatt says. "And you deserve it."

I swat at the tear threatening to break free and grab my laptop. "So do you."

His eyes turn anguished. "Brooke."

I slide my laptop into my purse, then sling it over my shoulder. "I'm going to finalize today's story. I'll send it to you when I'm done."

Wyatt stands. "Brooke," he says, his voice stern this time. "Don't go."

"It's fine. Really," I say, forcing a brave smile. Then I spin on my heel and hurry for the door.

I make it to the stairs before my eyes blur and my legs start feeling like noodles. By the time I reach my car, my hands are shaking and I can't breathe. I manage to get inside before a surge of emotion floods into me. I curl around my purse in my lap and try to fight the feeling that I'm drowning, that there will never be enough air to fill my lungs again. Great, heaving sobs erupt from my chest, shaking my frame. I squeeze my eyes shut as the emotions swirl inside me like a swarm of bees, stinging me with their hot needles.

Finally, the turmoil ebbs and I blink at the snowy parking lot and patchy blue sky. I grit my teeth and start my engine, then drive from the lot. At the Growly Bear, I take a long moment to stare at the wide porch and the polished log walls, the calico curtains in the windows, trying to settle my emotions. After cleaning up my face with a tissue, I push the door open and stride up the steps.

The older woman behind the register grimaces when she sees me. "I always knew something was off with that man."

"The youth pastor?" I ask. "What makes you say that?"

"The way the girls followed him around like he was the Pied Piper." She shakes her head.

"You know, normally it's pretty quiet around here, but lately, right about the time the paper truck shows up, there's a line out the door," she says. "Talking about what's in the newspaper's become like a national event."

I'm not sure what to say, so just smile.

"You having your usual?" the woman asks as a baker from the kitchen delivers a tray of muffins to the display. "A batch of Cowboy Cookies are about to come out of the oven, want me to bring one out when they're ready?"

The thought of trying to force food—no matter how delicious—down my throat makes my gut flip over. "No, just the tea, thanks," I say. The woman adds a blob of honey from the bear sitting atop the espresso maker to the bottom of my mug and pours the hot water. With shaking fingers, I slide a bill across the table, then walk toward the corner table—the one Wyatt and I always share. But I can't sit there. A wave of emotion washes through me again but I push it back.

"Here you go, hon," the woman says, arriving with my tea dolloped with the perfect amount of steamed milk. "Let me know if we can get you anything else."

"Thank you," I say, and move to a different table near the back. Through the open window behind an empty counter, I spot Annika talking to a tall man in a firefighter uniform. He reaches for a cookie and she swats his hand away. He feigns injury and she laughs. The tightness in my chest spreads to my shoulders. I look away.

I lower onto the bench side of the table and set my purse next to me. I stir my tea, my mind going round and round with the spoon. It seems to take an extraordinary effort to slide out my laptop and open the lid, but I do.

The story with the new witness's statement blinks to life in front of me. I try to read the words, but everything is fuzzy. I wipe my eyes and try again. I sip from my tea. The liquid fills my mouth with that perfect sweet and bitter combination blended with the creamy milk. It helps ground me.

Just because Wyatt got this job doesn't mean I'm somehow inadequate. It just means he was a better fit for the job. I take a breath and let that settle into my bones. I'll get another chance someday. Mr. Freeman promised me an opportunity if I succeed here, which I know I have. Maybe Mr. Thorne has another job somewhere else. Their other big news outlets are in Atlanta, Seattle, and Chicago. None of them have a warm ocean to swim in, but it would just be another stepping stone. I just need to work hard and be patient.

I gaze out the window at the snowy Sawtooths cut out against a pale blue sky. In a month, I'll be leaving. Back to the big city and the views of the Front Range. An ache spreads through my chest and I grip my mug, the heat of the liquid warming my palms.

I'm excited for Wyatt. Of course I am. But I'm angry too. At myself. I should have never let my guard down. This is my fault. I thought I could have it both ways—be with him and still reach my goal.

Will I ever learn?

I stare at the words on my screen again but they just wriggle around like a nest of hungry hatched caterpillars.

"Hey," a woman's voice says. "Mind if I join you?"

I turn to see Annika with her white apron tied around her waist and her blue eyes sparkling. She's carrying a plate of cookies in one hand and a cup of coffee in the other.

"Sure," I say. I snap my laptop lid shut and move it to the bench next to me. It's not like I was getting anything done.

She sits in the chair opposite me, then extends her hand. "I can't believe we haven't met yet. I'm Annika."

"I know," I say with a smile. "Your brother pointed you out to me on my first day here." Another pang of emotion sucker-punches me in the center of my gut. The memory of his teasing that day makes my hands shake. I put them in my lap.

"Cookie?" she asks, pushing the small plate my way.

I don't want to be rude, so break off a corner. I dip it into my tea and nibble it—it's crunchy and buttery and the coconut and butterscotch chips combine perfectly in my mouth.

"These are so good," I say through another bite. Maybe I was hungrier than I thought.

"I wanted to stop by because, well, to thank you, I guess," Annika says, dunking a corner of cookie into her coffee.

"Thank me for what?" I say, setting down my second quarter of cookie to wipe my lips.

She gives a subtle look around, as if afraid of being overheard. "Of being so careful about protecting the victims in your story."

"Of course," I say. "How is she doing?"

Annika sighs. "Pretty good, all things considered. I think she's glad she doesn't have to hide it anymore. But I worry that if people found out, it might not feel so liberating."

"It's so great she has such an understanding, loving family."

Annika beams. "I was eight when they were born, and my mom already had her hands full with Dylan, who was hell on wheels at three, so I ended up doing a lot. Changing diapers, feeding them, playing with them." She gives a wistful sigh. "I used to wish for my dolls to come to life so I could have a real baby to take care of. And then it was like a dream come true."

"That's a lot of work for an eight-year-old," I say.

Annika shrugs. "At the time, it felt magical."

"Was Wyatt close with them growing up?" I ask.

Annika laughs. "No, he was in college, swimming his brains out."

"It must have been so hard to give up his dream," I say, gazing up at her. "The Olympics."

She nods. "At the time, our family was in a pretty intense crisis. None of us wanted him to have to make that sacrifice, but he did it."

"He seems like such a natural with your sisters."

Annika takes another bite of coffee-drenched cookie. "It was a work in progress. His parenting style might be a little—" She scrunches her lips together. "—creative, but it's worked. Especially with Leah. The normal rules go out the window with that kid."

I finish off the last of my cookie and wash it down with a sip of my tea.

"So you're leaving at the end of December, right?" Annika asks, stacking her empty coffee cup on top of the now empty plate. "Back to Denver?"

I force a swallow but the ache tightens my throat. "Yeah," I say, but it sounds like a croak. "Another month, but I might…leave sooner."

"Oh?" Annika says, gazing at me curiously.

Until the words left my lips, I hadn't known they were there. "I miss my family." This isn't exactly a lie—the idea of laughing with Maggie in her shop after hours and sharing the holidays with my family pulls at me.

Annika's eyes cloud. "I'm sure that's hard. Well, if you do stay, we'd love to have you join us for Thanksgiving. Holidays at the Morgans can be crazy, but…it's awesome." She smiles, the joy in her expression making her eyes twinkle. "And eclectic, you might say. Everyone picks a favorite food and we draw up a menu. Some years we don't even have turkey. One year it was bison steaks. Another year it was Cornish game hens. When Peter's home, we always have Jell-O salad, even though he's the only one who eats it."

"Sounds really nice," I say. I picture myself in Wyatt's kitchen with his family swirling all around me, feeling warm and happy as I help make a salad or slice one of the pies. Holding hands with him as we say grace. Kissing him under the twinkling stars as we take an after-dinner stroll.

She slides her hand over mine. "I know Wyatt would love to have you there."

"Oh," I say, startled. "I…uh…has he said something to you?"

Her smile brightens her face. "He doesn't need to."

My stomach does a slow, painful flip.

"Well, I need to get back to the grind," Annika says, seemingly unfazed by my non-answer. She rises with the stacked dish in her hands. "It was really great to finally meet you. And thanks again for… well…everything you're doing for my family. And for being there for Wyatt. He puts on a brave face, but I know this has been hard on him too."

I paste on a smile. "Of course."

Annika raises an eyebrow. "Think about Thanksgiving, okay?"

"I will," I manage.

BY TWO O'CLOCK, I've done all I can with the story, plus written my other two assignments, a piece about Hazel's show at Cavendish Gallery and the other announcing the upcoming firefighter auction, a fundraiser for Northwest Burn Alliance. Unable to face Wyatt or anyone else at the Gazette, I drive to my cottage. They don't need me at the four o'clock meeting. Today and maybe not ever again.

Mrs. Genesee knocks on my door the second I'm out of my shoes.

She's cradling one of her cats, stroking its head while he purrs. "I thought we had an agreement. No nighttime guests."

"I'm sorry, Mrs. Genesee," I say as a hot ache pulses through my chest. "It won't be happening again."

"The neighbors will think I'm running some kind of flophouse," she says, her eyes fierce.

I bite my tongue. Defending myself will only prolong this conversation, and I just want to be alone.

"I'll expect you out by the end of the day tomorrow," she says with a curt nod, then spins away.

I stand there for a moment, stunned. I want to chase after her but I'm barefoot. "Wait! Mrs. Genesee, I'm sorry. It won't happen again!"

"Too late," she calls out over her shoulder. "You signed a contract."

I stand with my mouth open as she marches around the corner of her house. Moments later, her front screen door squeaks open followed by a door slamming shut.

It takes me only a few hours to pack because I don't take the time to do it neatly. I make sure to leave out a set of comfy clothes for the drive, and my toiletries. I throw out all the perishable food in the fridge and clean the shelves so they shine. There's no reason to do this —I've surely forfeited my cleaning deposit, but it gives me something do to with my hands. For dinner, I mindlessly devour a half a pint of vanilla ice cream and a vegan frozen burrito I bought that day I shopped with Hazel. It tastes terrible, but for some reason, I can't stop eating it. Then I pour the remains of a bottle of red wine into a pint glass and continue my packing and cleaning routine. If I leave first thing in the morning, I can be back in Denver by dinnertime. Tomorrow's a Saturday, so traffic through Ogden and downtown Denver will be light. I can eat dinner with my parents. They don't have to know about the L.A. job. I'll just say my assignment at the Gazette ended early and I was excited to see them.

I come across my kitschy baked potato salt and pepper shakers, the jackalope postcard I never sent to Maggie, and my Famous Potatoes hoody, and sink onto my bed. I fight the feeling that I'm running away. I'm not. I'm just...moving on.

Then why does it hurt so fucking bad?

I'm mid vacuuming the corners of my closet when a pounding startles me. I turn off the vacuum and walk to the door. Is it Mrs. Genesee coming to yell at me again?

But it's Wyatt, still dressed in his button-down plaid shirt and chinos, his breath making tiny clouds in the frigid night air. I see that it's snowing again, flakes so small they look like dust in the beam of my porch light.

"I've been texting you all day, where have you been?" he asks, his voice firm.

My hackles jump to life. "Working."

His gaze lands on something behind me, and he busts into the cottage and strides to my suitcase resting next to the couch. "What the hell, Brooke?" He turns back, his face pinched in a look of hurt. "You're leaving?"

"Look, we knew this would end this way. Your words, actually."

"But your assignment doesn't end for more than a month." He releases a hard sigh and puts his hands on his hips. "You don't have to go, just because of this."

"The Gazette doesn't need me anymore," I say.

His blue eyes flash. "What if I need you?"

I hug myself and blink at the ceiling. Did he really just say that? And what does he mean—need me as a colleague, or something else?

"Even if I stay, you're leaving," I say.

He gives his chin a hard scrub. "I turned down the job."

I stare at him. "What? Why? Wyatt, you earned it, fair and square."

"I told them to pick you instead."

A tingling rush singes my skin. "No, Wyatt, why would you do such a thing?"

"Because you're the one who's earned it. You were the one who helped me bring in Salbatore for the CJ story. You were right. I had gotten lazy." He walks toward me, his eyes blazing. "You're a better writer than me, Brooke. You're insightful and thoughtful and clever. You see things I don't. The job should have gone to you."

"I don't want to be some charity case, Wyatt!"

"This isn't charity, Brooke. I told them about how you busted my balls and how it led to unearthing the truth about CJ. That's not only good journalism, but you've made sure CJ won't get away with what he did. Don't you see what an incredible achievement that is?"

"I just reminded you of what you already knew. You would have done the same thing in my shoes."

He shakes his head. "What about the Rundell story? You knew to call his old church and get those valuable details before the police moved on it. And the way you've handled those witnesses, that took a delicate touch. There's no way they would have revealed so much to me."

"We were just playing to our strengths. We did this together."

"You're extremely talented, Brooke, and you deserve to be recognized for it."

"By stealing your job?" I say, my voice rising. "No, Wyatt. I won't."

"Damn it, you're stubborn. I'm willing to give this up for you, and you're not even going to think it over?"

"I don't want you to give anything up for me! You've already given up so much. You deserve this, Wyatt. Take the job. I want you to."

"I won't leave if you aren't coming with me."

"Okay, stop," I say, and it comes out bitter and harsh. "You aren't thinking clearly. I'm not moving with you to L.A. so you can take the job and I can sit around waiting for you to come home and tell me how great your day was."

"That's not what I meant!" he says.

"Then explain it to me."

"I don't know yet, damn it! I came over here to check on you but then find out you're running away! That doesn't give me much time to find a way through this!"

"I'm not running away," I say, swallowing the lie. "Mrs. Genesee evicted me."

He stares at me. "What?"

I sigh, my gaze drifting to the floor. "I signed a contract that I'd have no nighttime guests. She must have seen you."

Wyatt releases a laugh.

I give him a sharp look. "It's not funny, Wyatt. I've just lost my deposit and after tonight, I have nowhere else to go."

The laughter in his eyes fades, replaced by an intensity that sends a shiver down my spine.

"Come stay with me," he says. "You can have your own room if you want space."

I shake my head. "No, Wyatt, that would be a disaster."

"The hell it would," he says, slapping his hands against his thighs.

"With everything going on with your family, you don't need me there."

He steps closer. "If anything, I need you more than ever."

27

WYATT

Her glistening blue eyes are angry and hurt, but it only makes me more certain that I can't let her walk out of my life.

I close the distance between us and caress the side of her gorgeous face. She gazes up at me, her lips quivering.

"I can't let you do this to me," she says in a pained whisper.

"Do what?" I ask.

"Distract me. That's how I ended up in this mess."

"I disagree," I say, shaking my head. "You said it yourself, we're better together."

Her eyes tighten. "I don't want to need someone the way I need you."

"But you do and that pisses you off, doesn't it?"

"Yes," she says sharply.

I step closer. "Needing someone doesn't have to be a weakness, Brooke."

"I don't know how to believe that."

"Let me show you," I say.

I take her face in my hands and kiss her. Our lips touch in a soft embrace, her clove-honey spice enveloping me. I cradle the back of her neck and kiss her again. She releases a shaky breath.

I lean back and see that her eyes are wet, so I kiss the edges of them dry. "I'll be with you every step of the way. Just say you'll stay."

She grabs my shirt and pulls me to her.

I kiss her again, my hunger breaking free like a lion released from its cage. I may not have all the answers yet, but I have one of them.

I lift her into my arms and carry her to the bedroom, pausing to kiss her again before setting her softly on her feet. She kisses me back with eager flicks of her tongue. I tug off her t-shirt and her fingers work the buttons of my button-down. She guides it off my shoulders, then caresses my chest with her palms. Tingles erupt on my skin. I savor the silky feel of her touch, kissing her with a desperate need that feels aggressive, reckless.

I caress over her pink satin bra, tracing the embedded pattern to her hard peaks. She inhales a soft gasp as I circle here there with my thumbs, her hips pressing into me. Our breaths come faster and our kisses more urgent. I peel down her bra to take one of her nipples between my lips.

She whimpers as I suck and tease, grazing the edge of her with my teeth. I do the same to the other one, unfastening the bra so I can stroke and touch her everywhere. A shudder passes through her and her breathing quickens.

Her fingers curl into the waistband of my pants, so close to where I'm throbbing, sending an ache through me. She tugs at my belt buckle and, several agonizing moments of shifting clothing later, she's tugging everything down. Her smooth fingers wrap around me, making everything sharpen: the sound of her breath, her spicy-sweet scent, her warmth. She slides up, giving my tip a hard squeeze, and I curse inwardly because fuck, if she keeps it up I'm not going to make it and there's several dirty ways I need to make her come before we cross that line.

I slide her leggings to her mid-thigh and kiss my way down to the top of her panties, then slowly peel them down, grabbing her ass to pull her closer. She gives a startled cry as I glide my tongue deep into her soft folds. Everything is soft and wet and plush and fuck is it good.

"Oh, sweetheart," I say, tasting her raw sweetness again. I give her clit a soft caress with my tongue, inviting it out to play. "You need me right here, don't you?"

Her hands fly to my shoulders where she grips my flesh. "Yes," she says with a gasp. "Please, yes."

I wrap my lips around her and caress up her inner thigh to her folds. I glide and suck as she starts to rock with me. I love how I know her body, know exactly what she needs. I slide a finger inside her, caressing the special place that makes her shudder. Her heat wraps around me, clenching me hard. I start to thrust as I circle and glide with my tongue. Her fingers dig into my shoulders and her hips rock with me. I add a second finger, sucking hard on her clit while my fingers move with her, thrusting and stroking. Her little gasps fill the room, faster and faster until I can feel everything pulling tight. She comes in a series of beautiful cries, her warmth pulsing around me. I urge her to the bed and peel off the rest of her clothes, then kiss my way back up, parting her thighs as I go.

"Wait," she says, still breathing fast as I settle on my belly. "I can't possibly..." She gasps as I flick my tongue against her swollen folds.

"I'm not done," I say, caressing her again. She tries to buck away, but I grasp her around the hip and press her into the bed. Using just my tongue, I stroke her firmly, teasing her hard little berry until she's breathing fast and moving with me. I glide a finger through her wet folds to her backdoor where I circle slowly, caressing her most private place.

"Wyatt!" she cries, bucking hard against my mouth. I glide and tease as she comes, drinking in this feeling of being her entire world, of giving her everything.

But deep down, I know it's not everything. Hadn't she just told me so?

A shudder erupts from her core and she lies still, breathing hard. I take my time kissing up her body, climbing fully onto the bed so I can shift her to the center. She is splayed out like a goddess, her cheeks flushed and her soft, round breasts rising and falling with her fast breaths. I give myself a hard pull, watching her eyes light up. She licks her lips.

I straddle her shoulders. She looks up at me, her gaze full of heat, and then she grips the base of my shaft and wraps her lips around me. A rush of pleasure floods through me as her sweet mouth takes me inside. I ache for more—to thrust harder, deeper, but I focus on watching her pink lips stretching around me. I grip the top of the headboard and force myself to savor every inch of her wet heat griping me tight. She feathers her touch lower, beneath my balls where everything is buzzing and pulsing.

"Fuck," I utter, arching with as much restraint as I can muster as she glides and caresses. My desire builds until I'm getting dangerously close to the edge. Gently, I pull back and lie next to her, drawing her to her side so I can kiss her and my hands can explore. I caress her everywhere with soft strokes until she's panting and arching against me.

I reach down for my wallet and pull out a condom, but she surprises me by rising up and snatching it from my fingers. She tears it open, then using both hands, slides the condom down my length. I caress the scoop of her waist and kiss her, our tongues swirling until I can't take it another second. I urge her to her back and part her thighs with my knees.

"Say it, baby," I say, my voice urgent.

Her eyes have that desperate edge. She reaches out and tries to pull me to her but I resist. "You don't get what you want until you say it."

"Say what?" she whispers.

I kiss up her chest, pausing to taste her perfect breasts, then brace myself above her. "You need me too."

She gives me a tormented glance, her eyes glistening. "Yes, Wyatt, I need you."

I lean down and kiss her, my tongue dancing hungrily with hers.

"Say it again," I command.

She sucks in a shaky breath. "I love you."

"Fuck, Brooke, I love you too."

"What are we going to do?" she says in anguish.

I reach up and wipe her eyes and kiss her. "I don't know, but it's going to be okay."

"Promise?" she asks, caressing the side of my face.

"I promise," I say, and slowly, I drive inside her. She welcomes me, arching in tandem with my thrust. She's so tight and plush and warm. Her body gives me a little squeeze and I have to shut my eyes tight to keep from losing my sanity. I thrust again, savoring the intense, sweet pleasure of being so close to her.

I hook her legs around me and thrust again, sinking deep inside her. With a moan, she grabs my ass and pulls me closer. I kiss her neck, gliding the edge of my teeth against her ear. "This is where I belong, Brooke," I whisper, then thrust again. "Right here."

"Harder," she begs, her fingers digging into my skin.

I nibble the edge of her shoulder and plunge inside her, my hips meeting hers. She gasps. I arch again, thrusting deep into her belly. Her hips urge me faster, harder. I lift her arms above her head and pin them there. An aggressive urge takes over. How can she leave when we're sharing something so perfect, so intimate? This, right here, isn't something you can just run away from, no matter how difficult everything seems. We belong together, she has to see that.

I thrust harder, my fingers tight around her wrists. How dare she make me feel this way and then threaten to walk out of my life?

She gasps, arching into me, our hips crashing together. "Yes," she breathes, her eyes clenching shut.

I thrust faster and the heart of her tightens around me. I'm breathing fast, my release coiling at the base of my spine. I arch hard into her and she gives a needy, keening cry, her body gripping me tight. Her fingers curl around the slats in the headboard and she comes, her hips rocking against me and her soft cries ringing in my ears. I bury my face in her shoulder as my own release bursts and the freight train thunders through me like a rush from some powerful drug. I'm weightless in a cloud of joy that carries me off to some blissful place. As it fades, I collapse against her, my chest heaving, her fast pulse beating in tandem with mine.

· · ·

I WAKE to the sound of movement in the cottage and blink awake, startled that Brooke isn't in the bed. The only way I was able to sleep was the knowledge of what we'd shared. I promised her it would be okay and damn it, it will be. As long as she gives me time to figure everything out.

But as I slip into my boxers and pad into the living room, I see she's dressed in a pair of leggings and a hooded sweatshirt, her hair tied into a messy bun.

She's leaving.

"I was just going to wake you," she says, lowering her eyes.

I grab the door frame for support, my fingers digging into the wood. "I don't understand," I say, my voice tight.

"I need to do this my own way, Wyatt."

I shake my head. "I'm pretty sure we agreed last night to do this together."

She raises her chin in defiance. "I swore I wouldn't let someone make decisions for me again."

I walk into the tiny kitchen. "I won't do that."

"You did it yesterday," she says, her eyes blazing.

"I'm sorry," I say, rubbing the back of my neck. "You just can't expect me to see you miserable and not try to fix it."

"Do you really want me to go to L.A?"

"If that's what you want, yes," I say, gazing into her fierce blue eyes.

"Even though we'll be separated."

"That's what caring about someone looks like, Brooke, putting that person first. I want you to do what makes you happy."

"What if you make me happy?"

I shake my head to clear the flood of thoughts and fears rising through me. "I told you we'd work this out together. That's pretty hard to do if you're not here."

She braces her hands against the counter and gazes out the window. "I just need to think, okay? This doesn't have to be...goodbye."

I close my eyes. "It sure as hell feels like it."

"I need this, Wyatt," she says. "Please let me go."

It takes me less than two minutes to leave, and I don't look at her once. I can't. It'll break me. Once in the Suburban I grip the wheel and stare into the snowy street. I'm out of choices. I've told her how I feel. I've promised to honor her in all the ways she needs. What else is there?

I go to the pool and try to wipe it all away with a brutal workout. There are moments where I'm focused on the work, but my mind wanders to the time Brooke and I shared, and the turmoil heats my blood all over again.

When I get home, Leah's already gone. She left early for a back-country ski trip with her tribe and won't be back until late tomorrow. Vonnie is likely still asleep. She and Leah went to the football game last night, and once I knew I wasn't going to be coming home I begged Annika to pinch-hit curfew duty for me. According to Annika's text, they rolled in at 11:54 and Annika crashed in her old room. Next to her car is a set of tire tracks in the snow. Probably Grady's truck.

Inside, the scent of coffee and rising dough tickles my nostrils. I'm wrapped in a sensation of home and warmth and all things good. But behind it is the torment that I might never share it with Brooke. That she might be leaving me for good. An ache spreads through my chest, making me stop and take a deep breath.

"Smells amazing," I say, hanging up my coat and sliding out of my snowy boots. Gideon curls around my ankles. I reach down to scratch him on the back of the head. "Someone's happy you're here," I say as the cat leans in, purring.

Annika chuckles. She pulls a pan of cinnamon rolls from the oven, her cheeks flushed. "There's coffee ready," she says, sliding off a pair of calico-fabric oven mitts.

"You are an angel," I tell her, striding into the kitchen. "Did you and Grady hang out last night?" I ask, the haze of cinnamon and yeast wrapping me in a warm hug.

She spins away from me so I can't see her face. "Yeah."

"Why didn't he stay? You know he's welcome. We have plenty of room."

Annika pours two mugs of coffee and hands me one. "He's on shift today."

She always seems to have his schedule memorized. I've tried keeping track of Caleb's, but it's impossible. Twenty-four hours on, forty-eight off, then forty-eight on followed by four days off. Then there's something called a "Kelly Day" but I have no idea what it is.

"So, some kind of emergency last night?" she asks.

I sip from the mug and the liquid scalds my tongue, but it doesn't matter. I feel so completely numb inside that taste isn't registering. "I guess you could call it that, yeah."

"Everything okay?" she asks over her mug, the steam making her cheeks even rosier.

I set down my mug and peel off a section of cinnamon roll. "No."

"I'm so sorry, Wyatt. Can I help?"

I tear off the bite of the roll and chew slowly. The buttery sweetness wakens my taste buds, but swallowing the bite takes effort. I wipe my cinnamon-sticky fingers on a nearby napkin.

"I got the job in L.A.," I say.

Her eyes light up. "Wyatt, that's fantastic!" She starts rattling off her plans to help, like when she'll move in, how she'll make sure Leah keeps her grades up, but then stops mid-sentence. "You don't exactly look overjoyed."

"I turned it down."

Her eyes cloud. "Why?"

"Because it was going to make the woman I love miserable."

Annika's expression tightens in grief. "Oh, Wyatt."

"And to be honest, the thought of leaving right now, after what we learned…" I trace the rim of my coffee cup. "I don't want them to feel like I abandoned them. They've walked that road before."

"Mom," she says softly.

"And Dad," I reply. "I'm sure he didn't mean to die that day, but he did, and though it's a messed-up way of looking at it, he still left them."

"But you wanted this job," she says.

I shove my hands in my pockets and sigh at the ceiling. "I thought I did. But when that phone call came, I don't know…I wasn't excited at all. I knew it would take me away from you guys, from what I love. From the person I love."

"What are you going to do?" she asks.

"I don't know. Brooke left for Denver this morning."

Annika gives me a thoughtful glance. "I saw her in the bakery yesterday. I invited her to Thanksgiving."

The thought of her finding comfort at the Bear when she was hurting and sad somehow gives me hope. While I would have rather she come to me, this means something. "What'd she say?"

Annika shrugs. "Honestly, she looked like she was about to cry. What the heck is that all about?"

"She wanted that job too."

Annika closes her eyes for a long moment. "Shit."

"Yeah," I reply.

She grimaces. "You told her how you feel?"

I nod.

"Maybe she just needs time."

"I don't know, it felt pretty final."

"Be patient," she says, touching my arm. "If she immediately gave in to your charms you wouldn't have fallen so hard for her in the first place."

This rings true, but it hurts too much to explore any further. I heave a giant breath at the ceiling as my pulse flutters in my belly.

Annika wipes a crumb off the table and dumps it into the sink. "So, we should probably talk about Thanksgiving soon. Finalize the guest list, menu, etc."

Another pang of dread tightens my gut. Brooke. I can't stop picturing her here with my family, her eyes sparkling and her laughter filling the space. But that's a fantasy I need to shut down.

"I'd like to invite Hazel, if that's okay," I say.

"Pete's ex?" Annika asks, her brows furrowing.

"Yeah," I say, "she's also my friend."

"Of course she's welcome," Annika says, then tilts her head to peer at me. "Anyone else you want to invite?"

"No," I say with a deep breath that does nothing to clear the turmoil in my heart.

Annika gives me a tight nod, then slides into her coat and walks to her car. From the window over the sink, I watch her climb in and start the engine, then drive slowly down the snowy driveway.

2 8

BROOKE

As I pass the Growly Bear, the tears start again. I fight the craving to stop in for one last mug of tea or order a sandwich for the road. I'm not going to be tempted anymore. The streets have been plowed but I pass a car in the ditch, the front axle bent in and a layer of snow coating the windows. By the time I get to Galena Pass, the clouds have parted and the sun is rising over the ridges to the south, casting a golden glow over the snowy ground. In my rearview, the rough-cut Sawtooth Mountains stand guard over the valley in slate gray and stark white, their tips aglow with a fiery orange. I give them one last glance before descending the other side of the pass.

My phone rings as I reach the highway junction with Highway I-84. A jumpy flutter breaks loose in my stomach. "Good morning, Ike."

"What the hell kind of message is this?" he growls.

I swallow. "Um, well…"

"We're running the biggest story of the decade and you're quitting?"

"I'm just letting you guys enjoy the spotlight."

"I assigned you and Wyatt to this beat for a reason, Brooke."

"I…can't work with him anymore."

Ike curses under his breath. "Why? If he's being a pigheaded asshole, you should have said something so I could wring his neck."

"It's not anything like that. Wyatt's been extremely—" I stuff down the rise of emotions. "—accommodating."

"Does he know about this?"

"Yes."

"And he didn't try to stop you?"

Breathe. "He did, but I can't stay."

The line is silent for a moment. "This is bullshit, but...sounds like you've made up your mind. We'll miss you, Brooke."

My throat closes around the sob, stopping it just in time. "I'm going to miss you too," I manage.

I end the call and glance at the screen. There's a hopeful part of me that wants a message from Wyatt, but the hurt side of me is glad there isn't.

We said we'd do this together. That's kind of hard to do when you're not here.

But I can't be around him and keep my head on straight. Obviously.

As the jagged mountains fade in my rearview, I review my time in Penny Creek, searching for where I went wrong. For the moment I veered off the path I had set. It had to be the kiss on the dance floor that night. I suck in a breath as the memory floods in—the way he took my face in his hands, and his soft, urgent lips pressing eagerly into mine. In that moment, all my defenses vanished. I thought it would feel terrifying, but that's not what I felt at all. I felt free. But then I realized that I was slipping dangerously into that place I'd been before. The one where I gave up myself.

I thought cultivating a friendship would create a barrier, but it only made the pull between us stronger.

If I had let him take me to bed that night, would we have gotten it out of our system so we could return our focus to our jobs?

I shake my head. No, I was right to push him away, to draw the line. I just should have enforced it better.

In between the busy cities, the miles drift by. I listen to the radio as

I cut through the Wasatch Mountains and descend onto the plains, but it's just noise. I wait for the cloudy thoughts in my mind to clear, for my chest to stop aching, but the pang deep down in my belly won't go away. I try eating, but the truck stop sandwich tastes like sawdust. When I stop for gas, there's a Starbuck's across the street, and I use the drive-thru lane to order a mug of English Breakfast with steamed milk.

"Can you add a little bit of honey to it? You know, like, at the bottom before you add the milk so it can dissolve?" I ask the speaker at the order station.

"Sorry, you'll have to add it yourself. How many packets?"

I stare at the reader board, fighting the feeling that I should just cancel it. It'll be fine. "Just one please."

At the window, a girl with a narrow face wearing a green apron hands over my tea while talking into her headset. "Have a good day," she says, but I'm not sure it's intended for me.

I set my tea down and drive to the parking area, but the process of adding the cold honey from the little plastic packet when the mug is so full turns into a giant mess. I burn my fingers while trying to pour some of the scalding hot tea into a planter, and the honey somehow gets on my pants. When I finally get everything cleaned up and the lid back on, I've wasted a good ten minutes. Later, when the liquid has cooled enough for consumption, I risk a taste, hoping for validation that it's possible to get a decent cup of tea outside of Penny Creek, but the flavor that hits my tongue makes me wince. The milk must be nonfat or some other atrocity, and the tea tastes off—like it's been blended with peach. Who on earth would flavor a perfectly good black tea with fruit? I consider chucking the cup out the window, but at seventy miles an hour, that might not be such a good idea. Instead, I ignore the cup like the traitor it is until my next pit stop.

The plains are so barren and stark, the dead landscape covered with a thin layer of snow. The wind buffets my little car and sends white streams of spindrift over the pale concrete. *Go back*, it seems to say.

But I can't go back. Not until I can make sense of what happened and how I lost my way.

"COME HERE, TIGER!" my dad growls as he pulls me into a giant hug. "How was the drive?" he asks while Mom shrieks and grabs me.

"Not bad," I lie, savoring my mom's arms around me. I exhale a long sigh and let the warmth of my childhood home and the people who know me best fill me up.

"Mom's got dinner all ready, just waiting for you," Dad says, welcoming me inside.

I tuck into the bathroom to wash my hands and see my stricken expression reflecting back in the mirror. I splash water on my face, hoping to get some color back in my cheeks, or at least help put the last of the long drive behind me.

To my relief, the topic of why I left Penny Creek doesn't come up as we eat. Apparently, my simple explanation over the phone this morning had been enough, and we fill the time catching up, the conversation and warmth a welcome distraction from my tumultuous thoughts.

That night, back in my old bed, though my bones are road weary, I lie there, unable to find sleep. What is Wyatt doing right now? What new development came up today? Are more victims coming forward? What's happening with the investigation? A pang squeezes my chest, making an already painful knot cinch tighter.

If anything, I need you more than ever.

And yet I left him. The ache in my chest echoes through me. I curl into a ball and try to fight it, try to breathe, but the memory of his caresses and the fierce look in his eyes makes it impossible.

Say it, Brooke, say you need me.

Yes, Wyatt, I need you.

The walls seem to press on me, squeezing out all the oxygen in the room. Throwing the covers back, I get up for a glass of water. The house is dark but I know my way. There's a light beneath the door to my dad's office.

I knock and poke my head inside.

My dad twists around from his chair and lowers his glasses. "Hey, I thought you'd be asleep by now."

I shrug, then nod at the laptop open on his desk. "Are you writing?"

He closes the lid of his laptop. "A little."

I slip into the room. "Is it your book? Can I read it?"

"When it's ready, sure."

"Have you been writing more lately?" I ask as a little thrill zips through me. Maybe he's finally taking my advice.

He shakes his head. "I write when the inspiration strikes."

"But you could be so much more than a hobby writer. You're going to get a book deal someday, I know you will. You just have to keep writing, keep trying."

"Maybe." He stands from his desk and stretches, then comes over to give me a hug. "You want to tell me why you're really here?"

I collapse against his chest. "It's that obvious, huh?"

He rubs my back. "Only to me."

I force a slow exhale through my tight lips. "I didn't get the job in L.A."

He steps back and gives me a look of empathy. "I'm sorry, honey." He settles on the couch and taps the neighboring cushion. I sit down and draw my knees up.

"Do you know why?" he asks.

"I guess I...underestimated the competition." I decide to be vague, otherwise I'll have to listen to Dad rant about how Wyatt stole the job from me when I know he earned it fair and square. I got complacent while Wyatt kept true to his goals.

The pain in my chest burns hot like a blast from a torch. I resist the urge to rub the place where it hurts. It won't help. What's broken is deep inside.

Dad settles in next to me and drapes an arm over my shoulders.

"When you were about two, a story I had written before you were born won a prize. Me and four other literary writers were selected to be a part of a mentorship program. They were going to make us all bestselling authors. It was a year of training. Not just the writing, but all the research behind it, to make sure what we wanted to write was going to sell."

I turn so I can see his face. "You never told me this."

He shrugs. "It was legit and all that. They had the track record to prove it, but it cost twenty grand, and, well, we were broke."

"You turned it down?" This is starting to sound like history repeating all over again. First he switched from creative writing to teaching because of me, and then, he gave up his opportunity to make a living as an author?

"I didn't want to be a bestselling author if it meant I had to write what they told me to. It sucked the soul right out of it for me. Plus, I had just finished my student teaching and had a job lined up at Bridge Creek High."

"But you're a gifted writer. You could've been famous by now."

He squeezes my shoulder. "I didn't need to be famous. I had everything I needed."

"But you hate teaching."

He laughs. "I complain about it, sure, but it's meaningful, and important. I feel...I don't know, I guess you could say...that I've made a positive impact on the world."

"You absolutely have, Dad." I shift away from him so I can see his face. "Do you ever lie awake at night, wondering if you made a mistake?"

He raises his eyebrows. "Nope."

"Was it because of Mom? Was she worried that writing wouldn't earn enough to support us?"

"No. We weighed the pros and cons together and I haven't looked back."

Together. That's what Wyatt wanted—for us to work through this as a team.

You said it yourself, we're better together.

I wince. "I wish you could have had the ability to do both—follow your passion and do what's right for your family."

"Making you and your mother happy is my passion. Being your dad is the best thing that's ever happened to me."

"Even though I made you give up your dream?"

He reaches out and places his hand on top of mine. "My dream changed the minute I learned you were on your way."

Tears prick at the corners of my eyes.

"And, I would argue that I didn't give up anything," he says with a twinkle in his eye. "Sure, my goals shifted a little bit, but I'm still just as happy writing now as back then, plus I have you to share it with. That's all I've ever wanted."

I tuck back into his arms and he gives my shoulder a squeeze. "I love you, Dad," I say.

"And I love you."

Back in my bed, I turn the conversation over and over. Dad never gave me any reason to think he regretted his choices because of having me so young. My goal was to prove that I was worth his sacrifice. But now he's telling me it wasn't a sacrifice at all, it was a choice. An easy one.

THE NEXT MORNING, after a brisk walk with my parents on their favorite trail, I drive downtown to meet Maggie for breakfast. The minute I see her, I jump into her arms and she squeezes me so tight I see stars.

"I've missed you so much!" I say as she rocks me back and forth.

"Oh girl, you have no idea," she says, stepping back. She brushes back her thick curls and smiles, her brown eyes sparkling. "After breakfast we're getting our nails done, and if you aren't too pooped, there's a fab boutique I've been dying to check out, and then I booked us a table tonight at Matador with Becca and Evan."

"Wow!" I say as a rush of gratitude washes through me. It'll be good to see my cousins again, and Matador will be quite the change from quiet Penny Creek.

"And this morning I reserved us a booth, so you have no excuses not to spill your guts," she says, hooking her arm around mine.

Though I knew she wouldn't let me off the hook, my insides still flutter. As she leads me inside, I feel like she's dragging me to my doom.

A waitress comes by for our drink order as soon as we slide into the booth.

"Okay," Maggie says, licking her lips. "Your explanation of why you're suddenly here doesn't hold water." She reaches for my hand. "Did something happen with Wyatt? Is it his family? Is he too wrapped up in caring for them? Did he push you away?"

"No," I groan.

Her eyes darken. "Did that asshole cheat on you?"

I shake my head.

The waitress returns with my tea. Even though I love this place, I didn't order any steamed milk to go with it. I can't take any more disappointment.

Maggie wraps her fingers around her coffee drink. "Then what went so wrong you left Idaho like your ass was on fire?"

"He wanted me to go to California."

Maggie gives me a quizzical look.

I release a sigh. "He got the Times job."

Maggie's face falls. "I'm sorry, girl. That stinks."

"He turned it down and told them to hire me."

She sets down her mug and shifts to face me. "Why would he do that?"

"He said he couldn't take the job knowing it made me miserable. Told me I deserved the job and that I earned it."

"Wow." She blows across her coffee. "But...you going to California means no happy ever after for you two. And he still wanted you to go?"

The waitress returns for our breakfast order then hurries off.

"He said he wanted what was going to make me happy."

"Damn." Maggie stares into her coffee, looking pensive. "So are you going?"

"Maggie!" I say, sending her daggers with my eyes. "No, I'm not going."

"Because you love him?" Maggie replies, looking confused.

"Yes," I say. "I mean, no."

"No, you don't love him? Or no, you're not going because you do?"

I put my head in my hands. "I don't know," I moan.

Maggie inhales sharply.

"Right?" I say, snapping my head up. "Do you see now how sincerely screwed I am?"

Maggie's face softens and she reaches over to take my hand. "Honey, you're not screwed, you're in love."

I close my eyes and let my head fall back against the booth. "I never wanted this to happen. I swore I wouldn't let anything keep me from my goals this time. And look what happened? I'm right back where I started."

Maggie watches me, her gaze unwavering. "Are you, though? Wyatt's not limiting your choices. Sounds like the opposite."

My stomach drops.

"Love isn't something you can control, Brooksie. It's not a faucet you can turn off."

"But it's ruining my life!" I say.

She gives me a kind smile. "Only because you're not trusting it."

"What if I'm giving up my dream?" I say as my nose starts stinging.

"Look into your heart and tell me if it's changed."

I clench my eyes shut but the tears spill out anyway, tickling my cheeks. Maggie's right—those dreams I had months ago don't fit anymore.

"See?"

"Love sucks," I say, and try to laugh but it just makes me cry harder.

"Stop fighting it and it'll stop sucking, I promise."

This time, I do laugh. I blink at the ceiling and wipe my eyes.

Maggie slides close and wraps her arms around me. "I love you to pieces," she says. "But you are so freaking stubborn. I feel like I need a two by four sometimes to knock some sense into you."

"I know," I say, sniffling. "I'm sorry."

"There's a hunky journalist with a broken heart who needs to hear that, not me."

The waitress arrives with our breakfast, but suddenly, I'm no longer hungry.

29

WYATT

"Yo, anyone in there?" Ike growls.

I'm yanked from my thoughts and blink at Samantha, Quinn, and Ike staring at me.

"Sorry, I, um, must have zoned out there for a second," I joke, but nobody smiles.

"Samantha's going to jump in and help you with interviews," Ike says, still scowling at me.

"Sure," I say. "Great." Even though it's far from great. Samantha's a good reporter and a nice person, but she's not Brooke. But Brooke's not here and there are still stories the Gazette needs to tell.

Samantha and I hash out a plan, then get to work. So far, four women have come forward with stories like Vonnie's and Hazel's. Rundell paid them special attention, then asked to take pictures of them and after, manipulated them. None of them ever told anyone. Some say they were ashamed, some say he was too intimidating, blaming them for making him do the things he did.

The police question Renee Fuller, rumored to be the rich widow Rundell ran off with. After she's released I manage to get her number, but she hangs up on me, so I dig up an old friend of hers who offers up that Ms. Fuller had needed extra support from the church during the period after her husband's untimely death.

"According to our records, she left town right around the time Rundell disappeared," I say, holding the phone with one hand while I scribble notes with the other.

"Well, she was embarrassed, of course."

I pause. "Embarrassed by what?"

"Because he wouldn't sleep with her."

I sit bolt upright. "She actually told you that?"

"Not in so many words, but I know how to read between the lines. Pastor Fredrickson asked her to leave the congregation."

I raise an eyebrow, my mind working furiously.

"So she just up and left town," the woman says, her voice bitter.

"Do you think she could have been angry enough to commit a crime?" I ask, tapping my pen on the pad.

"Like bean him over the head with a rock? Heavens no."

I wince at the graphic image the woman just planted in my mind, then thank her and get to work on the story. My phone buzzes with a text and I snatch it up, my pulse racing because finally, *finally*, it has to be Brooke.

But it's Samantha telling me she's almost done with her research for the story.

After the call, I stare at the words on my computer screen, willing the magic to come to life and make something of the information. Everything I type comes out like mush. I switch gears and edit a follow-up story about the Zuniga family and the working conditions they've suffered. Samantha sends me her contribution, and I go back to my Rundell story and try to hammer it out, but it's no use.

I can't do this without Brooke.

Or maybe I just don't want to.

I send Ike a note of apology with the half-baked story, hoping he'll come to my rescue, then grab my coat and leave the Gazette. I should stay at the office and finalize the story, but I need to get away from the place that most reminds me of her.

After leaving the building, I walk to the parking lot. I guess I'll head home, even though nobody's there. Vonnie's at her Saturday nanny job, caring for a set of four-year-old twins until late. Leah's still up on the mountain at the high-country yurt.

Once I reach the Suburban, I slide out my phone and check the screen, but there's nothing from Brooke. The ache I've been staving off all day comes rushing back. I force myself to climb into the seat, but the tightness and sense of hopelessness roar and snap to life like a pack of angry dogs inside me. I punch the steering wheel hard. The pain in my knuckles feels strangely reassuring. I do it again until I've scraped off a layer of skin. When I finally stop I'm breathing hard and shaking.

I was willing to give her everything. The only thing I asked for in return was time, but she couldn't even give me that.

I drive to main street, past the empty newspaper boxes in front of the grocery store, past the turn to her cottage, past the pool.

There's a dull throb deep down in my belly, a gnawing, raw feeling. It makes me feel sick, and then so full of venom I want to punch the wall. A part of me is exhausted, but I know I won't sleep. I head up Cold Springs Road, slipping in the snow when I take the turn too fast. I can't even muster the energy to care that halfway up the road, there's a car in the ditch.

Then, I recognize the car.

My heart slams into my throat. I yank the wheel to the side of the road and jump out.

"Brooke!" I call out, but hear nothing in return.

I go to the driver's side and heave open the door, but the car is empty. "Brooke!" I call out, searching the twilight for any sign of her, then spot a set of footprints.

She's okay, I tell myself to calm my pounding pulse. But now I have to find her.

I set off at a run, slipping in my work shoes. The footprints seem to be spread far apart, like she was running.

Was she? And why? Is she hurt? Did she hit her head and now she's delirious, wandering around in the snow? I picture several unwanted scenarios of finding her frozen body, or worse, never finding her.

The footprints turn down my driveaway. This has to be a good sign. Please be okay. I race past the giant trees, their massive boughs heavy with snow, the icy air burning my throat. Then, our porch comes into view. To my relief, a figure is sitting on the second step.

Brooke.

She's scrambling down the steps as I hurry forward. By the time we meet, my chest is heaving.

She dives into my arms. "I'm sorry," she says.

My fears begin to melt away. She's here. She's mine. "For what?" I ask as a laugh bubbles up from my chest. I lean back and take her face in my hands so I can look at her, make sure she's all in one perfect piece.

"For not trusting you. For leaving." She gazes into my eyes. "For being a pigheaded assho—"

Before she can finish, I kiss her. It's aggressive and firm and I don't hold back. I tug on her lower lip and dance with her hot little tongue, swirling deep into her mouth. She responds with a soft moan and slides her hands into the back pocket of my pants to pull me closer. My growing erection presses against her belly, and she arches her hips against me.

I lift her up and carry her into the house. "Wyatt!" she shrieks.

"You're going to pay for that little stunt." I slip through the door and shut it with my heel, then kiss her again.

"What stunt?" she asks while unbuttoning my shirt, her fingers working fast.

It seems to take forever to get to my bedroom at the end of the hall. "Doubting me. I promised you I'd make it okay. That we'd be a team. That we could find a way through this. Together."

Her eyes find mine at the use of that word. "You're right."

I set her down at the edge of my dresser and kiss her. She unbuckles my belt and slides her fingers inside the waistband. A shudder of longing breaks free inside me.

I unzip her coat and toss it, then tug her sweater off. "When you left, it hurt, Brooke."

"It hurt me too," she says, her eyes filling with emotion.

"I need to be able to take care of you."

She slides my pants down and caresses my pulsing length. My hunger explodes. I peel down her leggings and very wet panties. Then I lift her to the dresser and press her back into the wall. I kiss her hard and wrap her thighs around me.

"I didn't understand before, but now I do," she says.

"I need you to trust me, to trust us," I growl, kissing down to behind her ear where she smells like clove and sugar.

"I do, I just...I was scared. Trusting hasn't worked out so well for me in the past."

"None of that matters now," I say, gazing into her eyes. "We're in this together."

"I know," she says, and pulls me to her for another kiss. She arches her hips so that I'm right there.

I try to break away to grab my wallet for a condom, but she's got a tight hold on me.

"Please, Wyatt. I don't want anything between us."

Joy flutters through me. "Really?"

She nods. "You're the only person I've been with for the last year."

I smile. "I'm clean too."

"So we can?" she asks, her eyes lighting up.

"You've got me in a death grip, Brooke, do I have a choice?"

Her eyes soften and she reaches up to stroke my face. "You always have a choice. And so will we. Together."

I lean in for a kiss, tasting her soft lips. Then I lift her thighs and thrust slowly inside her.

30

WYATT

"You made your cranberry sauce," Annika says with a grin. "I thought you said never again?"

I stir the sauce, watching the fat cranberries bubble. "There may be a certain guest I'm trying to impress."

Brooke dives under my arm and wraps herself around me. "Would that certain someone be me?"

I lean down to kiss her. "Maybe."

She pokes my stomach.

"Ow! Careful," I say, flinching. "I'm sore from that workout you punished me with this morning."

She gives me a sultry grin. "I've got plenty more where that came from."

"Here, taste," I say, dipping a spoon into the cranberry sauce and lifting it to her lips.

She blows on the fat berry on the end of the spoon, then lets me slip it into her mouth. Her eyes light up. "So good."

I kiss her again, my hunger igniting. I savor the hint of my cranberry sauce on her tongue and the spicy-honey scent of her skin. Yeah, there's a house full of people here to celebrate, but that might make it easy to sneak off. Just for a few minutes.

Annika smiles and shakes her head. "Get a room," she mutters as I kiss Brooke again.

Little does Annika know that we've already made good use of my room today—twice. Once when we woke up and again after the Turkey Day Workout That Nearly Killed Me.

Brooke laughs. "Don't encourage him." She spins from under my arm and tries to dash away, but I snatch her wrist and pull her back.

I wrap my arms around her. "I love you."

"I love you too," she says with a sigh.

I kiss her again and she presses closer to me.

From behind us, Annika clears her throat.

Brooke pushes off my chest, her cheeks flushed. I'm going to have to find a way to sneak off with her soon. Definitely before dinner.

"Grady's here!" Annika says, and dashes to the door, past Lori and Caleb who are setting the table.

Out of the corner of my eye, I watch Annika step back to let Grady inside, her face practically glowing. Grady sets a small cooler and a grocery bag down, then dusts the snow from his thick hair and removes his boots.

"You didn't have to bring anything," Annika scolds him. "I told you."

Grady shrugs. "I can't show up to Thanksgiving dinner empty handed."

Caleb and Lori join them at the door, exchanging hugs and greetings. Taylor races into the living room, dressed as a pirate complete with a homemade cardboard sword and eye patch, followed by Vonnie.

"Grady!" he cries. "Come see my pirate ship!" He grabs Grady's hand and pulls. Moments later, they're disappearing towards the rec room at the back of the house.

Vonnie comes into the kitchen.

"You ready for a break?" I ask her as she grabs a soda from the fridge and pops the top.

"Whew," she says, wiping her brow. "The pirate life is thirsty work."

"Let Grady have a turn. Go put your feet up by the fire for a minute," I say, turning off the burner and setting my spoon aside. Since I found out about Rundell, I've kept a close eye on her. She does great until bedtime, when she needs one of my stories. Her first visit with the therapist was just a few days ago. Vonnie shared that it was "good" though also "weird", but that she liked the woman.

Vonnie gulps another sip. "I'll rest later." She places the can back in the fridge and hurries back toward the rec room.

I help Annika prep the salad, then baste the turkey. Brooke unveils her giant appetizer plate with cheeses, apple slices, crackers, and figs. Caleb and Lori drift over, hand in hand.

Grady comes back from pirate-land. "Looks like it's cocktail hour," he says, rolling up his sleeves. He washes his hands at the sink, then unloads the grocery bag he brought.

"Glad you could make it, man," I say while Annika carries the salad to the table.

"Me too. I almost got pegged for overtime," Grady replies, and unloads the contents of his grocery bag on the counter. "But someone else volunteered to stay."

"Who would volunteer to work on Thanksgiving?" I reply, reaching to the appetizer plate for a cracker.

Grady shrugs. "Someone who doesn't have a family."

I slap him on the shoulder. "You'll always be family to us."

A tight look passes through his eyes, and he nods. "Thanks," he says simply. "That means a lot."

From the table, Annika glances at him, her eyes glistening, but Grady's busy shaving fresh ginger into cocktail glasses.

Hazel appears, bringing a gift of hand-thrown pottery bowls. "Just a little side project," she says. She's shy at first, but slowly gets swallowed by the welcoming vibe, and soon we're all laughing and sharing bites from Brooke's plate while sipping Grady's ginger rum cocktail.

Leah arrives from the mountain and soon the noise level in the house could make the walls bulge. But as I gaze around at all the rosy cheeks and sparkling eyes, drink in the laughter and banter and the joy flowing between us, I wouldn't have it any other way.

I'm tending the fire one last time before we sit down when Brooke appears at my side. "It's too bad your brother Peter couldn't make it," she says, settling on the couch.

I add one more log and shift it with the poker, squinting at the flames. "Yeah. It's a busy weekend in the E.R. and he's still the low guy on the totem pole."

"Will he come home for Christmas?" Brooke asks.

I lower onto the couch next to her. "Not sure. He doesn't always know his schedule."

"You two aren't close," Brooke says, her eyes clouding. She gazes back at the kitchen where the swarm of people are talking and laughing. "How is that possible?"

"We used to be tight. We had a falling out back in high school and it's been sort of tense ever since."

She touches my arm. "What happened?"

I coax a long breath into my lungs. "Remember how I told you Hazel was dating Pete?"

"Right." Her eyes widen. "Did he know about what happened to her?"

I shake my head. "She wouldn't let me tell anyone."

"So you had this big secret about his girlfriend and couldn't tell him," she says. "That's tough, Wyatt."

I nod as the fire cracks, sending crimson sparks up the chimney. "He thought I'd stolen her from him."

Her eyes fill with empathy. "Did you try to explain?"

"There wasn't much I could share, right? I just said that Hazel and I were friends. That she was going through a tough time and needed someone she could talk to." I scrub my chin with my fingertips. "That only seemed to make it worse because he wanted to be that person for her."

"And he couldn't let it go?"

"I'm not sure I'm ready to forgive him, either. I mean, he completely threw our trust out the window." I press my lips together. "I would never do that to him. Yet he cut me—and Hazel—out of his life, in a heartbeat."

243

"Sounds like he was hurting pretty badly," Brooke says, sliding her hand into mine.

"I think he really loved her," I reply.

"When I interviewed her, she told me she wanted to be a nurse back then. Maybe they were planning a future together. You know, going to college, then into the medical field."

"Maybe," I say.

"That's really sad," Brooke says. "Maybe now, if Hazel's willing to let you share what happened, you two can try to patch things up."

I glance at Hazel, who has Taylor in her lap at the counter, drawing something with him. "He's going to have to stop avoiding me first."

Leah and Vonnie hurry in the direction of the rec room, soda cans in hand.

Brooke scoots closer to me and lays her head on my shoulder. "How are they doing?"

I wrap my arm across her shoulders. "Good. Vonnie's back to straight A's and Leah's keeping up with her online work."

"That's great to hear."

I let the tension of everything we've been through wash through me one last time. Vonnie finally admitted her fears about me leaving her and Leah for the job. I'm pretty sure they're tied to when Dad and Mom both disappeared from her life when she was eleven. When I told her that I wasn't taking the job in L.A., she cried.

"After they graduate, I'm taking them to San Diego to celebrate."

"That's really sweet of you. Have they ever been to the ocean?"

I shake my head. "Nope. When we moved Mom to Seaside, it was just me and Annika. The twins were too young to be part of something like that."

Brooke nuzzles closer to me. I can feel her curiosity engine whirring to life, but she doesn't ask for more about my mom. Maybe because she hears the tightness in my voice whenever it comes up, or maybe because it's Thanksgiving and not a day I'm willing to tarnish. I'll share more about what happened sometime, if she wants to hear it. Just not today.

"Hey you two," Caleb calls from the kitchen. "This bird's ready."

A whoop comes up from the crowd, followed by cries of "Let's do this!" and "I'll get drinks!"

Once we're all settled at the table—the extra leaf added earlier to accommodate everyone—we all clasp hands.

"Who's saying grace?" I ask, gazing from the spread to a quick scan of the circle of family and friends.

"Thank you for volunteering, Wyatt," Leah says with a haughty expression.

"You're the eloquent one, anyways," Caleb says with a smirk.

I laugh. "No pressure or anything."

Next to me, Brooke squeezes my hand.

"I'm grateful for this amazing day filled with the warmth of family and friends and good food. I'm grateful for the close bonds we share. The way we support each other." My voice wavers a bit, and I can't help but take a moment to pause and try to get my emotions in check. Vonnie gazes at me, her eyes misting up too. I give her a smile to let her know that I believe in her and her strength, that what happened to her isn't going to get in the way of her dreams. I shift my gaze to Leah, who lifts her chin and smiles.

Under the table, I caress Brooke's palm with my thumb and gaze into her dazzling blue eyes. "And I'm grateful for the many challenges life throws our way because they help us see what's true, and remind us of what's important."

"Hear, hear," Caleb says from the other end of the table.

As platters get lifted for passing and conversations break the silence, I lean down to kiss Brooke, my heart filling with hope.

31

WYATT

After dinner, everyone gears up for a stroll before dessert. The entryway gets crowded with bodies adding layers and donning boots. Taylor grabs his sled from the porch and races down the steps.

Outside, it's snowing lightly. Brooke and I walk, our hands clasped. Behind me, Grady and Annika banter about something while Hazel and Lori talk and Caleb pulls a bundled-up Taylor on his sled. Ahead of us, Leah and Vonnie race ahead, laughing, scooping up snowballs to throw at each other.

"Any more thoughts about my offer?" I ask, swinging Brooke's hand.

"About moving in?" she replies. "Did you check with your sisters?"

"Of course. They're crazy about you."

She squeezes my hand. "How about this," she says. "We'll try it until my assignment ends, see if we still like each other."

I laugh. "I thought we agreed you were going to stop doubting me."

"I'm not sure you know what you're getting into."

"That's what makes this so fun," I say, leaning over to peck her on the cheek. "It'll be like an adventure."

"But what if it's too much? I'm a terrible cook. I hog the bed."

"I happen to like you hogging my bed. And I don't mind cooking."

She smiles. "I'm kind of a grump in the morning."

"Good thing I have the perfect cure for that," I say as a hot ache pulses through me. Though I managed to get her alone before dinner —a quick fix in the bathroom—it wasn't enough. I'm not sure I'll ever get enough. Not that I want to.

"Wyatt," she groans. "I'm being serious."

I pull her hand so she stops walking. "I'm serious too, Brooke."

A flicker of trepidation passes through her eyes, but then she draws a slow breath and it fades, replaced by a calm that softens her expression. "I like the idea of being close to you. Of waking up with you and cooking dinner with you and helping you with your sisters and talking through stories with you as we get ready for bed. But, Wyatt, what if it's too much?"

Annika, riding piggyback on Grady, and the rest of the group behind us pass by, ignoring us. Their banter fades, leaving us in the quiet. Snowflakes drift down, dusting Brooke's long eyelashes. I take her face in my hands and kiss her, our chilled lips quickly heating. "How could it be too much? I love you."

Her eyes twinkle. "As if that's the answer for everything."

"As far as I'm concerned, it is."

"But what are we going to do when my assignment ends?" she asks.

"I think you should apply for Ike's job," I say.

Her jaw drops. "Like, be editor?"

"Yes, ma'am," I say. "You'd still get to write too. You'd be so good at it."

She gives me a sassy little smile. "I would be. Plus, I'd get to boss you around."

I kiss her again, my skin tingling with the need to feel her body against mine. "Anytime, princess."

She leans back, panting, a hungry look on her face. "You'd have to stop calling me that at the office."

"True, though we could have plenty of private meetings."

"Wyatt!" she cries, laughing. "You have a one-track mind."

"So do you," I tease, giving her ass a playful tap.

She jumps away from me. "It's all your fault."

I take her hand and start walking again. "What do you think, though?"

She gives me a pensive glance. "That would give us both jobs here."

"Yeah. Is that bad? Would you rather apply elsewhere?"

"Maybe if we take a vacation every winter, I could be convinced to stay."

"Deal. Where should we go? Hawaii? Mexico?"

She laughs. "Whoa, that was easy. Maybe I should ask for more."

"Name it," I say.

She tugs me to a stop, her gaze turning serious. "I didn't mean that. I don't need anything more, Wyatt." She closes her eyes and kisses me. Her lips press tenderly into mine. I tug on her lower lip and flick my tongue against hers. She deepens the kiss and we stand there under the snowflakes, the energy between us sparking to life.

I break away and rub noses with her. "You don't have to take Ike's job. You know that I'll support whatever you want to do."

"Yeah, I know," she says, then grins wickedly. "But being your boss could be very entertaining."

"Maybe we should practice that tonight, see if it's all it's cracked up to be."

She raises an eyebrow. "You're kind of infuriating, you know that?"

"Yeah, I know," I reply.

On the return trip, Brooke and Vonnie get engrossed in a detailed conversation about a book they both loved and I end up walking in the back of the pack with Caleb. In the sled behind him, Taylor is humming "Rudolph the Red Nosed Reindeer" and eating snow off his mitten. A long string of friends and family extends ahead of us, their conversations muffled by the snow. Even Cold Springs Creek next to the road is only a gentle whisper.

"So, uh, I got a question for you, Oh Great One," Caleb asks in a muted tone.

"Oh Great One, huh?" I reply.

He smiles, but it's tight. "Am I crazy to ask Lori to...you know..."

I side-eye him. "Ask her to what?"

He puts his finger to hips lips and eyes the group ahead, where

Lori is talking with Hazel. "Not so loud." He huffs a sigh. "Marry me. On my birthday."

I practically tackle him with my hug. "That's awesome, man!"

"Quiet," he groans. After glancing back at Taylor, who has now moved on to "Jingle Bells, he gazes up at the falling flakes, as if gathering courage. "Am I crazy? I mean, we'll want to wait until she's out of school."

"That's only two years from now, though, right?" I ask.

"Yeah. She's away from me so much. Going to classes. Teaching undergrads. Writing papers. I just want everyone to know she's mine." He glances my way. "So, I'm not crazy?"

"Not in my book."

His shoulders seem to lower a notch. "Okay, good. I was kind of starting to freak out. I mean, my birthday is in three weeks."

"Does it feel right?" I ask.

He lets Taylor's sled leash go to tap a large branch, sending a flurry of flakes down. "Fuck yeah, it feels right."

"Then it is," I say, taking over pulling Taylor. "Do you have a ring?"

His face lights up. "Yeah. I actually bought it the first weekend she went back to school. Grady and I went all the way to Boise."

I raise an eyebrow. "Impressive."

He gives a sheepish little smile. "I wanted to do it the minute we got back, but I don't know, I wanted it to be special."

I bump his shoulder. "It will be, because it's coming from your heart."

We reach our driveway. I take the turn wide so as not to dump Taylor. He scoops up more snow. "Can we sled down the hill tomorrow?" he asks.

"Sure, bud," Caleb replies, then turns to me. "Looks like things are working out for you and Brooke."

My chest warms with a prickly, satisfying tingle. "Yeah."

"Look at you all glowy," Caleb says, punching my arm. "Is she moving in?"

I glance up the road and catch Brooke's face in profile. She's so fucking gorgeous. Lately I feel like my heart is going to burst. "Temporarily," I reply. "Her assignment ends in January. We'll see if we still like each other then. I told her she can have Pete's old room if she wants space."

"Yeah, like you're going to let her spend a single night in there," Caleb says.

"True," I say with a laugh.

Caleb grabs me around the neck and rubs the top of my head with his knuckles. "Just promise me I get to be your best man, okay?"

"Okay, okay!" I protest, jabbing him in the side.

"Get him, Uncle Wyatt!" Taylor calls from the sled. He throws a snowball at Caleb's back.

"Watch it, you little toad," Caleb says, releasing me. "Or I'll make a snowman out of you."

Taylor wriggles on his sled. "Do the hyperspace thing, Dad!"

Caleb gives me an exaggerated sigh. "Duty calls," he explains. He takes the reins from me and tears down the driveway while Taylor shrieks in delight.

I watch them go, replaying Caleb's demand. My stomach does a cartwheel. Yeah, it's soon to think about making Brooke mine once and for all, but I've never been more sure of anything in my life.

SIX MONTHS LATER, SAN DIEGO
WYATT

"Ohmigawd, there it is!" Leah cries from the backseat. Vonnie gives a shriek and the minute the wheels of our rental car stop they both burst from the car and take off across the parking lot, their hair whipping in the salty breeze. Ahead of them, the golden stretch of sand dotted with lifeguard towers meets the slate-blue Pacific Ocean.

"Don't go in past your knees until we get there!" I call out after them.

Leah flips me off before the two of them disappear over the sandy berm.

Next to me, Brooke giggles.

"It really is breathtaking," she says with a huge smile.

I lean over for a kiss and savor her soft lips and her warmth.

"We better go make sure they don't drown," I say, reluctantly pulling away.

"They're both champion swimmers," Brooke replies, giving me a look.

"True, but I've kept them alive this long, it would be a shame to start slacking now."

With a laugh, she pushes off my chest and we both step out of the car. The hot summer sun heats my shoulders as we grab backpacks, towels, and boogie boards, then hurry after the twins.

Though the beach is crowded, I spot Vonnie and Leah splashing in the waves fully clothed, their shrieks rising above the constant crashing of the waves. They run up the beach to get away from a wave, then run back down, their long hair already wet.

The crisp ocean air pricks my skin, cooling my core temperature in seconds. The air here is thick and moist, almost like I could chew it —completely opposite of central Idaho's that's so dry in the summer my skin cracks. Brooke and I pick a square of sand and drop our things. Our hotel receptionist warned us not to leave anything valuable unattended, so we've been careful to just bring food, sunscreen, and towels—no fancy cameras or expensive sunglasses.

Brooke peels off her shirt and slips out of her shorts to reveal a navy-blue bikini. My heart jolts inside my chest.

"Okay, um, can you do that again? Only...slower."

She rolls her eyes, but sends me a grin. "Later, cowboy. Right now I'm getting wet."

I rip off my t-shirt and race after her. "Hey, that's my job," I say in her ear as I catch up.

Brooke's musical laughter blends with the *shushhh* of the waves. Our feet slap the wet, smooth sand as we race each other into the water.

The instant my legs hit the warm ocean, I hoot like a moron. Two more steps and I'm diving in with a splash, the saltwater enveloping me. I come up next to Brooke, who is wiping her eyes, her beautiful face lit by a hundred-watt smile.

"It's so warm!" she says, laughing.

"Wave!" I shout, and we dive under. The wave's gentle current washes over us.

We come up again and I pull her close. Her tight curves fit perfectly against me. I lean down for a kiss but barely get started when Brooke breaks away to yell "wave!" and we dive again.

Vonnie and Leah have stripped out of their wet clothes to their swimsuits and are hurrying back to the ocean. I stuff down the comment that their bikinis are way too revealing—I don't have to play that role anymore. A part of me already misses it, but the other part is going to enjoy being there for them as a soft landing instead of the hammer. I'll always feel protective of them—that's not something I can ever turn off—and I'll always be there for them if they need me, but they're free to make their own choices now.

Brook and I duck under another wave, and when I come up, Vonnie and Leah are holding hands as they race into the surf, their feet kicking up water.

"It's great to see them so happy," Brooke says, watching them.

"They've worked hard," I say. "Celebrating that feels pretty good."

We dive under a wave, the warm ocean caressing my skin.

"This chapter in your life is closing," she says after we surface. "How's it feel?"

"Bittersweet," I say, laying back to float, sculling my arms at my sides. "They're moving on with their lives and I won't be in it so much, but I'm proud of what the three of us have accomplished."

"I'm glad you're acknowledging your success too," she says, treading water next to me. "You've earned it."

"I guess that's true. At times, it's felt like a long road."

"I'll bet. It's been a huge sacrifice."

I push off the bottom to bob over a wave. "Speaking of those, how's it feel to be here?" I ask, watching her face for a reaction.

She smiles. "You mean, am I sad that I didn't get the Times job so I could do this every day?"

I wince. "*Are* you sad?"

"We won an award, didn't we?"

A few months ago, Brooke and I were awarded the Milton Freer Award for excellence in investigative journalism for our series featuring Youth Pastor Jonah Rundell. Though the police ruled his death accidental, they credited our involvement in helping his victims find closure.

"Yeah, but it's still a small town paper."

Brooke tilts her head and gazes at me, squinting a little, which makes her already cute nose even cuter. "No, I'm not sad. Not one bit."

"Even though it was your dream?"

She closes her eyes and lifts her face to the sun. "Dreams change."

A week ago, Ike retired and officially turned over his office to Brooke, who landed the job of editor in chief of the Mountain Gazette.

I yank her to me. "If the Gazette turns out to not be enough, I want you to tell me. The last thing I want is for you to wake up some morning and hate me for holding you back."

She reaches down to stroke my growing erection through my trunks. "How could I possibly wake up hating you in the morning with this to look forward to?"

My dick pulses against her firm stomach. "Well, when you put it that way..."

She kisses me, her salty lips teasing, hungry.

"We better be careful or I'm not going to be able to walk out of here," I say.

She laughs. "Maybe we'll have to make creative use of some towels."

"Such a one-track mind, princess," I say, kissing the crook of her neck.

"Wyatt," she says in that needy little whisper. She wraps her legs around me and kisses me, her lips salty and warm and so soft.

"Ew! Parental PDA!" Leah calls from five feet away.

"Gross!" Vonnie echoes, splashing us.

"You're going down, both of you!" I shout, splashing them back.

THAT NIGHT, I take everyone to a swanky beachside café for dinner. The girls dress up for the occasion and they both look so pretty and perfect that my heart squeezes painfully. Fuck, I'm going to miss them. Miss corralling them for swim team practice in the morning and cooking with them at night. I'm going to miss watching them grow and change into the incredible young women they'll become.

Next month, Leah is leaving for New Zealand to film with Matchstick Productions—a contract she signed two months ago after her video of a wicked descent in Idaho's backcountry went viral and she suddenly had offers from filmmakers all over the globe. Even though it was hard for me to let go of wanting her to complete a four-year degree before she started her career in the ski industry, now it feels right. Leah has to make her own way, and college will still be there when she's ready. I'll worry about her riding around in helicopters and dropping into steep chutes while battling extreme conditions, but I trust her judgement.

Vonnie deferred college for a year to work full time for the family she currently nannies. They do a fair amount of travel, so Vonnie will get a taste of the real world before she continues on to the University of Washington next year. When she came to me asking if she could stay with me instead of leave for Seattle in the fall, I held her and told her she was welcome to stay as long as she needed to. She's sleeping better now, and laughs more. She even sort of has a boyfriend, though she claims they're just friends, but I know a spark when I see one.

As we walk through the lobby to our table, a rush of emotion surges through me and I grip it tight, savor the tenderness and grief and joy as the sweet moment it is, then release it to soar in the warm breeze.

Dinner is rowdy and lively and we catch several scowls from nearby patrons. From our table, we watch the orange sun melt into the dark sea, snapping selfies of ourselves and making silly faces and teasing each other.

After dessert, I suggest a walk on the beach. Vonnie catches my eye and I give her a wink. Leah's got her poker face on, but she knows what's coming too. I had to tell them. Not just because of buy in, but because it didn't seem right to plan something like this without including them. Team Morgan all the way.

"Definitely," Vonnie says.

"I'm in," Leah adds.

After I pay, we cross the boardwalk to the soft sand. Everyone slips off their shoes and the four of us stroll on the cool sand toward the black ocean.

"What an amazing day," Brooke says with a sigh. "Thanks so much for letting me crash your graduation trip," she says to Vonnie and Leah.

"Are you kidding? If you hadn't come along, Wyatt would have spent the whole day smearing sunscreen on us and correcting our grammar," Leah says.

"We wanted you here," Vonnie says, giving Brooke a thoughtful smile.

Brooke pulls Vonnie into a quick hug. "Thank you." She hugs Leah too, and when she steps away, her eyes are shining.

"I actually have an ulterior motive for inviting you," I say as the butterflies I've been able to keep tame all day break free, tickling my insides.

Brooke gives me a curious look.

Vonnie and Leah huddle close, holding hands, their excitement evident in their faces and the way Vonnie's rocking on her toes.

I inhale a shaky breath of ocean air for bravery and lower to one knee.

Brooke's eyes widen. She glances at Vonnie, who has her hand over her mouth, and Leah, whose wicked grin burns like a beacon.

I take Brooke's hand, willing mine not to shake, and gaze up at the woman I want in my life forever. "I love you, Brooke. I've loved you since that first night."

Vonnie gives a little squeal.

Brooke's sparkling eyes are so clear and blue and beautiful.

"I loved you even when you hated me, when you challenged me, even when you pushed me away."

From my left, Leah snickers. "Something we have in common," she mutters.

I laugh, and so does Brooke, her eyes beginning to glisten.

Our gazes lock. "I'll never stop loving you, Brooke. You're the first thought in my mind when I wake up and you're what fills my dreams when I'm asleep. I want to take care of you, laugh with you, support your dreams. I want to share all that I have to give," I say as my emotions surge inside me.

I slide the box from my pocket and open it.

Brooke covers her mouth as tears begin to fall.

I have to swallow hard to make way for the words I've been holding close to my heart. "Will you marry me?"

She smiles. "Yes, yes!"

I stand and pull Brooke into a bone-breaking kiss. Vonnie and Leah jump up and down and start hooting.

Brooke and I break away, breathless.

"I love you so much, Wyatt!" Brooke says, grasping my face to kiss me again.

I grab her around the waist and spin her, laughing. "I love you too!"

"Ring! Ring! Ring!" Leah chants.

"Yeah, put it on!" Vonnie adds.

I set Brooke down and slip the ring from its satin hold inside the box. My sisters crowd around. I take Brooke's left hand. My chest tightens as my emotions swirl inside me. I've imagined the sparkly gem flashing on her finger for months, and now I finally get to see it in real life.

I slide the silver band onto her slender ring finger. Brooke draws in a breath and extends her hand, her gaze fixed on the round diamond glittering in the low light. "It's gorgeous," she says, then looks up at me.

"We helped pick it out," Vonnie says.

Brooke smiles at my sisters. Vonnie sucks in a sob and Brooke hugs her.

"I'm just so happy for you guys," she blubbers. I tug her from Brooke and she squeezes me tight.

"Welcome to our crazy family," Leah says as she and Brooke hug. "You sure you know what you're getting into?"

Brooke reaches for my hand, and I fold her in a soft embrace. "It's a valid question," I say, brushing the hair back from her face.

She smiles up at me. "Yes, I'm sure. I love all of you, Wyatt."

"Even the disgustingly chipper in the morning part?"

She laughs. "Yes."

"What about our rivalry?"

She raises an eyebrow. "I think we've decided it brings out the best in us."

I kiss her again, savoring the warmth and the joy sparking inside me, knowing I'll never forget this moment. Hope rises inside me like a hot air balloon as I realize that this is only the beginning. We have the rest of our lives to challenge each other, to fight and make up, to surrender and give, to care for each other, support each other, listen to each other, love each other.

I can't wait.

***

Ready for more small town love with the Morgan family? Read on for a sneak peek of Annika and Grady's story, Falling for My Best Friend, coming in July!

FALLING FOR MY BEST FRIEND

A Friends to Lovers Romance

Chapter One

Annika

I'M SLIDING a pan of cinnamon rolls into the rising rack when across the room, my ancient Hobart mixer makes that same funny sound again. The whirring paddle slows to a silent halt.

"No, please," I whimper as I race over, the smell of burning rubber filling the air. "Not today."

I cut the power to the mixer then place my shaky hands on the top, as if I can read the problem with my fingertips.

I have three more batches of cookies to make before we open in an hour plus the many loaves of bread I'll need for lunch. But more than that, I hate this sudden disruption. These early mornings when the kitchen is my own, my senses filling with cinnamon and yeast and my body consumed with purpose, is the only thing keeping me from falling apart right now.

However, the mixer breaking down is totally my fault. For weeks, there have been signs that Gloria needed TLC. Why didn't I listen?

Because you're a horrible procrastinator, that's why.

Grady had even mentioned that it might be a belt—a simple fix.

I groan and push off the mixer, then hurry over to the phone. Hobart's service number is tacked to the bulletin board over my tiny desk. *See?* my conscience scolds. *How hard would it have been to call two weeks ago?*

I know the answer but shove it back.

The ring tone blares in my ears while I hug my middle with my free hand and wait. Outside the back door's window, the white stars burn against the still-black sky, but a pale glow coats the jagged horizon, a reminder that morning is coming whether I'm ready or not.

Finally, a man answers and I tell him my problem.

"We can send someone out by Friday," he replies after putting me on hold for the longest half-minute of my life.

"Friday?" I cry. That's three days from now.

"Well," he drawls. "You're pretty remote up there. My guy will have to make a special trip."

I slump against the edge of the desk and pinch the bridge of my nose.

"I'll tell you what, though. Sounds to me like it's a snapped belt. I can overnight one and you can probably fix it yourself."

I scowl at the giant gray mixer across the kitchen, as if she's testing me. "Well, I guess I'll have to give it a try, won't I? Did I mention that I don't have a backup mixer, and practically everything I sell here runs through the one I have?"

"Maybe you're ready for an upgrade," the man says with a chuckle. "Invest in one with gears instead of a belt. More reliable. Plus, your model is over twenty-five years old."

The skin on the back of my neck prickles. A new gear-driven mixer costs twelve thousand dollars. "I'll think about it."

A knock sounds on the back door, startling me. I peer through the window and sigh with relief; it's Grady in his uniform and thick coat. He's clean-shaven and his hair is still slightly wet, so I know he's headed for his shift.

The man on the phone confirms my address, then we hang up.

When I let him in, a cold gust of winter air comes with him, which feels good on my hot skin. Grady takes one look at me and frowns. Then, he glances at the mixer and winces.

"You need my help?" he asks.

I want to melt into his arms, but resist. He's my best friend, not some white knight. Though he's played the part plenty of times—changing my flat tire, climbing our giant pine tree to rescue Gideon, going with me to the vet when I had to put Juney down.

"The guy thinks it's a snapped belt. But I don't have a new one. It'll be here tomorrow," I say, pushing off the desk. I suddenly have too much to do in too little time, and my mind takes off with the rapidly unspooling list of tasks.

"That sucks," Grady says, following me over to the mixer. "What are you going to do in the meantime?"

I lower the bowl from the paddle and grab my biggest spatula. "Mix this by hand."

Grady's ginger-colored brows knit together. After a quick glance at the clock, he takes off his coat and rolls up his sleeves. "I can stay for a half hour."

"Come on, you don't have to do that," I say.

"What if I want to?" he replies.

I roll my eyes. "You just want free cookies."

He grins. "Busted. Do we have a deal?"

I laugh, and a pulse of warmth washes through me.

I scrape the last of the dough from the giant bowl of the mixer into a separate one. On his way back from the sink from washing up, Grady swipes the bowl from me and mixes the contents with a wooden spoon, his muscular arms making the work look easy. I set the giant baking pans in the middle of the island, then grab two ice cream scoops and pull out my digital scale.

"I was surprised to see your car out there," Grady says as we get to work scooping and weighing the cookies at the island.

I brush a hair from my forehead with the back of my wrist. "I gave Hellen the week off."

We scoop and measure in silence, trading off at the scale before we add the mounds to the pan in neat rows.

"Everything okay?" he asks.

I take the first completed tray to the oven and slide it in. "Yeah," I reply, catching his skeptical reflection in the glass of the oven door. I paste on a smile when I spin back for the second tray.

He dips his scoop into the bowl for another mound of dough, his face contemplative. "Good," he says.

I move to the other side of the island and pull out the ingredients for the chocolate chip cookie dough, keeping one eye on him. The light from the kitchen windows casts a soft glow over the frosty ground and paints the distant peaks with pink. I've always said I have the best view in town, and it's true. Watching Grady work while the light strengthens behind him fortifies me with a feeling I can't quite place—peace? Gratitude?

Just so long as it's not hope.

He finishes loading the tray and I add it to the oven. When I turn back, he's biting his lip, as if unsure about something.

It transports me back to when we were kids climbing trees or having spitting contests, that charismatic look he gets right before he gives me shit.

"I kind of need a favor," he says finally, exhaling.

I add the vanilla to the creamed butter and sugar and give the dough a vigorous stir. "I can only spare a half dozen now, but I can bring more later, after the breakfast rush."

His face tenses. "I'm not talking about cookies."

"Oh, do tell," I say, measuring and adding the flour.

"You can totally say no," he adds, leaning his hip against the side of the kitchen island, crossing his legs at the ankles.

I notice that his big boots are dusted with flour and make a note to loan him a rag before he goes. I never would have pegged him as such a rule follower before he became a firefighter, but I know him better now.

"Especially if it's going to cause problems with Brad," he adds.

My pulse leaps, which sends a painful throb to my temples. "We broke up," I blurt.

His face freezes and a look of compassion fills his eyes. "Shit, I'm sorry."

I start mixing again, throwing my shoulder into the work. I'm grateful he doesn't ask for details, but that's Grady—never nosy. "Thanks."

"You okay?" he asks.

"Of course," I say because it's true, or it will be, and measure out the chocolate chips.

He clears his throat. "Maybe this is a bad idea then."

I huff a sigh. "Would you come out with it already?"

He nods slowly, as if deciding. "You know the firefighter auction is coming up, right?"

I add the chocolate chips and start stirring again. "I still can't believe you participate. Letting yourself be sold like that. Like you're a piece of meat."

"You know why," he says.

I lift my gaze to his. "Yeah, I know, but still."

"Anyways," he says, brushing the tabletop with his fingertips. Back and forth. Back and forth. "You know Erica Slade, right?"

"The woman that runs the garden shop?"

"Yeah," he replies, then swallows hard. "Well...she's set on winning me."

I press my lips together to contain my laughter. "I see," I manage. "What have you gotten yourself into now, Grady Dole?"

The corners of his mouth arch down into a scowl. "Honestly, I don't know. Every time I go in there she...follows me around, and does this weird thing with her hair, flipping it over her shoulder, or finding these annoying ways to get close to me or touch my arm or whatever—"

I turn to him, hands on my hips. "I'm getting a very strong cougar warning, here."

He nods, exhaling a slow breath. "I don't want to say anything bad about her or anything. I'm sure she's perfectly nice. I just don't want to be on a date with her. I don't want to give her the wrong idea."

"Like that you might be into her?" I ask, a little thrill zipping through me because giving Grady shit is going to be the highlight of my shitty morning.

His mouth forms a grim line. "Yeah."

I bring the bowl over to the scale. Grady has already set out two baking sheets. "What does this have to do with me?" I ask.

Grady scoops a lump of dough and measures it, adding a tiny bit more to get it accurate, then drops the lump onto the pan. "I was thinking maybe you could bid on me instead."

I'm scooping dough but suddenly forget what to do with it.

"Okay, sorry, dumb idea," Grady says quickly. "Forget it."

"No," I say just as quickly while my breath rattles in my throat. "I'd be happy to help."

His eyes fill with relief. "Really? Fuck, that would be awesome. I'll pay you back and everything."

"You wouldn't have to pay me back," I say, because I pay my own way, always. Yeah, I need a new mixer, but I'll figure it out. "It's for a good cause, right?"

"Yeah," he says, the relief now making his cheeks glow. After a glance at the clock, he tugs me into a quick hug. "I gotta bounce, but we can talk more about it later, okay?"

I wrap my arms around his solid frame and sigh. He smells as good as he always does, like pine and spicy citrus. "Okay. I'll bring cookies to the station later."

He rests his chin on the top of my head, sending a tingle over my skin. Then he releases me and grabs his coat. "Tomorrow we'll fix your mixer," he says from the door.

"I can do it," I say.

He smiles, making his whole face brighten. "I know you can."

I roll my eyes as he slips through the door.

A tremor passes through me as silence settles over the kitchen once more.

Did I just agree to go on a date with my best friend?

Keep reading HERE.

ACKNOWLEDGMENTS

Thank you so much for reading this book and giving me a chance. I hope you enjoyed Wyatt and Brooke's story! If you haven't read the series prequel featuring Caleb and Lori's summer of first love, you can get it for free HERE.

I'm excited to bring you more stories in the Morgan family saga, including Falling for My Best Friend, Annika and Grady's friends to lovers romance, coming July 22nd.

While you're waiting, you might also enjoy my angsty friends to lovers trilogy, *Entwined Hearts*, featuring professional athletes Colby Fox and Anya Templeton.

Many thanks to my tribe of beta readers and fans of my Facebook and Instagram pages for encouraging me to publish this sexy new series.

Thank you to my insightful editor, Jana Stojadinović, for unearthing the gems in what was a rather messy first draft. Your skill and determination made this book shine.

Also, thanks to my author bestie Amy Olle, for always being there to listen, encourage, and make me laugh. To Rebecca Hamilton, thank you for your incredible support and knowledge.

A huge thanks to every reader, fellow author, or blogger who has recommended or commented on my books. Your support is such a gift. Thank you.

I also wanted to thank the wild mountains of the West for inspiring me. There is truly no place on earth as beautiful or inspiring, and revisiting the meadows, peaks, and rivers in my stories is nothing short of magical.

Don't forget to grab your FREE prequel to the Falling Hard series by joining my author community.

CLICK HERE to claim your freebie!

ABOUT DAKOTA

USA Today Bestselling author Dakota Davies writes hot romance stories featuring hardworking, broken heroes and the feisty women who break down their barriers. She is the author of the suspenseful Falling Hard family saga and the emotionally driven Entwined Hearts trilogy.

By day, she's a swim team mom, book addict, and nature lover, but inside the mind of the person packing her kid's lunches and going for a run with the dog is an alter ego brimming with passionate love stories. When not writing, Dakota takes adventures in the mountains, speed reads anything by Lauren Blakely, and bakes gluten-free bread.

Sign up for Dakota's newsletter for a free book plus receive news on releases, giveaways, and exclusive reader bonuses! Join Here.

Don't be shy, follow Dakota on all platforms:

ALSO BY DAKOTA

Entwined Hearts Series - Colby & Anya

A slow-burn, sensual friends to lovers trilogy

Entwined Hearts

Unraveled Hearts

Twisted Hearts

Falling Hard Series – The Morgan Family Saga

Falling for My Fling (prequel) – Caleb & Lori

Falling for My Fling - Caleb & Lori's duet

Falling for My Rival – Wyatt & Brooke

Falling for My Best Friend – Annika

Falling for My Plus One – Peter

Falling for My Ex - Leah

Falling for My Blind Date – Dylan

Falling for My Crush - Vonnie

Wild Hearts Series

Action and adventure romance novellas

Her Wild Coast Outlaw – Hunter & Petra

Her Wild Coast Haven – Cody, Jared, & Tasha

Her Wild Coast Rescue – Cooper & Sarah

Their Wild Coast Rebel – Martin, Luke, & Lexie

His Wild Coast Bride

Stand-Alone Titles

Hush: A Holiday Romance – Ben and Elise

Yours: A Virgin Romance – Brian & Darcy